PRAISE FOR VI(

The Secre

"A red-hot suspenser aimed at readers for whom a single serial killer just isn't enough."

—*Kirkus Reviews*

An Unreliable Truth

"A straight-A legal thriller with a final scene as satisfying as it is disturbing."

—*Kirkus Reviews*

A Killer's Wife

An Amazon Best Book of the Month: Mystery, Thriller & Suspense

"*A Killer's Wife* is a high-stakes legal thriller loaded with intense courtroom drama, compelling characters, and surprising twists that will keep you turning the pages at breakneck speed."

—T. R. Ragan, *New York Times* bestselling author

"Exquisitely paced and skillfully crafted, *A Killer's Wife* delivers a wicked psychological suspense wrapped around a hypnotic legal thriller. One cleverly designed twist after another kept me saying, 'I did not see that coming.'"

—Steven Konkoly, *Wall Street Journal* bestselling author

"A gripping thriller that doesn't let up for a single page. Surprising twists with a hero you care about. I read the whole book in one sitting!"
—Chad Zunker, bestselling author of *An Equal Justice*

THE
GRAVE
SINGER

OTHER TITLES BY VICTOR METHOS

Shepard & Gray Series

The Secret Witness

Desert Plains Series

A Killer's Wife
Crimson Lake Road
An Unreliable Truth

Other Titles

The Hallows
The Shotgun Lawyer
A Gambler's Jury
An Invisible Client

Neon Lawyer Series

Mercy
The Neon Lawyer

THE
GRAVE
SINGER

VICTOR METHOS

THOMAS & MERCER

Published by Thomas & Mercer, Seattle

www.apub.com

Amazon, the Amazon logo, and Thomas & Mercer are trademarks of Amazon.com, Inc., or its affiliates.

ISBN-13: 9781662507809 (paperback)
ISBN-13: 9781662507816 (digital)

Cover design by Faceout Studio, Molly von Borstel
Cover images: © Stephen Mulcahey / Arcangel; © Abstractor / Shutterstock; © Ravindra37 / Shutterstock

Printed in the United States of America

THE
GRAVE
SINGER

1

Mark felt the shattered glass cut his face as he was thrown through the upstairs window.

He landed with a thud on his snow-covered driveway. It knocked the wind out of him, and he felt cracks in his ribs. His hips were on fire, every joint radiating pain. His face, already bloodied from the beating he took, had left an imprint in the snow, ringed with blood.

He groaned, one hand holding his shattered wrist in place. He slowly rolled onto his back and took deep breaths—the exhalations like smoke in the cold winter air. The sky was black as oil, and flakes of snow, remnants of the day's storm, drifted quietly to the earth.

The double doors of his palatial home opened, and a man in black slacks and a black button-up shirt appeared. The man was a giant. Taller than Mark by at least a foot and huge. Like an NFL linebacker. The man was bald with the beginnings of a beard and brown skin the color of caramel, a mix of his Afghan father's and Cuban mother's heritage.

Even at night, he wore oversize black sunglasses.

He sauntered to Mark and stood over him. The man dipped into his pocket and came out with a cigar. He lit it with a solid gold lighter, the smell of tobacco swirling with the icy breeze.

He offered him the cigar. "Cuban."

Mark spit out a glob of blood and tongued a loose tooth. "Go to hell, Alonso," he said.

Mark was used to getting his way. Wealth could do that: bring a sense of power. He wasn't the insecure small-time hustler anymore like when Alonso got locked up. He was different now. He was a big-time player in the community, with the bank account to back it up.

"You've been gone eleven years. It's too long. You're out of the game. You don't know how it works. It's all lawsuits and lawyers now. A thug like you is a dinosaur in this game. Find some other sucker to play."

Alonso watched a car that drove past as he sucked on his cigar. He waved to the driver, who sped off.

"Eleven years . . . the thing about being inside is the time, Markie Mark. Time's your enemy, but I used my time. Studied law and philosophy and psychology. Everything that gives you power. Power, homie. That's what it's about. Men are animals when they're locked up, and you gotta be more than a man to survive. That's what I am to you. I'm a man, and you're a cockroach."

He squatted down, his fists covered in cuts and blood from Mark's teeth, and said, "Know what hurts the most? You didn't visit me once. I got locked up, and you pretended like you didn't know me."

With a deep groan and burning in his hips, Mark sat up. His mouth was filled with blood, and he spit it out into the white snow.

"When you ever visit anybody in the can?"

He chuckled. "Good point." He looked back at the home. "I lent you a hundred Gs in good faith. I find out you made it big and forgot about your friend Alonso. It's hurtful, Markie Mark."

"I'll get you a hundred grand."

"No, my man, you didn't pay a cent in vig for eleven years, and I was gonna use that money to make money. Compounding vig at twenty percent a month over eleven years is, what? 'Bout nine hundred Gs?"

Mark chuckled mirthlessly. "No way I'm paying you nine hundred. You'll get your hundred, that's it. No matter how many windows you throw me out of."

"Come on now, don't be like that. You got this fancy house, apartment buildings, that sleek Mercedes, the hot little filly with all that plastic in her face . . . you done pretty good for yourself." He sucked for a second on the cigar. "More than a cockroach deserves making with my money."

"Your money? I did this on my own. Yeah, you got me the down payment on my first building, but everything else is because of me. I did this."

Mark grimaced as he tried to stand. He got to his knees before he had to spit again so he could breathe and said, "You'll get your hundred grand and that's it. Write the rest off on your taxes, I don't care."

Alonso laughed. "Tax write-off. That's good, homie." He sucked a massive hit off the cigar before letting smoke stream out of his nostrils. "I'm not gonna lie; I'm saddened to hear that."

"Then do what you gotta do."

Alonso nodded. "What I could do is sue you."

Mark laughed, but the motion sent a shock of pain through his ribs, and he grimaced and stopped. "That's what Alonso Hafeez has come to, huh? Just another little punk going to the cops."

Alonso tossed the cigar into the snow. "You have yourself a good night, Mr. Webb."

Mark didn't move until Alonso was entirely out of view. Then, when he turned a corner and was gone, Mark breathed deeply with relief. He'd taken a risk being defiant, but sometimes that was the only thing that worked with thugs.

Alonso had never killed anyone as far as Mark knew. You kill someone that owes you money, you never get your money. He might still come around, but next time Mark would have his gun, and it wouldn't go down the same.

Prison affected everyone differently. Some men got out and didn't care anymore about anything, and others got out and acted like they'd rather die than ever go back. Alonso had mentioned filing a lawsuit, and Mark wondered if that's what happened to him. Alonso never thought of going through the system to get money owed him before he went to prison. Being locked up must've frightened him so bad it broke him.

Mark painfully rose and couldn't put much weight on his right foot. His hip was probably fractured. He took out his cell phone to call his girlfriend to take him to the hospital. The screen had cracked from the fall.

He started limping toward the house as he dialed her number. He got about halfway when he heard a car driving by on the street and glanced at it. An old Chevy. He ignored it as he focused on his legs. His knees ached, and one felt loose: like it was connected by spaghetti. When he was better, maybe he should be the one to go to court, except of course Alonso didn't have anything to take anymore.

The car roared as it made a sudden turn. Tires spinning in slush and the impact of rubber and rims against the curb made Mark look back right before Alonso slammed the Chevy into him, catching him midhip. Mark flew off his feet and thumped onto the hood of the car. His legs dangled over the hood, scraping against the driveway and lawn.

Mark felt the full force of the car as Alonso gunned it. Then deafening sounds and white flashes, but no pain. He thought maybe he'd fallen off the car. When his vision stopped spinning, he found he couldn't breathe but was somehow standing upright.

He looked down at the mass of metal smashed into him and felt the brick wall of the house behind him. He was caught in between the two.

The car had slammed with so much power it nearly cut him in half, and it looked like the twisted metal was growing out of him. The shock kept the pain away, but he felt the warmth of blood bathing his legs. He couldn't pull in any breath because there was nowhere to pull it into.

Alonso got out of the car and tossed the keys into the driver's seat. Blood cascaded down his forehead from a massive cut. He took out a handkerchief and dabbed at it.

"I don't know, Markie Mark. Suing you just didn't sound like fun. That's all life is, my friend, fun. That's what I learned inside, what I thought about for eleven years. Because for eleven years, I had the grim reaper whispering in my ear. You wanna know what he was saying?"

Alonso leaned close.

"He said, 'Have fun now, 'cause I'm comin'.'"

2

Solomon Shepard thought the defendant's attorney had made a mistake letting him take the stand.

The defendant, Charles Hill, was slim and mild mannered and wore glasses today. Over the past twelve days of testimony, the jury hadn't heard from him, so it was difficult to gauge whether they liked him. But anybody accused of murdering their wife while she slept would have to work hard at getting a jury to like them. It was a risk for the defense to have him testify and a stroke of luck for the prosecution.

"Anything further?" the judge asked.

The defense attorney, an elderly man in a tweed jacket, said, "No, Your Honor."

"Mr. Shepard, the floor is yours."

"Thank you, Judge."

Solomon used his cane to push himself up from the table. He went to the lectern but chose to stand in front of it, leaning on his cane and looking Charles in the eyes.

"Charles, you loved your wife, didn't you?"

"Of course."

"Been married almost twenty years, right?"

"Yes."

"In your version of events, you were lying in bed asleep when an intruder burst in and opened fire. Probably the most horrifying thing that could happen to someone, right?"

"Yes," he said, glancing down.

Solomon waited until the man was looking at him again. Eye contact during cross-examination, he believed, created almost a mind-to-mind connection and made people more malleable.

"I have here the statement you wrote to the police introduced during your attorney's direct examination. You wrote this the night your wife was murdered, correct?"

"Yes."

"So your memory of the incident when you wrote this was still fresh, right?"

"Yes, I suppose so."

"You state here that you and Wendy heard a noise, and you got up to get your gun from the safe, and that's when someone started firing shots that missed you and hit her, right?"

"Yes, that's right."

"Nowhere in the statement does it say you and Wendy talked?"

"Talked?"

Solomon nodded casually, as though speaking with a friend. "Yeah, talked. You didn't say anything to her."

He shrugged. "I don't know what you mean."

"So you heard the testimony of your two neighbors, right? Mr. and Mrs. Craft?"

"Yes, I did."

"They heard noises that night. Gunshots."

He nodded again and glanced to his attorney. "Yes, that's what they said."

"And the first thing that Mrs. Craft did was ask Mr. Craft if he heard something, right?"

"Yes."

"But according to your testimony today and the statement you wrote that night, you didn't ask your wife if she heard anything, and she didn't ask you if you heard anything when you woke up."

"We might've said something. I don't remember. It was last year."

"Again, your memory was better the night this happened than a year later, isn't it?"

Charles didn't answer.

"I'm sorry, Mr. Hill, is there something you don't wish the jury to hear? We'd appreciate it if you answered my question."

"Yes, my memory was better that night."

"And nowhere in your statement you wrote that night does it say you and your wife exchanged any words. Is that right?"

He glanced at his attorney again. "Yes. But . . . but I was told to write that statement hours after my wife was murdered. You can't expect me to—"

"To be accurate?"

"I wasn't going to say *accurate*. I was going to say *detailed*. I was a mess. I was very nearly killed, too."

"How many gunshot wounds did you have?"

He flexed his jaw. "None. The bullets missed me by inches."

"Yeah, that's amazing. We heard the ballistics expert testify that Mrs. Hill was shot from a range of twelve feet and that the doorway, where you say you were, was about half that distance. So someone shot at you from six feet and missed every single time. That's either the worst shot in the world, or you seriously pulled some *Matrix*-style moves to dodge the bullets."

"Objection," his defense attorney said.

"Sustained," the judge said without looking up from writing a note.

Solomon stepped around the lectern and leaned against it with one hand, his other holding the lion's head handle of the cane. "I don't want to get off topic, though, Charles. Let's talk some more about right before the shooting happened. Your neighbors heard the shots, rose, and conversed with each other. They talked. You claim you didn't talk to your wife right before the shooting."

"I heard something that woke me up. I didn't think I needed to confirm anything with her."

"But you just said you don't remember."

"What I said was—"

"Let's assume that your second statement that you didn't need to confirm the noise with her is true. You hear something loud enough in the middle of the night to wake you up. You're lying right next to her. As close as two people can be. You hear something that alerts you that there might be danger. So much so that you get out of bed to get your gun. She's lying right next to you and potentially in danger, but you didn't take a few seconds to say anything and warn her?"

He folded his arms. "I thought someone was in our hallway. My only goal was to get my gun from the gun safe."

"A rational person who wanted to protect his wife would have ensured she was safe, right? If she was scared or panicking?"

"I don't agree with—"

"You didn't establish if she was scared?"

He sighed as though dealing with an annoying child. "No, I did not."

"You didn't establish if she heard anything in the hallway?"

He unfolded his arms and put them on his lap. He appeared to be fidgeting with his fingers, though Solomon couldn't really see because of how high the witness box was.

"No, I did not."

"You wanted to arm yourself."

"Yes."

Solomon took a step closer to him. "That was the first thought you had, right?"

"When I thought someone was in my home, yes. I didn't have any other choice."

Victor Methos

"Well, that's not true, is it? There were a lot of other steps you could've taken if you had talked with Wendy, right? You guys could've escaped to the balcony, for example."

"The balcony was ten feet off the ground. We would've had to jump and risk hurting ourselves."

"So confronting an unknown number of people in your hallway seemed like the safer option?"

"I didn't have time to—"

"There's another door in your bedroom that leads to the bathroom, which has another door that leads to another hallway. So you could've escaped that way, right?"

"I had so many things running through my mind I didn't think about every possibility, Mr. Shepard."

"You just thought, *I'm going to grab my gun and start shooting*."

"I didn't think I'd start shooting."

"You got the gun out of the safe in your closet, right?"

"Yes."

"You flicked off the safety?"

"I did."

"You ran toward danger with a gun ready to shoot."

"I wasn't ready to shoot."

"You testified you had the gun pointed at chest level, right?"

"Yes."

"And what if you would've seen movement from someone? You would've fired."

"I don't know what I would've done."

"Then why get the gun at all? Why have the safety off? Why rush into danger with the gun pointed in front of you?"

He looked to the jury as he said, "All I wanted was to put myself between the intruder and Wendy."

"Yeah, but you didn't know at this point there was an intruder. You said you heard a noise like something falling."

"Yes. Like I said, it sounded like someone bumped something, and it fell to the floor."

"Did you wake up Wendy?"

"No, I didn't think—"

"Before you grabbed your gun, did you get your phone to dial 911?"

"No, there wasn't time."

"There was time to go to the gun safe, enter the code, get out your gun, load it, flick off the safety, and then go to the hallway, but there wasn't enough time to call 911?"

"I just . . . I wanted to protect my wife," he said, emotion in his voice. The sentiment felt forced to Solomon, and he hoped the jury saw through the act as easily as he did. "That was my only thought. You read about people breaking into homes and killing everybody and robbing them. I wanted to make sure that didn't happen to us."

"Did you shout for Wendy to call 911?"

"No."

"If you had, she would've called the police, wouldn't she?"

"I don't know what she would've done."

"Maybe the supposed intruder you claim was there would've run off, too."

"I don't know what they would've done."

Solomon took another step toward him. "In your direct examination, you stated that the intruder you saw was taller than you. Correct?"

"Yes."

"In your written statement you made that night, where you state your memory was better than now, you said you held the gun at chest height and pointed it at the intruder's chest. Indicating you were both the same height. When the police asked you how tall you thought he was, you said, 'Maybe five-nine or five-ten.' You're five-nine. You never said he was taller than you in this statement, did you?"

"No, but I told you, I had to write that statement hours after. I wasn't in my right mind."

"Yeah, maybe, but again, that's an important detail, the description of your wife's supposed killer, you got wrong hours after seeing him. Yet now, a year later, you mention a contradictory detail you didn't mention the night it happened."

He shrugged. "Yes, well, I apologize. It was a horrific night, and I was confused."

"You see, though, Charles, you can't make contradictory statements and then apologize for them. There's a reason people give contradictory statements."

"I just made a mistake."

"No, it can't be a mistake. It's an untruth. When you make up a story and have to stick to it over time, you start making mistakes."

"Objection!" the defense attorney said, rising to his feet. "Badgering, Your Honor."

Before the judge could answer, Solomon quickly said, "If catching a murderer in a lie is badgering, then what are we even doing in court, Judge?"

"Objection! That is grossly out of line. Mr. Shepard needs to be—"

The judge looked up from his notes and said, "Gentlemen, please approach."

The attorneys went up to the bench, and the judge hit a button that sent static through the speakers so the jury couldn't hear. Charles pretended like he wasn't paying attention or listening in.

"Mr. Shepard, I'm guessing this cross-examination is going to be contentious and will require some time."

"It will."

"So, how long do you anticipate it taking?"

"Probably two days, Judge. Maybe three, depending on how cooperative Mr. Hill is."

He nodded. "It's been seven hours of testimony today, and I'm noticing the jury losing concentration. I know it's right at the start of your examination, but I think it would be good for everybody if we broke for today and came back fresh on Monday."

"I think that's fine," the defense attorney said.

Solomon knew he had some momentum going, but what the judge said was true: he'd seen three yawns from different jurors in the past hour.

"No objection from me," Solomon said.

"Good. Let's get back on the record then."

When the judge turned off the static, he said, "Ladies and gentlemen of the jury, it's been a long day, and I believe we could all use some dinner and rest. Let's resume this on Monday morning. Mr. Shepard, the objections are sustained. Please move on when we continue. This Court is now adjourned until eight o'clock Monday morning. All rise for the jury."

When the jury filed out, the bailiff escorted Charles Hill to be transported to his holding cell at the jail. The defense attorney said nothing as he gathered his papers but came over to Solomon afterward and said, "You're a son of a bitch."

Solomon laughed. "Your client just needed to tell the truth," he said. "You know the great thing about the truth? When you tell the truth, it's somebody else's problem. When you lie, it's your problem."

"Up yours."

Solomon gathered his papers with a grin and turned to leave when he saw Sheriff Billie Gray standing near the door in a black suit. She opened the doors for him as he approached and said, "You just make friends wherever you go, don't you?"

"Must be my quiet charm," he said. "What are you doing down here? I thought you had court in Salt Lake?"

"Finished up. There was an incident near here I wanted to check out and thought I'd drop by and see how you're doing first."

They walked down the courtroom hallway, and a bailiff told them to have a good evening as they headed out the front entrance.

"I'm fine. Why are you worried?"

"You've been anxious and sleeping less. I can see it in the bags under your eyes." She paused a second. "Have you thought any more about calling my therapist friend? She's quite good."

"No, I don't need therapy. Junk in the mind doesn't matter. Plus, it's important to keep my edge, and I don't know how therapy would affect that."

"Nothing is important, Solomon, but everything is meaningful. Including the fact that you won't get help if you need it."

They went down the courthouse steps, and Solomon said goodbye to a bailiff he'd befriended.

They got outside and felt the chill of a breeze. The sun was out, but snow covered the ground and the air felt wet and cold. Solomon put his free hand in his pocket as he maneuvered the cane in his other one.

The courthouse was in the Justice Center building complex holding most of the city and county's government services, but it was surrounded by residential property, and he could see kids across the street building a snowman in front of an elementary school. A drab gray building with red doors.

"Enough psychobabble talk. I'm interested in this incident you're here for. Something juicy?"

"You'll hear all about it soon, I'm sure. A gentleman got crushed by a car against his own house, and whoever was driving fled on foot."

"Ouch."

"The vehicle cut him in half."

"Anybody see anything?"

"Nobody we could find yet."

"Could just be some drunk driver."

"Possibly, but I don't think so. The car was reported stolen the day before."

"That does sound juicy. Mind if I tag along?"

"You really wanna see that?"

"I've seen worse. Mostly I just wanna grab a chicken shawarma on the way."

3

Solomon offered a bite of his shawarma to Billie, who declined with a shake of her head. She stopped her truck at a light, took out some napkins from the center console, and handed them to him.

"Thanks," he said with a mouthful of food. "Place is so freakin' good."

She glanced at him.

"Don't worry. I'll leave the shawarma in the truck. You have to be a gloomy coroner to eat something over dead bodies. It's a rule I learned from *Law and Order* and *CSI* episodes."

He took another bite and then a swig of lemonade. "So, who is this guy?"

"Mark Webb. He's got a rap sheet, but it's mostly minor stuff. Some larceny and drug possessions. He was allegedly a gang member in his youth, so we think it might be gang related."

"In his youth?"

"Yeah, he's thirty-nine."

"How many thirty-nine-year-olds have you seen active in gangs? Gangsters either get out before their thirties or end up dead or in prison."

"True, but they also have long memories. Maybe he did something once someone hasn't forgotten about, and the opportunity just came up? We had a murder here involving a Russian street gang. Eighteen years after someone testified against the gang, one of the members saw the witness in another state. Both of them were on vacation in Yellowstone, of all places. The gang member stabbed him with a steak knife in the middle of the restaurant at their hotel. Don't underestimate how long people can hold a grudge."

"Eh. Humans have short memories. Dolphins have far superior memories to us."

"I haven't seen any dolphins involved in revenge killings, but I know sometimes things bury deep, and people don't know how to get it out."

She parked the truck near a police cruiser. The neighborhood was clean and had luxury cars in the driveways—the road looped around a small honorary statue on a patch of grass.

Solomon motioned with his head and said, "Who's the statue of?"

"The founder of this area. A gold miner. They're petitioning the county to incorporate their city and break off from Tooele."

Solomon opened the door. "Gotta keep the peasants like us away from the royalty that lives up here, I guess."

Near the home was a jumbled mess of metal and glass. There wasn't a body here anymore, and a tow truck waited to haul off the car. Splashes of blood had stained the car and wall.

"How fast would someone have to be going to cause that much blood to leave a human body? It even spattered up onto the roof."

"I know," she said, "but let's not jump to conclusions yet."

Billie nodded to a detective in a white shirt and brown tie, who came up to her and began speaking.

When they weren't paying attention, Solomon quietly wandered off, near where the blood was on the wall.

The wall had collapsed to the point where Solomon could see inside the home. Bits of metal, covered in a gelatinous substance, had embedded themselves into the bricks.

He glanced behind him, and Billie was still speaking with the detective. She nodded and had a look of concentration on her face, something she did when slowly getting upset with somebody.

Better stop whatever you're saying to her while you can, buddy.

The front door was wide open. Solomon went inside. The house smelled pleasant, something like the scent of warm grass. It was airy and decorated sparsely with a few discreet paintings and marble statues. A few of the paintings were held in what looked like real gold frames, and the doorknobs appeared to be actual gold as well—the ornaments of someone who had become rich and wanted everyone to know it.

"You like the house?" Billie said from behind him.

"I do. It's like if Martha Stewart got to decorate Al Pacino's mansion in *Scarface*."

She grinned. "Let's get out of here before you contaminate my crime scene."

As they passed the scene back to the truck, Solomon said, "Out of curiosity, what did the victim do for a living?"

"Real estate. Buying and flipping houses, renting out duplexes and such."

"Huh."

"What?"

He got to the truck, and they got in. "Seems weird for a gangbanger from the streets to have a three-hundred-thousand-dollar Floyd Gaul painting in his house, doesn't it?"

"Who's Floyd Gaul?"

"Sheriff, I am taking you to an art museum." Solomon looked back to the house as she started the truck. "But first, I wouldn't mind looking at the detectives' reports on this when they're done. It'll probably be my case anyway."

4

Solomon met Gesell at an Asian bistro. He was a burger-and-fries guy, but Gesell had opened his food horizons since they'd started dating a few months ago. When she was younger, she had been a chef in New York City at an upscale restaurant, and anything less than gourmet was offensive to her tastes.

Seeing her sitting at a table with her chocolate-brown hair pulled back with an elastic and wearing yoga clothes gave him butterflies. He hadn't dated for nearly a decade before running into her at a bookstore. He commented on the book she was reading about developing good habits. She asked about the book on cannibalism he had in his hand.

"Yo," he said, sitting down across from her. "Should I be wearing a suit or something? Everybody here looks like they're about to go to a wedding. Or a funeral. Which is like just two of the same thing."

She tapped him playfully on the arm. It made him smile, and he forgot what he was going to say.

"Get the sautéed noodles with peanut sauce," she said, picking up the menu again.

"Maybe just a salad. I ate shawarma on the way over."

"You ate shawarma on the way to the most exclusive restaurant in the city?"

"I almost ate it over a dead body. That's just how I roll."

The server took their drink orders. Gesell turned her phone off when he left and set it facedown on the table.

"What's wrong?" she asked.

"Nothing. Why?"

"You get this wrinkle in your forehead when you're thinking really hard about something."

"I'm that obvious? I need to change up my game and keep you on your toes. Women don't like obvious men." He took a sip of his water from what looked like a bowl. A man in a gray suit with a gold watch at the next table was slurping out of his own bowl and trying to act sophisticated as he did it with a straight back and holding the bowl with only two fingers of each hand.

"It's nothing," he said. "Just went with Billie to this crime scene on a case I might be handling. The guy was crushed by a car against his own house."

"Wow. Who did it? His wife? I bet it was his wife."

"No, no wife. It could be an accident or a million other things, but how much force was involved was odd. There's no way someone crashing a car at that speed into a brick wall wouldn't know they're going to get hurt, too."

"So, what does that mean?"

"Well, if it is a murder, this guy or gal was willing to injure themself just to make the biggest spectacle of the victim's death. People like that make me nervous. They have nothing to lose."

She unfolded her linen napkin as the drinks came and spread the cloth on her lap. Solomon just played with his, crumpling and uncrumpling it in his hands as he thought. She watched him, and he noticed out of the periphery of his vision as he looked around the restaurant. One of the first things she did when they'd first met was wipe a little foam off his lip from the espresso he was drinking at the bookstore. Then she apologized and blamed a nurturing disposition. It seemed she wanted to take care of him right away, and he wondered if she'd been that way with her ex-husband, too.

She said, "I think I might know how to get your mind off of such morbid thoughts."

"Really?" Solomon said with a grin. "And how would you do that?"

She sipped her drink slowly and seductively. "Oh, I can be creative when I need to."

Solomon lay in bed with the moonlight coming through the windows. He was bare chested and in black boxers, Gesell asleep next to him. Her hair fell lightly on his skin, and her hand was on his chest. He didn't want to move: it felt good to experience someone else's touch. He'd been alone so long he'd forgotten what it felt like.

Slowly, so as not to wake her, he rose from the bed, grabbed his cane, and went to the kitchen. His phone was on the counter. He took it and went out to his balcony and sat down. He liked watching the city early in the morning, that gray area of time when the actual city came out. The city that only the residents knew about.

Billie had emailed him the Marcus "Mark" Webb case reports.

Mark Webb was worth about $3 million on paper through investments in eleven properties. He'd bought his first property more than a decade ago, and it had doubled in value within three years. Before selling that first property, he'd apparently worked odd jobs in body shops. His rap sheet had several convictions, all minor stuff, even the felonies. Nothing violent. He'd never been married and had no children.

Solomon went to the photos Billie had included. A slight shock of revulsion went through him before he could prepare himself. The victim's body didn't look cut in half like Billie had said: it looked *torn* in half.

The car, an older Chevy, had been reported stolen by the owner the night before. The criminalist had done an excellent job with prints and trace evidence. Still, there was too much of it to find anything meaningful. The car owner was a college student, with his friends in and out of the car all day. They had compiled fingerprints from eighteen different individuals so far, but most were unusable because of their degradation or cross-contamination with other fingerprints.

Solomon's cat, Russ, rubbed himself across Solomon's calves and rested near the edge of the balcony, his paw lazily going over the bottom of the metal railing.

"You just think you own the place, don't you?" Solomon said.

"What are you doing?"

The voice made him jump. For a split second, he thought it had come from Russ. Gesell laughed and then immediately covered her mouth with her hand.

"Sorry, I shouldn't laugh."

"It's fine. I've been waiting for the day I go crazy and my cat starts talking back to me. Thought it finally happened."

She sat down in the chair next to him. "Not yet, but I'm sure one day."

"We can hope."

"What are you reading?"

"Some reports from the murder last night."

"Is that even your case?"

He let out a breath and put his phone facing down so she wouldn't see the photos. "Not yet, but it'll come to our office, and I can request it if I want."

"Why would you want to?"

He looked at the lights of the city. "Something doesn't feel right about it. The fact that they were willing to hurt themself as long as they killed this guy . . . I don't know. It's vengeful."

"Aren't all murders vengeful?"

"They vary. Most murders are shootings in drug deals gone bad or vendettas between gangs. They want to kill as efficiently as possible.

This is different. This was loud, much louder than a gunshot, and they still did it in a quiet, affluent neighborhood where they'd likely be seen. They just didn't care."

She leaned her head on his shoulder. The way she looked right now, with her hair flowing down and her pink nails, reminded him of someone he had a crush on in elementary school. A girl he only remembered as wearing a matching yellow shirt and pants with little bird decorations on them. He had accidentally hurt her at recess playing tag, and she had a red bump near her eye. He felt terrible afterward and didn't know how to make it up to her. Before he could, the girl moved one day, and he had never gotten to tell her that seeing her sitting in front of him in class was the highlight of his day, because after that was being picked on for being the nerdy kid who wasn't good at sports and then going home to whatever foster family he happened to be staying with. But for that first part of the morning, when they were in their homeroom, he got to sit behind who he thought was the most beautiful girl in the world. He would occasionally think about where she was now.

"What are you thinking about?" Gesell said.

"Just how long it's been since I've had good nachos."

"What?"

"Nothing," he said with a chuckle. "Just old memories." He ran a hand through her hair.

She sighed. "I better go," she said. "David's coming home from his father's early in the morning."

Gesell's ex-husband had joint custody of her son, David, and each took him for two weeks out of each month. They both lived close to his school, so it wasn't a significant interruption to his life, but Solomon wondered if they'd asked the boy who he would've preferred to live with. Most parents didn't ask their children that question in a divorce because they didn't want to know the answer.

It was the typical story: She'd gotten pregnant in high school and, under pressure from family, was forced to marry. Having to marry someone you didn't want to sounded like slavery to Solomon, and after years of emotional and even sometimes physical abuse, Gesell left with her young son and one bag of clothes. She'd told him she wanted normal in her relationships now. Quiet and calm. A man who preferred the intellect to thrills and whose idea of a perfect weekend was having pizza and binge-watching '80s sitcoms.

Solomon seemed like the perfect fit. *Seemed* like . . . but his life at times was neither quiet nor calm. The consequence of his work.

She rose. "Dinner tonight at my place?"

"Can't say no to that."

"Bring a dessert."

She kissed him and then left. Solomon watched her over his shoulder until she shut the door. When she was gone, he brought up his phone again and read the detectives' narratives on Mark Webb's death.

5

Solomon dressed in jeans and a white Rolling Stones T-shirt with a black sport coat. He and his boss, the county attorney, Knox Scott, had a relationship so contentious that they avoided speaking to each other as much as possible to the point of not saying hello when they passed in the halls. So Solomon dressed how he wanted and came in and out of the office as he pleased. As ideal a setup as he could imagine. He prosecuted the cases he was interested in, and his boss wanted nothing to do with him but knew he was too valuable to fire.

The gym was packed today, mostly with women in full makeup and men with gelled hair as if they were going to a club. Cologne and perfume choked the air, the music sugary pop.

A green-eyed girl in her twenties with tanned skin worked the nutrition counter. Solomon pulled up a chair and sat down. She smiled at him and asked what she could do for him.

"You're Ashley Simmons, right?"

"I am."

"My name's Solomon. I'm with the County Attorney's Office and helping the police look into Mark Webb's death."

She lost her smile. "What do you want?"

"I'm a little surprised to see you at work so soon after your boyfriend is killed."

She straightened up a few containers of protein powder behind the counter. "Yeah, well, not all of us can take off work whenever we want."

"I wanted to—"

A woman came up to the counter and ordered a protein shake. Solomon grinned and nodded to her as he waited while Ashley blended the drink and rang the lady up.

"Look, you gonna buy something or not?" she said. "You can't sit here unless you are."

"Oh, um, sure. Give me a mango . . . whatever that thing is in the picture."

She began mixing it for him. "The police already talked to me," she said, not looking up from cutting a mango. "I was the last person he called before he died."

"I know."

"Then what do you want? I don't know anything. Mark kept that part of his life away from me."

"What part?"

"The sketchy part. He wasn't into it anymore, but he did some business with shady people. And no, I don't know who."

"Were you two close?"

She shrugged as she put the ingredients in a blender. "We'd only been dating a couple months, but I liked him. He was cool. Not like a lot of the losers I was dating before. I think I might stay single for a while. Dating's not even worth it anymore."

The drink came in a large plastic jug and had a colorful straw. Solomon tasted it: liquid sugar. Almost like fire in his throat.

"Wow. That is . . . interesting."

"And it's like a bazillion calories." She leaned her elbows on the counter in front of him. "What do you want from me? I don't know anything."

"Sometimes people know things they don't realize are important."

"I told you, he kept that part of his life away from me."

"Hey, I'm not here to interrogate you. I just wanna get a sense of who Mark was."

She took a moment to think. "He was really nice. You'd think someone rich and good looking would be a total douche, but he was always nice to me." She grinned at a memory. "He used to squeeze me as hard as he could when we saw each other for the first time any day. He was older than me, but he always wanted to do stuff like go hiking or on trips. He was cool to be around . . . I'm gonna miss him."

Solomon guessed he wouldn't be able to learn much from her that would be helpful. Still, he liked to speak to witnesses himself rather than relying on police reports. The way a person spoke, the look in their eyes, or the movement of their hands was just as important as the actual words they said. And the impression he got from Ashley was that she was someone who cared for Mark but knew almost nothing about who he really was.

Solomon looked down at his drink and the bits of fruit in the frothy liquid settling at the bottom. The concoction made him feel nauseated.

"It's on the house," she said, seeing the disgust on his face.

"Thanks. And thanks for talking to me."

"No worries."

He rose to leave, and Ashley said, "Hey? You know, there was something."

"What is it?" Solomon said, leaning on his cane with one hand.

"We were supposed to meet up that night, but he canceled."

"Did he say why?"

She shook her head. "No."

"Did he often cancel last minute?"

"If he had a meeting or something, yeah."

Solomon took a step closer to her. "Ashley, we don't know why this happened. So to be on the safe side, you should maybe be on the lookout for anybody strange that you don't know coming around."

"You mean like you?"

He grinned. "Yes." He took out one of his cards and laid it on the counter. "Call me if you notice someone like that. And maybe start carrying around some pepper spray. Lotta weirdos out there."

Solomon went into Cup of Joe's and sat at one of the tables with a chessboard set up. The weekly chess meetup at the coffee shop had become a favorite ritual of his since last year, when Billie had shown up at his door and asked for his help on a case from his past, the Reaper. Before that time, he spent his days in his apartment, having groceries delivered by the girl down the hall.

Kelly had been young, sixteen, and possessed a keen intellect that he admired. He pictured her growing up to be an investigative journalist or photographer, though she had once told him she wanted to be an attorney like him.

Occasionally, when walking by her apartment, which was now occupied by a quiet couple from North Carolina, he would stop and look at the door a little too long.

The thought of her pained him, and he decided to focus on something happier, like beating Ivan for the first time today.

He had both hands on his cane as the barista, Jodi, came over and brought him his tea with honey.

"Thanks, Jodi."

"You bet. You gonna take Ivan out today or what?"

"Stranger things have happened."

"Where'd you learn how to play so good anyway?"

"My dad. He was obsessed with chess. Playing with him is probably the only good memory I have of him."

"Shit, don't that sound familiar. My daddy loved fixing old cars, and sitting out in the driveway handing him tools is the only good memory I got. Some people just shouldn't be parents, huh?"

"Amen to that."

She lightly touched his shoulder and said, "Lemme know if you need anything, sweetie," before walking back to the counter.

Solomon checked the clock on his phone. Ivan, a retiree who had once been a chess grand master in Ukraine, liked to show up fifteen minutes late. Never fourteen, never sixteen, always fifteen.

As Solomon set the phone down, he noticed someone in a booth across the coffee shop near the windows. He was a giant; even sitting down, he was taller than people walking by. The man's beard was neatly trimmed, and he dressed nicely in a polo shirt with a Las Vegas Raiders cap. A tattoo said *THUGGIE* on his forearm, and he wore sunglasses indoors. He was reading a book until he looked up.

"Counselor, that you?"

The man rose, the muscles in his arms swollen like boulders. He pulled out the chair across from Solomon, and the chair creaked as he sat down.

"I thought that was you," he said. "Small world, isn't it?"

Solomon said nothing.

"Yeah, there it is," he said with a wide smile. "You do remember me. I'm flattered."

Solomon gripped his cane tighter. "When did you get out, Alonso?"

"Six days I've had my freedom back, and it's never tasted as sweet. You look good. Eleven years hasn't hurt you at all."

The door opened, and Ivan came in. He strolled over and stood by their table.

"My chair," Ivan said.

Alonso's eyes didn't move, but he lost his smile as he said, "Oh, I think Mr. Shepard and I wanna catch up. Find another game."

Ivan looked at Solomon, who nodded. "Next game."

Ivan looked puzzled and didn't move.

For the first time, Alonso looked at him. "Go away."

He said it with such an underlying menace that Ivan left. Of course, it also probably didn't hurt that Alonso was big enough to use the man as a belt.

He turned back to Solomon as though they hadn't been interrupted and smiled again, and his eyes softened. "Friend a' yours, Counselor? I didn't think you had any friends."

"They come and go."

"Yeah, they do. You know when they really go? When you see who has love for you and who has a knife for your back? When you're in prison. My wife and son ran like I had the plague when I got locked up. The boy don't know I'm out. She told him I was dead."

"I'm sorry to hear that."

"Are you?" Alonso leaned back in the chair, and it creaked even louder. "You know what book that is over there that I'm reading? *A Historical and Stochastic Analysis of Violent Crime*, by a Mr. Solomon Shepard, JD, LSW, MSc. Damn, boy, that's a lotta letters after your name. A man I admired used to say too much education pollutes the soul. But if that many letters after your name is what got you to write that book, it was worth it."

"Glad you like it."

"I don't just like it; it changed my life. You see people differently after reading that. 'Smarter but more vicious chimps.' Isn't that what you said about humans? If aliens came down and started classifying all the species, humans wouldn't be our own species. Instead, we'd be classified as a type of chimpanzee because we're almost the same." He pulled a cigar out of his pocket and smelled it but didn't light it. "The chapter on the Druids is my favorite. You remember the grave singers, Counselor?"

Solomon pushed on his cane and rose. Alonso looked hurt and said, "Where you goin'? I thought we'd play a game."

"Not in the mood anymore."

6

"Alonso Hafeez."

Solomon lay on Billie's couch in her office, tossing an autographed baseball into the air with one hand.

"Never heard of him," she said without looking up from her computer.

"He was a fence and a loan shark."

She stopped what she was doing and leaned back in her chair, making it creak. "Connected?"

"He had some ties to organized crime, but he wasn't part of that world." He tossed the ball into the air again and caught it. "Honestly, I think he probably just couldn't stand the thought of someone telling him what to do and preferred to go lone wolf."

"So what's got you spooked?"

"I'm not spooked."

"Don't do the mental gymnastics that men do where you pretend you're not scared. It's annoying. I hate pretending."

"All right, I'm a little spooked."

"Why?"

"He's one of the most dangerous people I've ever encountered. Extreme violence coupled with charm and intelligence. He started work at an oil refinery when he was a kid, getting paid under the table. He worked there for a decade, and they paid for him to get a degree in economics. He graduated college with honors when he was nineteen. You take that type of intelligence and put it with a volatile temper and a six-foot-seven, three-hundred-and-fifty-pound body, and you've got an out-of-control Mack Truck. And he was impossible to prosecute because he knew how to choose his victims."

"In what way?"

"He only loaned money to people who couldn't go to the cops, like felons on parole or people who would use the money to buy drugs or gamble. Something where they couldn't go to anyone else for help. That way, Alonso could hurt them if they didn't pay, and there was no one the victims could turn to. We're talking about thugs and drug dealers. And if one of them made the mistake of attacking him, he made sure they knew no one was safe. Not their children, not their parents, no one. He wasn't intimidated by anyone."

He caught the ball and lowered it, then tossed it between his hands as he stared at the ceiling. "The beef I got him on was attempted murder. A man borrowed some money from him for gambling debts. You should've seen what Alonso did to him when he couldn't pay it back."

"Sounds like a charming lad."

Solomon thought back to the last time he had seen Alonso Hafeez. It had been at his sentencing. Once he'd lost the trial, Alonso had to be taken down by the bailiffs and cuffed because he'd lost it. Solomon found out later both his shoulders were dislocated because he was fighting so hard.

Billie kicked her feet up on the desk and tilted her head back as she said, "So what are you nervous about? I'm sure you've put away men like him before."

"Yeah . . . I don't know. Something about him never sat right with me. Being around him was like being in the presence of a predator."

"Maybe it was just a coincidence that he was at the coffee shop at the same time?"

"Yeah, maybe." He sat up and put the baseball back on her desk. "So, what do you have going on today?"

"Just meetings and reviewing some reports. You?"

"I got a couple hearings next door." He stretched his arms overhead and used his cane to stand. "Lunch?"

"Can't. Have a lunch meeting with a county councilman. Life of the politician."

"I liked you better before you were a big shot."

"I'm not, but I care about paying my employees, and the county council determines our budget. Why don't you come along?"

"Nah, politicians make me feel greasy. I'll see ya later."

Solomon left her office and nodded goodbye to the receptionist at the front desk. The air outside was cold, but the sun was bright. The streets were filled with cars carefully maneuvering through thick slush. He changed into a black suit in his office and then headed to court.

The Tooele County Justice Complex housed most city and county government-services buildings. The court had recently moved in as well. It made going to court convenient, and now the courtrooms were huge. Still, it also felt like walking into a factory, like he was a small cog in a giant wheel.

The bailiffs waved him through the metal detectors, and Solomon headed to Judge Bevita's courtroom. An older Latino judge with thick glasses that reminded Solomon of soda bottles, Bevita liked to chew on carrots during court and didn't turn off the microphone. So whenever Solomon needed a recording of some hearing from his courtroom, quiet crunching was always in the background.

He froze as he walked through the double doors to head to the prosecution table. Seated in the front row was Alonso Hafeez.

Solomon at first wondered if he was here on an unrelated matter. But he knew that wasn't it. Running into him once, he could believe—not twice.

"What are you doing here?" Solomon said.

Alonso gave him a warm smile. "I'm just here to observe our justice system in action, Counselor. I didn't waste my time inside. No, sir, not me. I studied. Mostly law. Gave me a new appreciation for our justice system."

"If you don't have a hearing, you shouldn't be in here."

"Oh, now, I think the Sixth Amendment says otherwise. You do remember the Sixth Amendment, don't you, Counselor?"

Solomon took a breath and sat down at the prosecution table. Over his career, defendants had tried to scare him before, but he never took them seriously.

"All rise," the bailiff said. "Third District Court is now in session, the Honorable Raymond Bevita presiding."

"Please be seated."

Solomon watched as the judge sat down. The public defender, a younger guy named Will, was already seated at the defense table. He leaned back with a loud exhalation, glanced at the judge, and shook his head to Solomon. They bet each afternoon on whether Bevita would bust out the carrots.

"I say yes," Solomon whispered.

"Ten bucks?"

"Yup."

You had to make court enjoyable however you could.

"Ladies and gentlemen," the judge said, "thank you for making your court date today. My name is Judge Bevita, and I'll be handling your matters. We move through the calendar alphabetically and will get to your case in a reasonable time. So please don't keep asking my bailiffs when your case will be called."

Solomon heard a plastic baggie from behind the bench.

"Not looking good for you, Will," he whispered.

"Could be chips or something."

The crinkling noise stopped, and the judge continued. "Today, we will be addressing matters known as pretrial conferences. These conferences . . . excuse me a moment."

Solomon bit his lower lip.

A crunch of a carrot echoed into the microphones.

"Damn," Will whispered.

Solomon smiled and pulled up the first file on his phone.

After two dozen pretrial conferences, court finished early. Solomon got his ten bucks from Will and promised to spend it on lunch for them during the week. As he turned to leave, he saw Alonso Hafeez sitting in the same spot he occupied before court began.

Solomon didn't say anything as he made his way out of the courtroom.

He returned to the County Attorney's Office and sat at his desk. The desk and computer had collected dust, since he was rarely here. His main office was an old storage room near Billie's office at the sheriff's station.

"Solomon Shepard, as I live and breathe," Knox said, suddenly appearing from the hallway and leaning against Solomon's door with his arms folded.

Solomon glanced at him and then back out of his floor-to-ceiling windows. "I won't stay long, Knox. You don't need to get your feathers ruffled."

"Actually, believe it or not, I need something from you."

"What?"

"A sealed warrant on a case, and someone told me you're in good with Judge Bevita."

"He knows my name, if that's your idea of in good with somebody."

"Just get it done. The case file is emailed to you. You still have access to your intraoffice email, don't you?"

"I'll figure it out."

He turned to his computer as Knox left. This was why he never came to the office.

Solomon tried four passwords to log on to his computer, and they were all wrong. The machine locked him out for an hour.

"Damn," he said, turning back to the windows and staring absently out at the building across the street. His eyes drifted down to near the entrance of the courthouse. Standing outside was Alonso Hafeez, smoking a cigar and looking right into his office.

7

The parole board in Utah consisted of eight members from various criminal justice, sociology, or social work backgrounds. Solomon knew a few of them but considered only one a friend. Gary Russell. He was a younger man who practiced law for a year and hated it but had the connections to land a cushy job on the parole board.

His office was in the Justice Center, two buildings down from the court, and Solomon went there now. The office building was government in every sense of the word, looking like it had been built by bureaucratic committee: brown, ugly, with elevators about as far away from the entrance as possible and labyrinthian hallways where you had to walk around the entire building before finding the offices.

Gary's door was open, and he was at his desk with a young woman seated in front of him.

"Yo," Solomon said.

"Sol, hey, man."

"Sorry to interrupt."

"Nah, we were finished anyway. Have a seat."

The woman exchanged a few more words with Gary before she left without acknowledging Solomon.

"So what's up, man? You hanging in there with Knox, or you about to go postal?"

"Not postal yet, but the day's young."

He chuckled. "I never liked the dude. He's the kind of guy that tells you how hot your girl is and then talks shit about her behind her back."

"Speaking from personal experience, I take it?"

"Punk is lucky I didn't feel like getting arrested that day." He glanced at his computer screen when it dinged with an email. "So what makes you drop by?"

"I had a favor to ask; I wanted some info on someone you paroled recently. Alonso Hafeez."

"Don't tell me he got himself in trouble again. He barely got out."

"No, not yet. Just need some info on him."

He leaned back, tapping a pen he had in his hand against the arm of his chair. "Nothing much to tell, man. He was a model inmate."

"Seriously?"

"Yeah. He even got his ass kicked once and didn't defend himself."

"What do you mean?"

"Exactly what I said. Some little dude decided he didn't like him and messed him up. Alonso put his hands behind his back and let the guy kick the shit outa him."

"He didn't defend himself at all?"

Gary shook his head. "No, nothing. Dude broke his jaw, too. Alonso didn't even get payback. Like it never happened."

"Huh."

"What?"

"That's really strange. He's one of the most violent men I've ever prosecuted."

"Didn't seem like it when he was locked up."

Solomon tapped his cane on the carpet between his feet. "In your interviews with him, did he ever mention me?"

"Mention you? No, why?"

"Just curious."

"This guy bothering you?"

"He's shown up a couple places I've been at. I'm worried it's more than a coincidence."

"Well, I could give him a call and tell him to keep clear of you if you like."

"No, I don't think that would do much. It's fine. I'm more curious than anything."

"Up to you, brother. But lemme know if you change your mind."

"I will."

Solomon was at the door when he turned and said, "Hey, outa curiosity, what happened to the guy that beat him up?"

"Nothing. He served his time and was released a few years ago."

Solomon thought a moment as he tapped his cane. "Mind giving me his name?"

Ricardo Duran lived in a section of the city Solomon rarely visited, full of ramshackle houses run down with time and lack of upkeep. The Uber dropped him off, and the driver said nothing while Solomon got out. The house had two kids in front, and as he went to the gate, the older boy ran inside. A young man in shorts and a tank top came out a second later.

"You Ricardo?" Solomon asked.

"No. Who is you?"

"I'm a friend. Is he home?"

"I ain't seen him."

"Since when?"

The man stepped up to him. He was bigger than Solomon, but Solomon didn't feel any fear. The man had a look in his eyes that told him it was a show based on distrust.

"I know all my brother's friends, and I ain't know you."

"I need five minutes to ask him about someone he knew inside at Gunnison. I can even just talk to him on the phone if you wanna call him."

The man glanced back to the kids and said, "Go inside." When they didn't move, he yelled, "I ain't kiddin', go inside!" Then, after the kids had left, he turned to Solomon and said, "I ain't seen him for a minute."

"How long?"

"Since Monday."

"Is it unusual not to see him that long?"

The man nodded. "Ain't answerin' his phone neither. That's his boy back there, and he ain't even checked up on him."

"Did he say anything to you last time you spoke to him? Mention someone following him or something like that?"

"Nah, man. Nothin' like that."

"Does he work?"

"Yeah, but he ain't shown up for work."

"You didn't call the police?"

He chuckled. "Man, the police aren't gonna give a shit 'bout some missin' con."

Solomon took out a card. "Well, I do. He served his time and isn't any different from anyone else. Will you call me if you get ahold of him?"

He took the card and stared at it for a second. "Yeah, aight."

"Thanks."

Solomon waited for an Uber at the curb, staring at a plastic bag drifting with a breeze across the pavement and then floating into the air before disappearing around a corner.

He felt his unease growing. Something he didn't understand was just getting started.

8

Sheriff Billie Gray chatted a few minutes with the county medical examiner before leaving the Justice Center to head home.

Since her breakup with her boyfriend Dax last week, she went home to an empty house and preferred it. Always quiet, always everything left precisely where she remembered it. Sometimes she wondered what it would be like to come home and hear children there, to have someone run up and hug her and tell her they missed her and discuss their day, but she didn't dwell on it for long. She believed some people weren't meant to have children, and she was one of those people.

The country station played some Johnny Cash, and she hummed along. Music was the art form she related to most: the one that took her back to better times and helped her feel cheerful when she should've felt anything but. For Solomon, she knew, it was books. Books were his constant companions, his best friends, but she'd never found comfort in them. Probably one of the reasons she didn't finish her graduate degree.

She got home and noticed a white Corvette at the curb, parked about fifty feet away. Definitely not part of the neighborhood. She knew every neighbor and every car on her street. As the sheriff, a female sheriff to boot, she had received her share of threats and liked to keep a constant vigilance of her surroundings.

It was possible her neighbor had guests over, but she'd never seen the car before. The windows were too tinted to see inside. She stared at the Corvette for a few seconds and then went inside.

The inside of the home was clean and clutter-free. She took off her boots and tossed her keys into a bowl on a table. She went to the bedroom and undressed before getting into the shower. Leaning her head against the tile, she let the hot water run over her until the skin on her back hurt. Sometimes, when it was boiling hot, and she was in there long enough, she felt like she'd peeled off an old layer of skin.

When she got out, she put on sweats and went to the kitchen to make something to eat. When she tossed a few expired condiments out, she noticed her garbage was full and lifted the bag to take it outside to the can. The neighborhood was quiet except for the wind, which was a constant background noise much of the winter. The can was around the house. After she tossed the bag in, she noticed the Corvette again. It hadn't moved.

She hiked over to the sidewalk and headed to the car.

The lights flicked on and startled her.

The car started and quickly pulled away, leaving her watching the taillights disappear in the darkness.

Billie went to the neighbor's home the car had been parked in front of and asked them about it. They hadn't noticed any unfamiliar cars. Billie put out a BOLO call for a white Corvette in her neighborhood and then sat in her truck and waited.

The call came in from dispatch only minutes later that a deputy on patrol had spotted a white Corvette less than a mile from her house.

Billie pulled out of her driveway. Slowly, she went up her street, checking all the parked cars. She circled back around and saw the car parked on the side of the road. The driver was in there, and she could see the glow from a cell phone he had his face buried in.

She parked the truck far behind the car and got out. She checked her firearm, which she had in a holster on her hip, and pulled her sweatshirt down over it. Then, trying to stay in the shadows, she snuck up to the car. The driver wasn't paying attention. Billie knocked on the window and startled him so bad he dropped the phone.

"Dax?"

He rolled down the window. "Hey."

"What the hell are you doing?"

"Just in the neighborhood and wanted to show you the new ride."

"I saw you sitting in front of my house."

"Yeah, I know. I thought I'd stop in and say hi. But I saw you and panicked."

"That's all that happened? You weren't watching my house?"

"Of course not." He paused a second and looked away. "I do miss you, though. I still can't believe we don't see each other anymore."

"Dax—"

"I know. It's over. I get it. But sometimes these things take several times to work. A buddy of mine broke up with his wife three times while they were dating before they got married."

"We're not getting married, Dax. I told you."

"Yeah, I know. But . . . it doesn't make sense. We're perfect for each other. I mean, do you wanna grow old alone?"

"Yes."

"I . . . don't even know what to say to that. That's just stupid, Billie."

"I'm tired and hungry, Dax. I'm going home."

"Wait, I haven't eaten either. Come with me."

"No."

"Just a freaking sandwich and soup over at Mulligan's."

"No."

He shook his head. "This doesn't even make sense. I love you, and I know you love me. Is there someone else? Is that why you said no?"

"Go home, Dax."

She got into her truck and drove off. In the rearview, she could see him watching her.

9

Solomon waited for Gesell outside the symphony's main entrance. The Utah Symphony, for how small it was, had surprisingly good talent, and the drive to downtown Salt Lake wasn't far. Gesell had introduced him to chamber music when she found him listening to death metal while he read. She'd studied cello for twenty years and played part-time in various symphonies around the world before she decided she preferred being a chef more, though she had told him once cooking was an art form extraordinarily similar to music.

He had never been to the symphony before but had been to nine Metallica concerts.

She walked up to him and straightened his tie.

"Oh my gosh, you are so adorable in a suit."

"I can occasionally clean up nice."

She gave him a quick peck on the lips and said, "You'll love this. Do you like Mahler?"

"What? Mahler? Who doesn't like Mahler? You'd have to be a culturally clueless buffoon not to like Mahler."

"You don't know who he is, do you?"

"No idea."

"You'll like him, I promise. He was a romantic. Like you."

The symphony hall was packed, a mix of those in suits and jeans. The people in suits looked down on those who showed up in jeans, and the ones in jeans mocked the ones in suits in quiet whispers. Solomon mentioned it to Gesell. He was surprised she'd never noticed.

An elderly woman in a black dress scanned their tickets and let them into the hall. They had balcony seats.

Solomon liked the balcony. He had a view of all the murals on the walls, including an epic scene out of *Madame Butterfly*, depicted almost like a Renaissance painting.

Out of all the music Gesell had introduced him to since they'd been dating, *Madame Butterfly* was his favorite. A story about the pleasant numbness of self-destruction.

A figure caught his eye. Alonso Hafeez was sitting on the opposite balcony with a woman on his arm.

Alonso stared right at him and smiled.

"Be right back," Solomon said.

"Sol, it's starting," Gesell whisper-shouted.

"Just two minutes. Promise."

He hurried out and took the winding staircase down past a massive chandelier. He went across the hall to the other staircase and made his way up to the balcony seats. Alonso was in front with a young woman holding his arm and whispering something to him. He still wore his black sunglasses even in the quasi-darkness of the symphony.

Solomon went up to them, and Alonso said, "Counselor! This is a surprise. Didn't think you were the opera type."

"What are you doing here?"

"I brought my lady friend to see some culture. Been eleven years since I experienced any culture."

Solomon leaned on his cane. "Stay the hell away from me."

"Small world, Counselor. Never know where we might run into each other. It's maybe . . . what do you call moments where a coincidence is more than a coincidence? It was in your book."

Solomon glanced at the woman Alonso had with him. "Synchronicity."

"That's right, synchronicity. Can't help it if the universe wants us to run into each other, can I?"

They held each other's gaze a moment before Solomon turned to leave. He heard the young woman say, "Who was that?"

"Just an old friend," Alonso said.

10

Gesell had her son tonight, so she didn't sleep over. Solomon stayed up late watching television, flipping through true-crime documentaries and one on ancient Egypt. Billie texted and asked what he was doing. "Nothing," he replied, and she said she would be over. A few times a week, she used to come over and bring food because she'd been worried that he wasn't eating. She hadn't visited as much since Gesell came into the picture.

She was at his door in half an hour with a pizza. He got some plates and a couple of beers. They sat down on his couch and watched television, debating whether it was best to fold a pizza slice or bite it at the tip of the triangle.

"So, how was your day?" he finally asked with a mouthful of pizza.

"Shitty."

"What happened?"

"Dax showed up at my house."

"The ex can't get you out of his head, huh?"

"Guess not. He was waiting down the street, watching my house. Then he lied to me when I confronted him."

"I mean, the guy did ask you to marry him, and you said no. It's expected he'd be a little weird for a while."

"See, what is that? If I were a man and a woman was displaying this behavior, you would've called her crazy. But a man doing it is just *a little weird?*"

"Hey, I just live in the world. I didn't make the rules." He could tell this wasn't a joking matter only after he spoke.

"You're right," he said. "I'm sorry." He put the slice of pizza down on a plate and paused the television. "What scared you about it?"

"Nothing scared me. It was just . . . his demeanor was different. I think anyone outside the conversation would've said it was perfectly normal and calm, but I know him well enough to read between the lines. He was aggressive."

"Maybe you get a protective order to be on the safe side?"

"No, he hasn't done anything worrisome. Just acting odd. I don't know. Maybe I'm the one acting odd."

She leaned back on the couch and put one arm behind her head, revealing her firearm underneath her sweatshirt. She usually didn't carry it with her, and Solomon wondered if Dax had her more spooked than she wanted to admit.

"What about you?" she asked. "Anything exciting?"

"Saw Alonso Hafeez again."

"Where?"

"The symphony."

"In Salt Lake? He followed you up there?"

"Maybe. There's only one symphony. It's within the realm of possibility it was a coincidence."

"Solomon, there is no way that's a coincidence."

He ran his tongue along his lower lip, which was dry. "No, there's no way."

"I think I should pay a visit to him."

"Huh?" he said, his thoughts somewhere else. "Oh, no, no, don't do that. I mean, he just got out of prison. It'd be pretty irrational of him to want to immediately go back."

"Who said people are rational?"

After a movie, Solomon said good night to Billie and lay in bed with the lights off. Gesell called, and they spoke briefly about mundane things that didn't require deep thought, focusing on things that had happened to them during the day or current shows they were binge-watching. The banter of two people falling asleep on the phone. When he hung up, he let the phone rest on his chest as he stared at the beams of moonlight coming through the open window.

There was an alley between his building and the next, and sometimes the homeless would sleep there, as police rarely came to this neighborhood. He heard a clearly drunk man singing, and when he realized it was a Britney Spears song, he laughed.

Solomon went to the window. He couldn't see anyone but could hear the voice. "Hey, man, it's cold out. You need a blanket?"

"I'll take a beer if you got one," a voice said from the dark.

"Okay, hang tight."

Solomon dressed in sweats, grabbed a beer and a blanket, and headed down. The elevator was quiet, and he didn't hear anyone else up at this hour in his building. Outside was chilly but luckily not freezing. He found an older man in tattered clothes seated and leaned up against his building. Solomon handed him the beer and the blanket, and the man said, "Thank you."

"No worries. You need some food?"

"I'll take whatever you can spare," the man said. He had a broad smile on a weathered face.

A Vietnamese café was nearby that was open late, and Solomon went there. Unfortunately, the lights were a little too bright, and he didn't like how they reflected off the tiled floor. Bright lights could give him migraines, and he had to be careful what stores he went into.

He ordered some pho and waited at the counter. A waitress with a bob asked him if he wanted anything else, and he asked for hot water with lemon. Behind him, he could hear a group of teenagers talking about a recent football game, and one of the boys was bragging to the girls about his work on the field today.

A hand on his shoulder startled him.

One of the teenagers stood there with a credit card and said, "You dropped this."

He handed Solomon the credit card Solomon had paid with.

"Thanks."

Solomon put the card back in his wallet, his heart pounding. He stared out of the windows into the darkness, wondering if someone was staring back at him.

11

Gesell Prescott tucked her son, David, into bed and then went to the living room and turned off all the lights except the lamp next to the couch. It was still a relatively new home to her. When she had finally been able to get away from David's father, she couldn't stand the thought of sleeping in the same house she'd lived in with him, so even though it had been the home of her dreams, she sold it at a loss and moved into something much more modest. More modest, yes, but hers and hers alone.

David had some friends over and left a mess. Unfortunately, teenage boys seemed incapable of cleaning up after themselves.

She picked up some bags of chips and empty cans of soda, tossed them in the garbage, and then straightened up the kitchen. A pile of dishes was in the sink, and she sighed as she began to rinse them off and put them in the dishwasher.

After the dishes were done, Gesell went back to the living room, collapsed onto the couch, and picked up the remote. Out of the corner of her eye, she saw something outside the window behind the television directly in front of her. Across her lawn, near the curb, was a glowing red light. A pinpoint of red in the darkness that occasionally moved up, grew in brightness, and then lowered again.

The person wasn't moving or walking past the house. Instead, they were standing right in front, staring through the windows at her.

She went to the window. It was a man. He was dressed well and stood casually, leaning against a telephone pole as he smoked what looked like a cigar.

The man was huge. He seemed like he could rip the telephone pole out of the ground.

She closed the blinds, then turned off the lamp and peeked out. He was still there.

Gesell took a deep breath and decided she would have just ignored him if David weren't here. She had an alarm and felt safe with it, although she knew a woman who had been attacked in her home, and the man had managed to severely injure her in a few minutes. Too small a time window for law enforcement to respond to an alarm.

She went to the kitchen and got her biggest knife and tucked it into her waistband, then pulled her shirt over it before she went to the front door and opened it. The man stared right at her. No change in facial expression, as though he had been waiting for her to come out. He was wearing oversize sunglasses.

Gesell walked to the driveway and then down to the sidewalk. A streetlight was about ten feet away and gave enough illumination that one of her neighbors or someone driving by would see if he tried anything.

"Can I help you with something?" she said.

The man lowered the cigar and shook his head. "I'm admiring your home. It doesn't look like the other homes in the neighborhood. Custom build?"

"Yes," she lied, "me and my husband designed it." She emphasized the word *husband*.

"Is your husband inside? I'd love to meet him and ask him a few questions about it."

"Maybe some other time."

He took a puff of the cigar. It had a hint of sweetness but smelled like rotting wood. "What's your name, honey?"

"Gesell. And don't call me honey."

He held up his hands in a gesture of surrender. "Didn't mean anything by it. Where I grew up, that's just being polite. But I do like that name. Gesell. I knew a girl once named Gesell-Unique. Doubt her mama named her that, but that's what she liked to hear." He inhaled another puff and let it out through his nose. "Pardon my saying so, but you seem unique, too."

"I think I'd like you off my property."

"I'm not on your property. I'm on your curtilage. Do you know what curtilage is? It's the property attached to your house. See, the police used to think it's not part of your house, and they can search it whenever they want, but the Supreme Court disagreed."

She looked down at his hands. They were the size of baseball mitts. "You're a lawyer?"

He chuckled. "No, ma'am. I wouldn't lower myself to that station in life. But I do know the law. I studied it for many years. There's a lot there if you know what to look for."

He inhaled off his cigar and then lowered it again.

"Did you know threats aren't protected free speech, but poetry is? So if I were to say that I'm gonna saw your head off with that knife you got under your shirt, that would be illegal. But if I wrote a poem and said the same thing, that's protected speech. Everything is how you frame it, isn't it?"

She took a slow step away from him. "I'm calling the police."

He let out a last puff of smoke and tossed the cigar. "You're free to do whatever you like, but as I said, I was just admiring your home." He looked over to the house again. "You have yourself a good night."

He walked several feet away before he turned and said, "Oh, and that window on the second floor? I would get some bars put on there. Someone could climb the roof and break in through there. Folks try to save money and don't get alarm sensors on their second-floor windows."

She watched him walk away for a while, then ran back into the house, shut and locked the door, and quickly turned on her alarm. Then she ran up to David's room. He was sleeping soundly on his side.

The window the man had mentioned was in the hallway on the second floor. She checked the lock and decided she would call her alarm company tomorrow.

12

Solomon was woken up by his phone vibrating on the nightstand. It was Gesell.

"Hey," he said, trying not to reveal the grogginess he felt.

"Hey, I'm sorry to wake you up. But I don't know who else to call except the police."

Solomon suddenly became wide awake. "What happened?"

"There was this guy outside my house. He was smoking and staring at the house."

"What guy?"

"I don't know. I've never seen him. I went outside to ask him what he was doing, and he threatened me."

Solomon sat up. "What did he look like?"

"Really, *really* big with sunglasses and a beard. Bald head, mixed race maybe, I don't know. He was dressed really nice and had a gold watch on his wrist."

"Stay inside and keep the doors locked. I'm coming over right now."

He hung up and called Billie.

When they arrived at Gesell's, it was almost midnight. Billie looked wide awake, and Solomon wondered if she wasn't sleeping again. Lengthy bouts of insomnia had plagued her since childhood.

They went to the front door and knocked. Gesell looked out of the blinds and then turned off the alarm and unlocked the door.

"I'm so sorry," she said to them both. "I feel stupid now that I see you both here."

"You were right to call," Billie said. "Where's your son?"

"Asleep upstairs. I checked on him. He's fine."

Billie turned to Solomon and said, "I'm going to take a look at the backyard."

"You armed?"

"I am. Why? Don't think I can handle myself without a gun?"

"Not if the other guy has one." He turned back to Gesell. "Where was he standing?"

"Over here."

She walked him over to the telephone pole, and Solomon looked around with the flashlight function on his phone. When he didn't see anything, he logged in to the prison website and looked up mug shots for Alonso Hafeez. Then he turned the phone to Gesell.

"This him?"

"Yes! That's him. How'd you know?"

"His name's Alonso Hafeez. He got out of prison recently on an eleven-year stint and blames me for his incarceration."

"Why?"

He put his phone away. "They always gotta blame somebody." He glanced back to the house and saw Billie coming around the side. "I'm going to ask Billie to have some extra patrols come by here."

She folded her arms, and he could see the gooseflesh on her skin. "Sol, you're scaring me. Are we in danger?"

"No," he said matter-of-factly, "absolutely not. People that serve long sentences and get out don't want to go right back. This is about me."

"Has this happened before?"

He nodded. "People get fixated on the person arguing to a jury they should be locked up, but it passes."

She shook her head and looked down the street. "He talked about how if you say something in a poem, it isn't a threat, and he talked about sawing my head off."

"What?"

She nodded. "He didn't say *cut* my head off but *saw* it off. It just sounded so . . . sincere."

He put his arms around her. "I know it's scary, but this is part of the job. The victims like me and the defendants hate me. If I was a defense attorney, it'd be the other way around."

"Be honest. Should I take David back to his father's?"

Solomon wished he could say no. He didn't want to panic her any more than she was already, but he knew that was the right move.

"Yes."

"Solomon!" she said, pushing him away. "You said we're not in danger."

"Just until I get some protective orders in place."

"Protective orders?"

"Just a precaution. With those in place, he won't be able to come near you."

He could see the pain in her face. She was concerned about David.

"I'm sorry," he said. "I'd understand if you wanted to—"

"What, dump you?"

"I was going to say *take a little break*."

"As long as David's safe, it'll take a little more than an ex-con smoking in front of my house to scare me away from you."

Solomon held her and said nothing, but his eyes drifted over the neighborhood. The streetlamps were old and dim, giving off more of a foggy haze than bright light. Though he saw no one, he was certain eyes were staring back at him from the dark.

13

The following day, Solomon met Billie in front of his building. He got into her truck, and she shoved a bagel into his hands before pulling away.

"You know, you don't have to keep feeding me. I'm a big boy."

"You forget to eat sometimes. I think you get lost in your thoughts. What's that saying: 'If you're in your head, you're dead'?"

"I was dead at like five then." Solomon glanced at the GPS on his phone and said, "It's up here a few miles."

The tire-and-service store was connected to a gas station. They parked in front. Solomon could see two men smoking outside. They eyed Billie a moment and then Solomon. He was used to men staring at Billie, but the look they gave him afterward always bothered him. As if they couldn't believe that she would be with someone like him.

The men wore uniforms with name tags, and Billie said, "We're looking for Thomas Hicks."

"He's back in the office."

"Thank you."

They headed to the shop, and Solomon could hear the noise of bolts pulled from tires, compressed air released like the buzz of a chain saw, and the clanking of metal on metal.

An older man in a blue button-up shirt with bright-white hair was seated behind a desk in the office. He looked up from some papers, and Billie held up her shield and said, "Are you Thomas Hicks?"

"I am."

"I'm Sheriff Billie Gray. I need a moment of your time."

"What's going on?"

"It's about one of your employees, Ricardo Duran."

"Is he in trouble?"

"Not with me." She glanced at a photo of his family on the desk. "In fact, we believe he might be the one in trouble. When was the last time you saw him?"

"Last week. He worked a full shift on Friday and then didn't come in again."

"Has he ever done anything like this before?"

He shook his head. "Never. He's one of my best workers."

"Did he mention anything about someone following him or getting into a confrontation?" Solomon asked. "Anything like that?"

"I don't think so, but we didn't talk much. He's got some buddies here, you can talk to them if you want, but I don't think so. He was a straight arrow. Prison really changed him. He wanted to get his life together for his kids."

Solomon tapped his cane against the floor.

"Mr. Hicks," Billie said, "it's crucial for us to know that Mr. Duran is safe. So I'll leave my card with you and need a call as soon as you have any contact with him."

"Yeah, yeah, of course. I'll do whatever to help. If he really is missing . . . I mean, I can't even think about it. He's the sole support for two young kids. His family doesn't have much and can't raise them without him."

They exchanged a few more words, and then Solomon and Billie approached a couple of the employees and spoke about Duran, but outside a handful of visits to bars, they didn't spend much time with him and didn't even realize anything was wrong. One of them mentioned that he thought Ricardo might've taken off with a girl he'd been seeing.

Back in the truck, Solomon stared silently out the window before Billie said, "There's a possibility they're right. He might've taken off."

"And this just coincidentally happens right after Alonso gets out?"

The freeway on-ramp was closed due to an accident, and she had to drive through a residential neighborhood to get to the next one. "Would Alonso really get revenge on Duran after all this time?"

"He's smart and patient. A bad combination in a violent personality. He beat two aggravated assault charges before and then wised up. The two times I actually had enough evidence to move forward, the witnesses immediately changed their stories."

"Except when you convicted him."

"Yeah, well, apparently, that didn't teach him as much as I'd hoped."

They stopped by the sheriff's station and got out in the parking lot. Solomon was about to head to the County Attorney's Office a few buildings down at the Justice Center when Billie stopped in her tracks.

"What?" he said.

"That's Dax's car," she said, nodding to a Corvette parked near the building.

Solomon looked at the car and said, "That's a midlife crisis car if I've ever seen one."

She continued staring at the car in silence as though she hadn't heard him.

"There you are," Dax said from behind them. He had been waiting on a bench in a patch of grass near the entrance. His nose and ears were red from the cold. "Thought I'd missed you for the day."

"What are you doing here?" she said.

"What do you mean? It's the tenth."

"So?"

"So it's our monthly 'try a new food' lunch."

She folded her arms. "Dax, that was when we were together. We're not together anymore. Do you understand? I need you to understand."

"No, I get it," he said, "but I thought you said you still wanted to be friends? Friends can have lunch, right?"

"I need you to leave."

He looked confused. "I don't understand. You're acting like we don't even know each other."

"Goodbye, Dax."

She went toward the entrance, and Solomon followed her. When they were at the doors, Solomon looked back and saw Dax standing in the same spot before going to his car. He looked over to them with a scowl and then got into the driver's seat.

"The first time I met him," Solomon said, "he confused *Star Wars* and *Star Trek*. You can't trust someone who does that." When she didn't respond to his joke, he looked at her and said, "But I guess you don't really know someone until you break up with them, huh?"

"Guess not." She exhaled, and her breath was like smoke in the frosty air. "Anyway, what do you have going on today?"

"Not much. I convinced the judge in Charles Hill's trial to give me a couple weeks' continuance. The defense attorney was probably bouncing off the walls since he hadn't prepped him well for the stand." He looked back to Dax's car, pulling out of the lot and onto the street. "Grab lunch with me instead. I promise we can go somewhere we've been to before. We can start a tenth-of-the-month 'try something you've already had a million times' lunch."

She grinned. "You convinced me."

"I'll meet you back here at noon."

He turned to leave, and his cell phone buzzed. He recognized the number, coming from a defense attorney trying to work out a plea deal for his client who'd stolen a car from a rental agency. Solomon was about to answer when he got a text. It was his neighbor Angela.

Did you know your door was open? I closed it for you, but it was wide open

Solomon's guts tightened up into a ball. He summoned an Uber. "Extra twenty-buck tip if you get me there in less than ten minutes," he said to the driver as he got in.

14

The driver didn't get him there in ten minutes, but Solomon gave him an extra twenty dollars anyway. He got to the front entrance of his building and rushed to the elevator. He moved too fast, and his foot slipped out from under him. The cane caught his fall, but someone he hadn't seen, a woman he recognized from a get-together for the building tenants, hurried over and grabbed his arm, helping him straighten up.

"Are you all right?"

He felt the blush in his cheeks. "I'm fine. Just got ahead of myself. Thanks."

The elevator ride up filled him with dread. What would he do if Alonso was actually in his apartment?

His door had been shut but not locked. He opened it and stood at the entryway, listening. The sound of traffic couldn't pierce the high-end windows, and the apartment was quiet. He stepped in, suppressing the urge to ask if anyone was there. A couple downstairs had kids, and he had found them in his apartment once when he forgot to lock the door. They were too young to be malicious and instead were playing with his '80s VHS collection. Solomon gave them Dr Peppers and walked them back down to their apartment. But they were anything but quiet. They couldn't be still for this long.

He shut the door behind him, thinking he didn't want someone to escape, but then realized that wouldn't be the worst thing and opened the door again. He pressed his cane lightly against the floor. A creak came from his bedroom, and he tried to recall if the floors in there creaked.

His phone buzzed, startling him. It was Gesell. He sent the call to voice mail and opened a voice-recording app, just in case he needed a recording, and set the phone on the counter. It was only now, standing here with the light from the hallway as his only illumination in a darkened apartment, that the fear really set in. The realization that he'd had a knee-jerk reaction and acted impulsively, almost like an animal that rushed toward another animal that wandered into its territory. At least he'd had the clarity to text Billie and ask if she would send a patrol over.

Solomon took a few steps in and looked behind the counter in the kitchen, making sure no one was ducking down back there, even someone as big as Alonso.

The only rooms left to hide in were the bedroom and bathroom. He went to the bathroom first. Using his cane, he slid open the shower curtain. Nothing.

The bedroom was large and the door wide and thick. The building was old, and he wondered how much of its construction had war in mind when it was made. He'd read an article once that many buildings dating from the '70s were built with the idea to try to protect residents during a nuclear blast. Though what thicker doors and double-reinforced beams would do to negate an atomic explosion, he didn't know.

"Hello?" he finally said.

It was cold, but the sun was out, shining through the windows in the bedroom and lighting up his bed. He examined the hardwood floors, hoping he could see a shoe print if there were any.

A knock came from his front door, making his heart jump. Two deputies stood there, one male, one female, both in beige sheriff's department uniforms. The woman smiled and said, "Solomon Shepard?"

"Yeah, thanks for coming by. I was just having a look around."

The male looked annoyed and said, "I'll look with ya."

The male deputy began briskly going through the apartment. Solomon wondered what Billie had called him away from that he was so bugged about leaving. With the last name Call on her uniform, the woman said, "The sheriff said you've had someone maybe stalking you."

"I don't know if *stalking*'s the right word. He's shown up to a couple places I've been at. I think he's trying to rattle me."

"You're a prosecutor, right?"

"I am."

"Well, we gotta take these seriously. If people got the idea that they could scare law enforcement without any repercussions, it would make our job a hundred times more dangerous."

The other deputy came back around and said, "All clear. Did you leave the door unlocked?"

"Yeah, I guess I must've."

"This building have a camera?"

"No, the older residents like their privacy and had it removed."

He nodded. "Well, there's nothin' here now. What about a neighbor snooping around?"

"My neighbor's an eighty-year-old woman, and she's the one who told me it was open. There's some kids one floor below I caught playing up here once. Might be them. I'll check with their parents."

The female deputy glanced around and said, "Well, don't hesitate to call us if you see or hear anything."

"I will. Thanks for coming."

"No problem. I'll let the sheriff know everything turned out okay."

Once the deputies had left, Solomon turned back to his apartment. He leaned against the kitchen counter and read a text Gesell had sent, asking him where he was. He was about to reply but instead went online and ordered a doorbell camera.

Fear stopped him immediately and turned his blood to ice.

Russ.

The cat was usually lounging on his sun-speckled bed. Solomon hurried in there and didn't see him.

"Russ? Russ, come here, boy."

He didn't know why he'd called out since the cat had never once come to him after being called. But Solomon did it anyway.

"Russ, you here, buddy?"

Solomon searched the entire apartment from top to bottom. Even pulling out the contents of his closets. Nothing.

He ran out into the hallway and went up and down to each neighbor, asking if they'd seen Russ. No one had. Then he went to the floor above and the floor below his. He went out to the fire escape, the small garden attached to the building, and then the front entrance, calling out Russ's name.

His fear and dread slowly morphed into anger. He summoned a car and then paced impatiently while he waited for it to arrive.

15

Solomon got out of the car in front of the Buena Vista motel. The two-story building looked run down, and the parking lot was cracked, chunks of concrete lying out in scattered piles. A dumpster overflowed near the back, and some kids played nearby. They gave Solomon suspicious glares as he strode past.

The address he'd gotten from Alonso's parole officer listed him as staying in room 2C. Solomon climbed the stairs and found the room. Two large windows looked in, and they were closed with curtains. Solomon pounded on the door and took a step back.

Alonso answered, wearing a red polo shirt and slacks. He was so large that Solomon couldn't see the top of his head, and he had to duck to step outside, forcing Solomon to take another step back and push himself into the railing.

"Come to shoot the shit, Counselor?"

"Where is he?"

"Who?"

"Don't bullshit me. Where's my cat?"

He chuckled. "Your cat? How the hell am I supposed to know where your cat is?"

Solomon took a step toward him. "This is over the line."

"I don't know what you're talkin' about. I been here all day."

Solomon attempted to swallow down his anger. He took a step back against the railing again and said, "What's the endgame? Why do all this? You'd have to be an idiot to land yourself back in lockup after you just got out, and there's a lot of things I would say about you, but *idiot* isn't one of them."

Alonso reached back to a table and ashtray in the room and lifted a lit cigar. The earthy scent wafted into the air, and he blew a ring of smoke into Solomon's face.

"I tried to see my son, and my parole officer wouldn't let me. Said they've moved on and don't want contact with me. Did you know that?"

"No."

He inhaled from the cigar and, this time, blew it out through his nose. "I talked to his mama on the phone. He was eight when I went in. He's a man now. A junkie living on the streets somewhere in San Francisco. He needed his daddy, and his daddy wasn't there."

"You beat that man to within an inch of his life. He had kids, too, and had to go on disability because he couldn't work to provide for them anymore. You deserved your eleven years. That's not on me."

He nodded and leaned on the railing. "Our bodies ain't meant for constant stress. You need to control that temper a' yours."

"My temper? You haven't even seen my temper yet. And if my cat isn't returned to me in one day, I'm coming after you."

"You threatening me, Counselor?"

"Yes."

Solomon left without looking back.

"You're kidding me," Billie said over her burger.

Solomon shook his head and took a bite of fries, though he wasn't hungry. "If he hurt Russ . . ."

"That's idiotic if he has. Your door was open. I'm sure he just ran out, and cats have a tendency to come back. We'll find him."

"Maybe that's all he did: open my door and let him escape." Solomon leaned back and took out an old pen he kept in his pocket. He chewed on it as he said, "He wants to get inside my head but stay within the bounds of the law. He knows if I had anything on him, I could get his parole revoked."

"I'm going to pay him a visit."

"It won't do anything."

"Won't hurt."

Solomon exhaled and looked down at the food. The thought of eating made him nauseated.

"Solomon, we'll find him, I promise. I'll get a couple deputies, and we'll go around your neighborhood."

"They have better things to do than find my cat. I'll go search as soon as we're done."

"You could've canceled lunch if that's where you want to be."

"You kidding? I wouldn't miss our monthly 'I've eaten it a million times' lunch."

She put her burger down. "I'm clearing my schedule. Let's go."

"You don't have to."

"What are friends for?"

A light snow had started falling, and the sky turned gray. Solomon wore a black overcoat, and Billie had on a puffy blue North Face jacket. They walked through Solomon's neighborhood, paying particular attention to alleys with dumpsters in them, which were few. A small park was nearby, and they went there and called out Russ's name. A stream was behind the park, and Solomon got a hit of panic at the thought that Russ might have fallen in. He'd never shown any interest in going outside the apartment and probably didn't know how to avoid getting hurt.

They stopped at an intersection and waited for the walk signal. Billie had specks of snow on her eyelashes, and they didn't fall off when she blinked, so she wiped them with the back of her hand in a way that reminded Solomon of a child. He wondered what she had been like in youth and if they would have gotten along. Most of his childhood was a test of isolation. But it had made him come to see isolation as a gift. It allowed a person to think through problems that required energy to solve. Thoughts, he had always believed, were just energy, and to work through a problem was a matter of putting in the right amount of energy.

He contemplated this as they crossed the street. The problem of Alonso Hafeez. How much energy would it take to solve this problem? Whatever it was, he wasn't sure he had enough.

After hours of searching, they were back at Solomon's apartment building. Evening was falling, and the darkness was coming quickly. The streetlights were on, and snow drifted into and out of the yellow beams.

"I'm sure he'll come back," Billie said. "We had a cat when I was a kid gone for three days and then wandered back. We have no idea where he went or what he did."

"Yeah, well, we won't make any progress in the dark anyway. I really appreciate you helping me."

She brushed some snow off his hair. "We'll find him."

Solomon looked out at the darkening streets and didn't answer.

16

The next day, Solomon woke without an alarm and got dressed. He went outside and was grateful it had stopped snowing, though it was still piled at the curbs from the plows. The sun was out, and the cars driving by made a pleasant whooshing sound on the wet streets.

He circled the neighborhood again and then went to the park, a little farther out than he and Billie had the previous day. He asked a group of kids if they had seen an orange tabby cat. They said they hadn't.

When his leg began to bother him, he called an Uber.

Most weekday mornings, he stopped at Bagel n' Things Café and got the same breakfast: eggs Benedict drenched in Tabasco sauce. When he was a kid in foster care, one family he'd stayed with gave their foster kids—of which they had several to collect the monthly checks the state sent them—food that was left over or old. Solomon had learned to soak the food in Tabasco sauce to get it down. The habit had stuck with him.

The café was packed, and he waited in line to get a table. Seated near the front with an empty plate in front of him was Alonso.

"Counselor, we really do have to quit running into each other. People will get the wrong idea."

Solomon ignored him. He could tell Alonso had been there awhile from the crusted food on the plate. Waiting for him.

Solomon left the café without getting anything.

Alonso had been watching him. That didn't disturb him; what bothered him was that he hadn't noticed. Alonso wasn't exactly someone who blended into a crowd. So the fact that he had been able to watch Solomon undetected didn't sit well with him.

Solomon took an Uber to the sheriff's station. The driver asked him what was wrong.

"I'm sorry?" he said.

"You look anxious."

Solomon said, "That's just always how I look."

"If you say so."

The driver dropped him off right in front of the building, and he went inside. He went to Billie's office, and she looked up from some paperwork and said, "Hey."

"Hey."

He lay down on the couch and stared up at the ceiling tiles. A few sharpened pencils were stuck in the holes. His goal was to fill all the holes in a single square.

"You look like hell," she said.

"Thanks."

"Didn't sleep?"

"Nope." He took a pencil off her desk and tossed it at the tiles. It didn't hit a hole and fell back onto his stomach. "I haven't eaten. Wanna grab a bagel or something?"

"Sure. Lemme just finish this one thing."

When she was done, they went outside to go next door. A bagel place catered to the police by selling pastry bagels; a substitute for doughnuts, Solomon figured.

They spotted Alonso Hafeez standing against a black Cadillac as they got outside. Sheriff's deputies and court personnel made their way around him and into the buildings.

"What the hell are you doing here?" Solomon shouted. He went up to Alonso and shoved his chest with one hand.

"Easy, Counselor. I have an appointment with my parole officer."

"Bullshit."

Billie grabbed Solomon's arm. "Come on, Solomon," she said, not taking her eyes off Alonso.

Solomon started backing up as Billie pulled him away. "Stay away from me, Alonso. Last warning."

When they were far enough away that Alonso couldn't hear, Billie said, "What are you doing?" Her voice was seething.

"What? You've seen it. He shows up everywhere I am."

"You were trying to goad him into a fight."

"I wasn't."

"Don't lie to me. I'm on your side."

Solomon breathed out through his nose and looked back to Alonso, who still leaned against the car. "Okay, maybe I was. And the fact that he didn't do anything isn't good."

"Do anything? We're in front of the sheriff's station. What do you think he's going to do?"

He leaned on his cane. "I don't know. Snap."

"He's really in your head, isn't he?"

He glanced back. Alonso had moved away from the car and was headed into one of the buildings. He held a door open for a young woman with a child and then winked at Solomon before going inside.

Without looking at her, Solomon said, "Billie, I need you to do me a favor."

17

After a couple of brief court appearances, Solomon met Gesell in front of the sheriff's station. She hugged him and said, "Are you sure we have to do this, Solomon?"

"It needs to be done."

"He didn't really do anything."

"Doesn't matter. We can pull him in for the lineup and see if we can bring charges later. Maybe for trespassing or something. At least for the threat of sawing your head off."

"He wasn't trespassing, though."

"We'll worry about it later. You just have to show a bully you're not scared of them."

He walked her through the station and to the back, where they held the lineups. The room was dark, and the detective Billie had asked to help him out, a man named Hirsch Johnson, was already there.

Johnson looked at Gesell and said, "You ready?"

"I guess so," she said, glancing at Solomon. "You sure they can't see me?"

Johnson shook his head. "No. And we don't need to tell him what he's in here for, so he'll have to guess." He pushed an intercom button on the wall and said, "Let 'em in."

A door behind the glass opened, and several men were brought in. Some were white, and one was Asian, though all were tall.

"Seriously?" Solomon said to Johnson.

"If you know a lot of seven-foot-tall Middle Eastern guys who live in Tooele, Utah, let me know next time."

Gesell folded her arms. "Obviously, that's him."

Johnson said, "Which one?"

"Number four."

"That's the man outside your house two nights ago?"

"Yes."

Johnson hit the button. "Take 'em back," he said.

He looked at Solomon as he said, "Well, you're the prosecutor. What do you wanna charge him with?"

"Trespassing."

"All right," Johnson said. "I'll cite him. I can make the paperwork go slow and hold him until tonight if you like."

"I would. Anything that rattles him. He needs to know I'm willing to push back."

"Not for nothing, Counselor, but I don't think a guy like that much cares about guys like you pushing him back."

Before Alonso was out of view, he peered at the glass with a smirk, and though Solomon knew he couldn't see him, the look still gave him a ball of cold tension in his chest.

"Come on," Solomon said to Gesell, "I'll walk you out."

When they were at the car in the parking lot, Gesell held his hands and looked down to the backs of them. Then she ran her thumbs over the skin and said, "You have soft hands. Not a worker's hands."

Her ex-husband had been a construction foreman and a rough-and-tumble hunter and ex–football player. The fact that she was comparing their hands gave Solomon a slight tinge of insecurity.

"This man, he's really dangerous, isn't he?"

Solomon had tried to calm her fears, but without knowing what Alonso wanted, he wasn't sure he should do that. Better for her to be prepared than calmed.

"Yeah, he is."

"Is he going to try to hurt me and David?"

"I don't think so. All he's done so far is try to scare me."

"Is it working?"

"Yes."

She glanced at a police officer walking by. "What does he want?"

"I don't know."

"Solomon, if you need to leave for a while, I understand."

He shook his head as he looked down at her hands. They weren't wrinkled, and the nails were shiny from polish. He ran his index finger gently over a scar on her thumb. "It wouldn't do anything. He would find me. But I think it might be best if we . . ."

"What, took a break?" she said with a grin. "He was already at my house, remember? He knows we're a couple."

"I don't know what else to do. I mean, your dad has that ranch near Wendover. Maybe it wouldn't be the worst idea for you and David to go there for a while."

She let go of his hands and folded her arms. "Do you really think it's come to that?"

He nodded. "He'll slip up and get his parole violated. It's just a matter of time. Until he does, I think that would be best."

She nodded. "Okay. If that's what you think."

"There's . . . um, something else."

"What?"

"I want you to carry a gun with you everywhere you go. I can take you to the range to teach you how to use it."

"What? Are you crazy? I'm not carrying around a gun."

Solomon leaned on his cane and felt the smooth silver of the handle in his palm, a usually calming sensation that wasn't working.

"Gesell, I've seen what this guy does to people. We found a body in a warehouse once. A guy that owed him money and refused to pay. He had his hands cuffed behind his back and a tire soaked in gasoline around his neck before it was lit on fire. The rubber melted into his face as it killed him. And there wasn't a shred of evidence linking Alonso to the killing. But I knew it was him, and *he* knew that I knew. This is all a game to him."

She didn't say anything. He almost never talked about his work around her, and now he was reminded why.

"If anything happened to you . . . ," he said.

She let out a breath and looked at the horizon. The sun reflected off the snow in sharp pinpoints of light. Solomon thought she looked beautiful in the afternoon sun, the way her skin and hair shone, the sparkle in her eyes. Eyes that held a sadness now that it pained him to see.

They held each other's hands a long time in silence before she said, "What do I need to do to get a gun?"

18

Solomon sat on a bench in the county justice building, trying to read a book on Carl von Clausewitz, the author of *On War*, a title that he knew was required reading at West Point.

Clausewitz hated Napoleon but studied him intensely and even called him a genius. He admired him and hated him simultaneously and derived a lot of his theories on war from Napoleon rather than the ancient generals like Hannibal and Alexander the Great, which was the traditional education for a Prussian general at the time.

Admiration and hatred.

Solomon had never had those two emotions involved with a single person before, but Alonso came close. He was psychotic and shouldn't have been loose in society, but he was also intelligent and a self-made man. Growing up in an apartment with no power or hot water, surrounded by nothing but drugs and gangs, he managed to pull himself out and get into college, where he graduated with perfect grades. Then he applied the business and economics principles he learned in college to the streets.

A bookstore wasn't far from the building, and Solomon walked there now, enjoying the crunch of snow underneath his shoes. He got some Dostoevsky and sat at a table with a coffee and sipped slowly as he read. None of the words would penetrate. Like reading a cereal box.

His mind was elsewhere—on Alonso, on Gesell, on Russ—and only his eyes were reading.

When it finally started getting dark, he left.

The bar was called the Ex-Wife's Place, a dive frequented by cops that wasn't far from the Justice Center. Solomon went inside. He leaned his cane against the bar and sat on a stool. The bartender, a young woman in a tank top with her left arm sleeved in tattoos, smiled at him.

"What're you having?"

"Just a Heineken, please."

The bartender put a bottle in front of him and popped the top.

"I've seen you before," she said. "You work with the city police, right?"

"No, I'm a prosecutor. I can't be a cop. It's the uniforms. I look more like I should be running a ride at the county fair than enforcing the law."

She chuckled as she wiped the counter down. "So, how's your day been treating you?"

"Like a baby treats his diaper. Yours?"

"About the same."

It took less than half an hour for Alonso to walk in. He got a table near the front and didn't look around. A cocktail waitress exchanged a few words with him and then went behind the bar.

"You know that guy?" he said to the bartender.

"Who?"

"Big guy that just sat down. Near the front."

"No, never seen him before. Why?"

"He keeps staring at you."

"Can't stop people from staring."

Solomon took a sip of beer and put the bottle down. He let out a slow breath in anticipation of what was coming.

"I don't like the way he's looking at you," he said as he rose. He got his cane and went over to the table. Alonso put a cigar between his lips but didn't light it as he leaned back in the booth.

"You wanna join me for a beer, Counselor?"

"Quit staring at her," he said loud enough for people at the next booth to hear.

"At who? The bartender? Who's she to you?"

"None of your business."

He looked over at her. "She ain't bad. She a little side thing you got goin' on?"

"I told you to stop staring at her," Solomon said, stepping closer.

The waitress came over and set Alonso's drink on the table and said, "A seven and seven with a glass of water."

"Thank you." He lit the cigar.

Solomon knocked his drink over, and the whiskey and water splashed onto Alonso's clothes.

Alonso rose to his full height, towering over Solomon like a colossus. Anger filled his eyes, and his face contorted unnaturally. Then it softened, and he laughed.

"Oh, shit," Alonso said with a smile. He sat back down. "You're not pulling me into anything, Counselor."

Damn it.

Solomon leaned on his cane. He glanced around. Several tables were checking out the commotion. Now would've been a perfect time for Alonso to hit him. Assuming he survived the blow, he would make sure his parole was violated.

"Go home, Counselor. You're not getting what you want."

"Neither will you."

He blew out a puff of smoke. "Don't bet on it."

19

Billie was sitting at her desk when one of her detectives, Johnson, walked in wearing an ugly green sweater with Santa Claus on it that she knew his daughter had given him.

"Sheriff, we got something on the guy that got pancaked against his—"

He glanced up from the papers he had in his hand and saw the look she was giving him. Then he cleared his throat and said, "We got something on Mark Webb, the victim killed at his home."

"What is it?"

"A neighbor. I guess she heard Mark mention something to his accountant on the phone about someone getting out of prison he was worried about. An Alonso . . ."

"Hafeez."

"Yeah, that was it. Hafeez. The one ID'd in the lineup."

"Why was he worried about him?"

"I don't know. I'm heading over there right now to speak with the accountant."

Billie thought a moment. "I'll go."

"Why? I can take care of it."

"No, I want to go. I'll record it for you. You go have a long lunch with that beautiful little girl of yours."

"Don't have to tell me twice."

Billie got the name and address and then put on a black jacket and a scarf. She went out to her truck and was surprised at how much colder it had gotten since the morning. The weather in the Tooele Valley sometimes seemed to work in reverse, with the mornings warmer than the afternoons.

The building was in an office park near an empty lot where a strip mall was going up.

Another strip mall, she thought. The libraries were all closed, and the nearest one in Salt Lake was half an hour's drive away, but strip malls seemed to be filling every space where a store could fit.

The building looked clean but old and had no signage indicating what it was.

The accountant had an office on the second floor overlooking the parking lot on one side and the back lot on the other. A busy street wasn't far from the entrance, and the sound of cars speeding past was loud. There was no receptionist, just an open door into a front area with a few chairs and an office in the back.

The accountant wore a tracksuit and had a calendar up of women in bathing suits.

"Are you Filip?" she asked.

"Yeah."

She showed him her shield, and he stopped what he was doing and leaned back in the seat. Then he reached over to a drawer and took out a business card, laying it on the desk in front of her.

"Call my lawyer. Now please leave unless you got a warrant."

She picked up the card. "Wow. You've been through this before, haven't you?"

"I asked you to leave."

"You must have a fascinating client list."

"One of a kind. And I don't talk about any of 'em. So feel free to see yourself out."

She held up the card and grinned. "Right. Thanks for your time."

As she walked out, she could feel the man staring at her.

Billie waited in her truck for the information she had requested from her assistant. She got it within five minutes.

As a kid running around the sheriff's station, she learned a lot about law enforcement, and she remembered how getting information—even something simple like running a license plate—could take hours or even days. Some of the old-timers in the department couldn't keep up with the speed of technological innovation in law enforcement, and she'd seen a lot of early retirements the past couple of years, even though the work was more efficient now.

The address for Filip's former employee, of which he had only one, an assistant who quit last year, was one town over in Grantsville. Billie started the truck and headed to the freeway.

She found the townhome just off the interstate and parked outside. A playground was nearby, and she watched a few children swinging. Once, she had contemplated what a life with children would be like, but something was always there that told her it wasn't for her. No matter how much she had tried to convince herself that it was something she wanted, a voice told her it wouldn't happen.

Then, at the age of twenty-three, she found out she couldn't have children even if she'd wanted to. At the time, the news didn't seem to affect her, but now, it was something she thought about almost every day. A weight around her neck that was too heavy to lift.

She knocked on the door of the ground-level condo and waited. Lucinda Herrera didn't have a listed place of employment, and Billie hoped she wouldn't have to camp out here until Lucinda came home.

A woman in a sleeveless print shirt and shorts answered the door, though it was probably forty degrees outside.

"Lucinda Herrera?"

"Yes," she said with a hint of an accent.

Billie showed the badge. "Do you know why I'm here?"

Lucinda stared at her for a second. "Come in."

The home was decorated with religious icons and smelled like peppermint. Lucinda led Billie to the kitchen table.

"Is it about Filip?" Lucinda said.

"Good guess."

"I been waiting for the day the police show up at my door. The man was more a thief than the thieves he was helping."

"I'm guessing by the reception I received at his office his clients aren't the type to go to normal accountants."

She shook her head. "Unless you think human traffickers and pimps go to normal accountants. That's his bread and butter. People that can't go to no normal accountants. And I mean, some of 'em are straight-up psycho. I felt like someone was gonna come in shooting one day at the office."

"Is that why you quit?"

"That and he has a crazy temper. But he pays well."

"I'm guessing you know a lot about the inner workings of the tax side of things, but honestly, that's not my avenue. It's not why I'm here."

"Why you here then?"

"There's one particular client of his I'm interested in. Marcus Webb. Do you know him?"

Her smart watch vibrated, and she glanced at it as she said, "Yeah, I remember him."

"What can you tell me about him?"

Lucinda shrugged and said, "I only met him two times. He was nice."

"What type of business was he doing with Filip?"

"I don't know. Some people would come in, and you knew they were just dirty, and other people come in, and you know they're legit. Filip isn't a bad accountant. He's just greedy. I thought Mark was one of the legit ones. I think him and Filip used to hang together when they were kids."

"Did Filip ever have dealings with a man named Alonso Hafeez?"

"I don't know. That doesn't sound familiar. But honestly, there were so many people coming through I don't remember them all after this long."

"You'd definitely remember him." She thought a moment. "Lucinda, would it be possible for you to get me access to his client list?"

She had gum in her mouth and chewed for a moment. "What's in it for me if I do it?"

"What do you want?"

She checked her watch again and then leaned back. "My boyfriend, Sean, is in county lockup for some bullshit car-burglary charge. They hardly even took anything, like some cash and an old iPhone. The judge hates him and set the bail so high I don't have enough to get him out. You get him outa lockup, and I'll get you Filip's client list."

When Billie was back at her office with the client list Lucinda had given her, she had to take a break and rub her temples. Lucinda had a copy of all of Filip's files that she'd made the day she quit, probably in anticipation of exchanging them for some special favor from law enforcement. Her boyfriend was awaiting trial for six counts of vehicular burglary, but the amount taken was less than a thousand dollars. Not a huge case. Billie got him out with one phone call. Sometimes you had to help the little fish to get the big fish.

The reams of printouts had begun to blur. She hadn't become a cop because she was good at math. The printouts explaining who the client was, their assets and liabilities, amortization tables, and portfolio analyses with their goals hardly made sense. Like the brilliant, unethical accountants the big Wall Street investment banks and the Mafia hired, Filip wrote in a shorthand only he could understand in case his files were ever confiscated by law enforcement.

What she could piece together wasn't much, but she did figure out that the investment numbers were likely accurate.

The investment she was most interested in was Mark Webb's first. Her father had told her once on investigating white-collar crime to always look at the first transaction of anyone being investigated. Of course, they could have investments later that legitimately made them money, but how did they get there when they initially didn't have any money?

Webb's first property was an apartment building that required a down payment of $100,000. Where could someone who had a criminal history and couldn't get a traditional loan go if they needed that kind of money?

A small fridge was behind the desk, and she took out a Diet Coke. Some ibuprofen was in a drawer, and she popped several and then leaned back in her seat with a sigh. Gently turning the can in her hands, she focused on a space on the wall as she thought. Finally, after a minute, she put the can down, got her jacket, and left.

The motel was run down and far out of the city. Someplace where sex offenders who were ordered to stay away from children could go and live in relative peace without worrying about constant arrest. Alonso's room was on the second floor. No one answered. As she was leaving, a black Cadillac came to a stop in front of the building. The man inside glanced up at her and got out.

He was massive, easily dwarfing the tallest person she'd ever known, a basketball player who lived in her neighborhood growing up.

He had a prodigious belly and a thick beard with a cigar pressed between his teeth. She went downstairs and met him at his car as he lit the cigar.

"Howdy, Sheriff."

"You know who I am?"

He pulled deeply off the cigar, his eyes on her, before letting the smoke out. "Maybe. Or maybe it's that big-ass billboard you got on the freeway for your reelection."

He twisted one way and then another with a scowl, and his back sounded like dry cereal being crushed.

"Back injury," he said as he noticed her curiosity. "Played college ball one year and broke my back. Huge Samoan dude hit me from behind and took me down."

She leaned on the railing across from him. "Is that why you never went to the NFL?"

"Can't run with the ball if you can't run. Ain't that just life, though? You let your guard down for a second, and fate takes it all from you."

He held the cigar between his fingers and used it to point at her. "I know you, Sheriff. Not just from your billboard, neither. I knew your father."

"How?"

"He's been arresting my ass since high school. He took me for a burger once when he nabbed me for shoplifting. He's a good man. How's he doin'?"

"He's retired."

"Well, shit, I gotta send him a gift then."

"You don't hold any resentment for him arresting you that much?"

"Far as I can tell, he was just doing his job."

"So was Solomon."

He chuckled. "I like your balls. You must be really brave or really stupid to come out here by yourself. The people here, they're the people society throws away. The people y'all want out of your lives but can't just kill. If something were to happen to anyone out here, no one would see anything, no one would hear anything. Silence."

"You couldn't be stupid enough to be threatening the sheriff to her face."

"Not at all. I'm telling you how much I admire you. Not like that cockroach you spend your time with that locked me away."

"You seem like you could've taken care of yourself inside. Was it really as bad as that?"

"There's not much anyone can do when six jacked dudes run into your cell while you're sleeping." He lifted his shirt. "They tried to set me on fire."

He had looping scars over his belly and chest that went up to below his neck. Though he had a thick layer of fat, she could see striations under the scars from the bulging muscles. He looked like he could lift a car.

She noticed notches on his pectoral muscles: scarring from sharp instruments.

"What do you want, Sheriff? You didn't come here to shoot the shit."

"How do you know Mark Webb?"

"Don't know anyone by that name."

"You sure? Because someone told me you do."

"Then they're lying." He took a drag off the cigar and then blew it out in a ring of smoke before sucking the smoke back in and letting it out through his nose. "Anything else I can help you with? I got a meeting to get to in a bit and wanted to get some sleep."

"With who?"

He grinned. "Have a drink with me, and I'll tell you all about it."

She saw someone look around the curtains of a room, and then the curtains slid closed when she noticed them. "What do you want with Solomon, Alonso? No bullshit."

"*Bullshit* . . . you know where that word came from? Bulls don't have good manure for farming. They eat weeds and grass, where cows only eat grass. Weeds got too much salt, and their manure is worthless. But the shit sellers used to mix 'em together 'cause they got paid by the pound. When people found out they got sold bullshit, they'd hang the dealer."

"Is that your business? Selling people bullshit?"

"If that was my business, I wouldn't be in business long, would I?"

She pushed off the railing and started heading to her truck. "Stay away from Solomon Shepard."

Alonso took the cigar out of his mouth and said, "You have yourself a good day, Sheriff," before heading to the stairs and up to his motel room. As she walked to her truck, she heard him shout, "Sheriff?"

She turned and saw him near his door.

"Lemme know if you change your mind about that drink."

20

Solomon finished his work and left. Court had been grueling today. An arraignment calendar where cases were just starting and offers weren't going to be made, so nothing could be resolved. There were three hundred cases on the calendar. They all consisted of defendants saying *not guilty* and Solomon making a note in a paper file. An assembly line.

He came out into the night air. Court hadn't concluded until almost seven, and the sky was dark. Winters in this part of Utah meant short days, sometimes shortened by several hours.

He had little food in his apartment, so he stopped at the Vietnamese café nearby and ordered pho with meatballs. The pho was hot, and the Tsingtao beer he'd ordered stung as it went down. He regretted that he had no one to share it with. Gesell was with her son, and he didn't want to intrude on their time. His introduction into David's life would have to be slow and careful. Gesell had told him the last man in her life had been cruel to the boy, jealous of the time she spent with him and her stout devotion to prioritizing her son above everything else. She cut the boyfriend out immediately, but it had made David cautious of anyone who cared about his mother.

Solomon grabbed tea from the local coffee shop and then walked the neighborhood when he was done. He pictured Russ, and then something his mother said ran through his mind: *He could be dying in a ditch somewhere.* Solomon had no recollection of what had inspired this comment. Possibly a neighbor's dog. But it was all he could think about now: Russ hurt and alone, wondering why Solomon wasn't helping him.

A cold wind blew. Solomon lifted his collar and walked until his legs hurt. Checking alleys and parks and behind businesses hadn't been fruitful. He'd read somewhere that the best place to search for a missing cat was in bushes because they were likely scared, and cats had an instinct to hide when afraid. The other alternative was that Alonso had done something to him, and that alternative was something that Solomon didn't want to think about.

The harsh winter had taken care of most of the bushes, turning them into slim, leafless skeletons, but he checked where he could, each time getting excited he would see Russ's face when he spread the branches apart.

He made it several neighborhoods over before glancing at the clock on his phone. It was almost eleven.

The walk back had been more painful than the search. With his spinal injury and the resultant dysfunction of his leg, walking for prolonged periods caused SI pain. It shot from his hips to his ankles and seemingly into his head, causing migraines no doctor could explain. Though he recalled getting headaches as a child, they'd become more pronounced since his injury.

His apartment building was a welcome sight, the warmth of the lobby feeling good. But when he got to his floor, he found Billie knocking on his door.

"Problem, Officer?" Solomon said, thinking she'd come over for one of their late-night Netflix sessions when one of them couldn't sleep.

"I've been calling you for two hours," Billie said.

"Turned my phone off. Rots your brain if it's on all the time." He noticed the look on her face, and her lack of reaction told him something was wrong. "What is it?"

"It's Alonso. Solomon, he's in the hospital."

"For what?"

"He was struck by a car."

Solomon unlocked his door. "Is he hurt?"

"Some deep lacerations and fractures. He claims the car struck him as he came out of a Walmart and crossed the parking lot. He managed to jump out of the way, but it caught his hip and sent him flying."

Solomon opened his door and flipped on the light as he went inside. "Probably someone he hurt before. If you sleep with dogs, you get fleas."

He turned to see she wasn't coming inside with him. "What is it? What's wrong?"

"He says you were the driver."

Solomon sat on his couch as Billie went into detail as to what Alonso had said. The car was an old Jeep, and he had said he'd gotten a clear view of the driver, though it was dark and he was farther out from the lights of the Walmart in the recesses of the lot. There were witnesses, a father and his son, who were going to their own car when they heard screeching tires and looked over to see a Jeep come careening through the parking lot like "a bat outa hell."

No one but Alonso claimed to have seen the driver.

"I don't understand his endgame," he said. "He's got to know nothing will come from this."

Billie looked down at her hands and didn't say anything, and Solomon knew what was wrong.

"You need to interview me, don't you?"

"Knox asked that we conduct a thorough investigation."

"Of course he did. How does he even know about it already?"

"I told him."

"You what?! Without coming to me first?"

"He's the county attorney. One of his prosecutors is accused of attempted murder. I had to let him know."

"You didn't *have* to. You *chose* to so you could cover your own ass."

Billie slightly tilted her head and took a breath. Whatever she was about to say, she chose not to and instead calmly replied, "That's not fair, and you know it. Everyone knows we're close. Can you imagine what it would look like if I worked this without telling anyone? I let Knox know and told him that I wouldn't be part of the investigation. That's it. That's my involvement."

"Tell me you don't believe I did this."

"Of course not. How could you even ask me that? But the fact is, he's in the hospital because someone tried to run him over, and last night at a bar, you assaulted him in front of witnesses."

He exhaled and ran his hands through his hair, letting them rest on top of his head as though he were too tired to move them again.

"Solomon, what the hell were you thinking?"

"I was trying to piss him off. He's got rage issues, to put it mildly. I thought if I could provoke him to hit me, I could get his parole violated."

"And what happened?"

"He didn't bite."

She took a moment to collect her thoughts. Then said, "I think it best if you come in."

"Come in? You mean be interrogated?"

"No, no one is interrogating you. The best policy is to come out in front of something like this and vehemently deny the allegations and maybe even grant an interview with the media before the story breaks. Tell them how Alonso has been stalking you and blames you for his prison sentence."

He shook his head. "I can't believe I'm hearing this from you."

"What do you expect me to say? First, you threatened him, and then he gets run over the next day. What would you think if this was a case on your desk you were screening?"

He put his face in his hands and rubbed before grabbing his cane and standing. "Fine. Let's get this over with."

21

The sheriff's station didn't appear as friendly as it usually did to Solomon, almost as though the lights were darker, the halls more ominous, the voices less jovial as he walked by. Billie led him to the back interview rooms, where a detective was standing with Knox. The glee on Knox's face disgusted him.

"Mr. Shepard, please have a seat inside," Knox said while barely holding back a smile.

He went past him into the small, claustrophobic room and sat down at the table. The detective, a man in a beige sport coat with a balding head, sat next to Knox across from Solomon. Knox interlaced his fingers and said, "Detective Andrews, would you please read Mr. Shepard his rights."

"I know my rights, Knox. Let's just do this."

"Very well," he said, leaning back. He nodded to the detective.

Andrews said, "Did you want a drink, Solomon? I can run and get—"

"Quit the good-cop/bad-cop bullshit and ask me about Alonso."

Andrews cleared his throat and said, "Mr. Shepard, do you know an individual by the name of Alonso Hafeez?"

"I do. I prosecuted him eleven years ago for the crime he went to prison for."

"And you're aware of Mr. Hafeez's accusations against you?"

"I am."

"Would you please tell us about your recent involvement with him?"

"I have no involvement with him. He was released from prison and has been stalking me. Showing up places or arriving a little after I get there."

"Has he made any direct threats to you?"

"No. The threats are in between the lines. You'd have to know him to understand them."

"Did you have any contact with him while he was in prison?"

"Absolutely not."

"Outside of prosecuting him for that crime some time ago, have you had any interactions with him?"

"Yes. For years, he was on the county attorney's radar—the previous county attorney's radar. But we couldn't build a solid case against Alonso because he'd intimidate cooperative witnesses. When I finally had a cooperative witness, he was furious he got convicted and clearly hasn't let that anger at me go."

Andrews glanced to Knox, who nodded. "Where were you this evening, Mr. Shepard?"

"What time?"

"About eight."

"Out for a walk."

"By yourself?"

"Yes. I recently lost a pet and was looking for him."

"What about before that?"

"At a café near my building eating dinner."

"And you can prove that?" Andrews said.

"You can verify the credit card transaction. But look, this isn't about evidence for him. He knows this will never stick. It's about harassment. I'm not the one that should be sitting here, Knox."

Knox said nothing, but a slight smirk came to his lips before he said, "Can you drive, Mr. Shepard?"

"Can I drive?"

"Yes. Are you, with your injury, physically capable of driving?"

"Yes, I'm capable of doing it. But I don't have a car."

"Did you have access to a car this evening?"

"No."

"You're sure?"

"Yes, I'm sure," he said with anger, "and I'm not going to sit here and be interrogated so you can get your rocks off, Knox. I'm leaving."

"You're not under arrest. You're free to go. But we'll have to note in the reports that the suspect was uncooperative. You know how bad that looks in the police reports, don't you, Mr. Shepard?"

There was a knock at the door, and Billie stuck her head in. "Knox, can I speak to you for a second?"

"Later," he said without removing his gaze from Solomon.

"Now, please."

Knox sighed, and they went outside into the hall. Solomon looked at Andrews, flipping through some papers in a file he had in front of him to avoid eye contact.

"You know it's bullshit, right?" Solomon said.

Andrews didn't respond. When Knox came back in, he looked frustrated, and Solomon wondered what Billie had said to him. He folded his arms and leaned against the wall before clearing his throat.

"Mr. Shepard, you're free to go. But you're on indefinite suspension from the County Attorney's Office until this matter is resolved."

"What? You can't do that. You need approval from the county council."

"I have approval. I emailed them as soon as I heard. Best to be on the up-and-up in this matter, wouldn't you say?"

He shook his head. "You want it to be true, don't you? You know I didn't do it, but you're hoping there's just enough evidence to get me fired."

Knox came over to the table and leaned down, whispering into Solomon's ear so the camera's audio wouldn't be able to pick it up.

"Don't kid yourself. I'm hoping there's enough evidence to lock you up for a long time, Solomon." He took a step back and straightened his tie as he said, "Don't leave the jurisdiction, if you'd be so kind."

Solomon used his cane to stand and stared at Knox, the mutual distaste for each other like an acrid fog that filled the room. Finally, Solomon brushed past him and left.

Billie was still there, sitting on a bench against the wall with her eyes closed, her head leaned back against the wall. When she heard the door open, she opened her eyes and stood. They both walked out without a word.

Once outside, Billie said, "I'll give you a ride."

In the truck, Solomon didn't speak. His thoughts whirled. Usually, it was like a storm of ideas that he could pick and choose from and then pursue the idea obsessively until he came to an agreeable judgment. Exchanging energy to solve problems. But there was no energy now, just exhaustion.

He hoped there wouldn't be charges filed like Knox wanted. Walmart had cameras in the parking lot that could have, fingers crossed, picked up someone else in the driver's seat. But if Alonso hired somebody to do this, he would've taken precautions. If there was nothing conclusive on the video, Solomon wouldn't be allowed to work, and if news got to the media, he would become a pariah in the legal community. He didn't need to be convicted. Just the allegation that he'd tried to kill a prior defendant would give other lawyers and judges pause before relying on him for anything. He'd be unemployable.

"You okay?" Billie finally said.

"Super."

"Dumb question. *Do you need anything* would have been a better one."

He shook his head but didn't turn his gaze from the window. "He's going to ruin my life, Billie."

"So, what do you want to do about it?"

"What *can* I do about it?"

They came to a stoplight. "I'm not going to stop looking into this. I think he killed Mark Webb."

"Webb? Why?" Solomon said, turning to her now.

"I'm not sure yet. But I'm thinking maybe Webb needed money for his first real estate deal and, as a convicted felon, had few options to get a loan."

"That was Alonso's favorite game. Loan money to a new entrepreneur who can't get a traditional loan and do it at insane interest they can't possibly repay. Then take a part of the business as payment. That way, he has money coming in every month forever instead of a onetime payment. If we could find a link between Alonso and Webb, it'd be enough for a warrant on Alonso's property and storage unit."

"I'll look into it, but you have to stay out of this, Solomon."

"You know there's no way I can."

"You have to. You can't be seen anywhere near this. And even if we did find anything, it would be tainted because of your involvement. So let me handle it."

She dropped Solomon off and said she would call him tomorrow. A light snow was falling, and the moon was out. After Billie left, he stood on the steps of his building for a few minutes and watched the snow. Snow immediately quieted a city. Was it something psychological? Some evolutionary relic that had human beings grow quieter when it snowed? Or was it something physical? Snow dampening sound and muffling the constant noise of a city?

He scanned the surrounding streets one more time and called out Russ's name.

Only the falling snow followed his words, so he turned to go inside the building. The sound of his cane was loud on the concrete steps.

22

Solomon awoke to pounding on the door. He found his cane leaned against the nightstand.

The pounding on the door didn't stop. Solomon contemplated getting his gun down from the shelf in the closet before looking out the peephole. A man with shaggy hair and a jacket that was wet at the shoulders stood there. The man waited a few seconds and then pounded again with the back of his fist.

"Can I help you?" Solomon said.

"Solomon Shepard?"

"Yeah."

"Got a rush delivery for you."

"From who?"

"Some court."

He unlocked the door and opened it but only as far as the chain would allow. The man stuffed a stack of papers through the opening and said, "You've been served."

Solomon watched him walk away and said, "You could've been polite and come a little later than six in the morning."

"Blow me."

Solomon shut the door and read the summons. Alonso had filed a request for an emergency protective order hearing, which was granted for this afternoon. The allegations were that Alonso needed an immediate protective order to ensure his bodily safety. The evidence listed included medical reports from the emergency room and a statement by the father and son witnesses in the Walmart parking lot.

Solomon couldn't sleep now and sat on the couch, watching the sunrise through the windows.

Another knock on the door. He quietly went over and looked out of the peephole.

Gesell was in her work clothes. Sometimes she came by before going to work, and they went to the bagel shop down the street or sat on his balcony and had tea. He didn't feel like being around anyone right now but opened the door anyway.

"Hey," she said. "Thought I would come by and check on you."

"Come in."

She came inside, placed her bag down on the leather recliner like she always did, and then sat on the sofa. Solomon sat next to her. He could smell her bodywash and the hint of strawberry-scented shampoo. He loved the way she smelled right after a shower.

More than any other sense, smell connected directly to the human unconscious and formed impressions that influenced the conscious. Someone might be repulsed by another person who might seem like a good match for them rationally. Usually, it was because scent had picked up something that the conscious mind hadn't.

He got the opposite sense from Gesell. A quiet comfort came over him when he was in the same room. But the comfort was shattered by the realization that she was in danger as long as she was near him.

"You shouldn't come by here anymore."

"Why?"

"If you're around me, he'll see you as a target, too."

"Too late for that."

"I don't want to fight. You need to listen to me so he—"

"No, you need to listen to *me*. I'm not going anywhere. I don't abandon people I love because having them around is a little hard."

She had never said she loved him before. The word hung in the air, and he didn't know how to react. Whether to say it back or ignore it and pretend it wasn't important. Unable to decide, he sat still as glass.

"Yes," she said, reading his discomfort, "I said *love*. I wish we could've talked about it in better circumstances, but I love you, so I'm here."

She had milk-white flesh with just a touch of red on the tip of her nose from the cold. Her lips were usually the color of raspberries, but she didn't have on any makeup today. Though lovely, she looked tired. Not frightened but tired.

They kissed, and he stood up. "Let's go."

"Where?"

"To get you a gun and show you how to use it."

23

Billie sat in her truck and waited for the car to pull into the home. Since childhood, Ricardo Duran's best friend, Hector Lopez, lived in the center of the city next to a dry cleaner and a thrift store. Billie thought she would have a tough time finding him, mainly because Duran's family didn't even have a phone number for him. So she had to go down the list of Hector Lopezes who lived in Tooele. Luckily, there were only two, and the other one was elderly.

A red car with a fin and bright chrome rims rolled to a stop in front of the garage as the door lifted. Hector looked over at her. He was pudgy with a goatee and brittle hair from gel or hair spray. Billie got out of the truck, and he rolled down his window.

"Hector?"

"Yeah."

"My name's Billie Gray. I'm the sheriff for Tooele County. I'm looking into the disappearance of Ricardo Duran. Do you mind if we talk?"

"Lemme pull in."

He parked the car. A door was in the garage with a few stone steps that led to the kitchen. Billie followed him up. The home smelled like floor polish and cinnamon, and Hector yelled out, "Yaya, I'm home."

An elderly woman's voice shouted, "I'm making dinner, don't eat anything," from somewhere in the house.

He motioned to the kitchen table with his head and then got two beers out of the fridge, popping them open before putting them down.

"You found him yet?" he said, taking a long pull after sitting down.

"No. That's why I'm here. His family has no clue what's happened to him or why. The one impression I got from them is that Ricardo would never run off and leave his kids."

He shook his head. "No way. No way he would do that. My homie's solid that way. Family before everything else."

"So, assuming he didn't run away, what do you think happened to him?"

He inhaled deeply and leaned back in the chair. She could see remnants of grease underneath his fingernails, though his hands were clean. "Some dude took him. That's for real."

"Who?"

He drank his beer and shook his head. "Don't know. He told me he messed up some Afghan dude inside, and he was gettin' out. He weren't scared, though. Ricky ain't scared a' nobody. Tough little homie."

"Did he mention any details about this man?"

He shook his head again. "Nah, he wasn't like that to bitch about somebody. He told me what the dude was in for, though."

"What?"

"Almost killed some guy that owed him money. Broke his back 'n' shit. Said the dude was huge—that's why Ricky messed him up. You gotta prove yourself inside when you small like Ricky was. He found the biggest dude and started some beef with him. Ricky used to box and can hold his own."

"Did he ever mention somebody named Alonso Hafeez?"

"Nah, I don't think so. I'd check with his girl, though."

"I was told he wasn't dating anybody."

"Yeah, but he still talk to his baby mama. People tell them things they don't tell their boys."

The warehouse was in the factory district near oil refineries and storage facilities, a stretch of desert between Tooele, Ogden, and Salt Lake City that some of the police called no-man's-land because of how barren it was. Dozens of bodies had been found buried here, dating from the '60s on up.

When the businesses were closed at night, the only light came from the flames on long cylinders jutting out of the refineries. Fire instead of artificial light. As though civilization had collapsed and people were back to using flames to see.

She drove past the dull gray deserts and watched tumbleweeds blow in a strong wind. The sky was the color of smoke, and snow had stopped falling only in the past hour. The cold wind made her truck rattle, and she was glad she had four-wheel drive because the road was slick as greased glass.

The warehouse sat on a vast stretch of land that had nothing else near it. Some organized criminal elements that ran legitimate businesses preferred the remote locations. Most modern organized crime had profit streams from lawful industries like alcohol, tobacco, and clothing, as these were easy to launder money through. But the businesses themselves, other than the accounting, ran like any other business, and most of the employees had no idea that a biker gang or Mexican cartel was the actual owner.

Billie parked and got out. The wind hit her like a burst of ice water. It made the exposed skin on her face burn. She bundled up her coat and hurried to the front entrance as bits of hard snow chipped at her flesh.

Inside, the warehouse had a front office and reception area before a hallway leading to the main floor. She could see several factory workers sorting clothing in front of a big machine that sifted the clothing and spun it around to the other side of the floor, where some other workers wrapped the articles in thin sheets of plastic.

A short woman in tight jeans walked over to meet her.

"Can I help you?" she said.

"I'm looking for Sheri Ali?"

"That's me."

"I'm Billie Gray. I'm the sheriff of the county. I was looking into the disappearance of Ricardo Duran and was told you might be able to help me."

She made a clicking sound with her tongue against her teeth. "Now you interested in help? When my ex wouldn't pay me child support, the police didn't do shit."

"I'm sorry to hear that. This was Ricardo?"

"No, I never married Ricardo. This is from who I was with before Ricardo."

"You have two kids with him, right?"

"One of them is from my ex, the other is Ricardo's."

"You know Ricardo's missing, right?"

"Yeah. His brother called me and asked about it."

"Do you have any idea where he could be?"

She shook her head. "He ain't never done this before. He loves those kids more than anything. He wouldn't leave them without tellin' nobody. Especially me. He's a shit boyfriend, but he's a good father."

"Sheri, I'm going to be honest. I'm at a loss of where he could be. One of my detectives checked with his cell phone provider, and they said his phone hasn't been used in three days. No credit cards have been used, his bank accounts haven't been touched, and nobody's heard from him. So after speaking with you, I don't really have any more leads to follow up on."

She shook her head. "He's a damn fool. Always fightin'. It's little-man syndrome. He always thinks he got something to prove."

"Have you heard of a man that served time with him named Alonso Hafeez? I was told Ricardo injured Alonso in prison."

"Yeah, he told me about him. Alonso was crazy AF."

"How so?"

"Ricardo said the guy didn't talk the entire time Ricardo was there. Just read books. And when people messed with him, he didn't do nothin', even though he was huge."

"Did he ever mention he was nervous about Alonso or that Alonso had contacted him?"

"No, he never said nothing about it. He wouldn't say nothing anyway. Ricardo always had to act gangster."

"Do you maybe know someone I should talk to that could have any idea where he is?"

She shrugged. "Other than his homies and his family, he don't have anything to do with anyone. Maybe he's got some hood rat somewhere, but he would've told his brother."

Billie nodded. "Well, thank you for your time."

Once Billie was in the truck, she called Solomon and told him what she'd learned.

"What I'm hearing about Alonso's time in prison," she said, "doesn't jibe well with how violent he is."

"He was focused on parole," Solomon said. "He didn't want even one infraction, to ensure he would get out as soon as possible. I would rather he be violent and uncontrollable than able to restrain himself so much he could take a beating without lifting a finger." He sighed. "So that's it on Duran?"

"I'm happy to talk to whoever you'd like me to talk to, Solomon," she said, annoyed.

"What about Webb?"

"I'm waiting for the neighbor's Ring camera video. It's from the house directly across the street, but the owner is an unpleasant man and has been fighting us tooth and nail to prevent getting that video."

"Huh. Must have something juicy on it."

"Maybe. Sometimes people are just curmudgeonly and don't want to help the police."

"Yeah, well, I'll hit him up."

"You will do no such thing. You can't be a part of this investigation in any way."

"Yeah . . . all right. Fine, I won't talk to him. But let me know what you find as soon as you get the video."

24

Solomon hung up the phone and reclined on his couch. He didn't like being home during the day. After his injury, he hadn't gone out, even to get food, preferring instead to have it delivered. Whenever he was home for prolonged periods now, it reminded him of that time. A time of his life when he had disconnected from everything and everyone, even himself. Maybe especially himself.

Alonso's emergency protective order hearing against him was in an hour.

When Solomon got to the courthouse, he said hello to a bailiff he knew, and they talked briefly about oil prices. Something Solomon neither knew anything about nor cared to. Still, he was polite and listened while the man railed against this or that politician for driving up energy prices. Finally, when the hearing was fifteen minutes away, Solomon excused himself and went to the courtroom.

Alonso was already there. He sat in a wheelchair at the plaintiff's table and had a massive brace around his back. His arm was in a sling, and deep lacerations over his face were held together with stitches and medical glue. With his gargantuan size, he looked like Frankenstein's monster.

Solomon knew the attorney he had hired, a young woman named Lisa. She was in a black suit with her hair pulled back, flipping through some photos of what looked like the parking lot at Walmart. She saw Solomon and came over.

"You look well."

"Thanks. I'd look even better if I was getting a smoothie right now instead of being in here explaining why I'm not a murderer."

She folded her arms and said, "I want you to stipulate to the protective order," like she hadn't heard him.

"I'm not stipulating to anything."

"You're going to lose."

"Yeah, but I'm going down fighting. Your client just wants to use it against me."

"Opinions differ."

She went back to the table, and Solomon saw that Alonso grimaced from pain. He wasn't sure if it was real or forced.

The judge was a woman near retirement who used to be a rancher, and Solomon remembered she always wore cowboy boots to court. The bailiff announced her, and she came out. She sat down, put on thick glasses, and smiled at Solomon and then Lisa and Alonso.

"Good afternoon, everyone. We are here for the matter of *Alonso Bashir Hafeez v. Solomon Joseph Shepard*, case number 2288872. The petitioner is represented by Ms. Lisa Scout. Mr. Shepard, do you wish to represent yourself in this matter?"

"I do."

"Excellent. Then let's get started."

It was customary for the petitioner, the person requesting the emergency order, to present their case first. Then the respondent addressed why there wasn't enough evidence to impose a protective order.

Lisa presented the Walmart crash and then put Alonso on the stand. He filled the witness box, as tall sitting down as Lisa was standing up.

Protective order hearings were informal affairs where the rules of evidence were whatever the judge or commissioner said they were. Few rules were codified, and it was done purposely by the legislature to ensure that all relevant evidence was heard. But since almost anything could come in, it was tough for respondents to win these hearings.

"Tell us about your injuries, Mr. Hafeez."

"I was coming out of the Walmart two days ago after I picked up some groceries. I was walking up the rows of cars when I heard tires behind me. I barely had time to do anything. I jumped outa the way, but it hit me in the right hip and sent me flying into some metal banisters they had, like one of those things where you return your shopping carts. That's what injured my face. Fractured my cheek and orbital socket."

"Did you see who was driving?"

"I did." He pointed at Solomon. "Mr. Shepard, right there."

"Why would he want to run you over?"

"Ever since I got outa prison, he's been hounding me. He wanted me in prison for life, but I got twenty years and was let out after eleven for good behavior, and if you'll excuse my saying so, Your Honor, he's got a real bug up his ass about me."

"Please don't use profanity," the judge said as kindly as anybody could.

"Sorry, Your Honor. This whole thing has got me messed up. I'm scared all the time. This morning I jumped when my phone rang. I think I'm probably going to have to leave town to be able to sleep at night. Mr. Shepard's got the power of the law behind him. I'm a poor man, Your Honor. I don't have much, and what I did have, I used to hire this fancy lawyer to make sure I could stay safe while I got enough money to move."

"May I show the Court some photos, Your Honor?" Lisa asked.

"Certainly," she said, holding out her hand. She took a moment to look at each photo and then introduced them into evidence herself, as was the custom in these sorts of hearings.

"Alonso, you said Mr. Shepard has been stalking you. What has he been doing?"

"At first, I didn't pay no attention to it. He would show up places I'd be at and things like that. But then it started getting worse, and he started comin' up to me and saying things. Then we were at this bar, and one witness from the bar is here today to testify if she needs to, but Mr. Shepard assaulted me and then threatened me that he would hurt me. I got hit by that Jeep in the parking lot that night."

"How did he assault you?"

"He hit me in the chest."

"I hope you don't mind my saying so, Mr. Hafeez, but you're massive. Mr. Shepard is easily half your size."

"I mean, I could beat him man to man, but so what? I'm on parole. Touching the prosecutor that put me away would revoke my parole and send me back. Mr. Shepard knows this. He's got all the power." He looked at the judge and said, "I wanna be a good man for my boy. I've got a son I haven't seen in eleven years. I served my time. I just want this behind me."

"Your Honor," Lisa said, "I have here the timeline of events, Mr. Hafeez's statement, and signed affidavits from six witnesses to the assault Mr. Shepard perpetrated against Mr. Hafeez. And I do have a witness on standby who observed the assault should the Court wish to hear from them."

The judge took the documents and read them while everyone waited. The bailiff helped wheel Alonso back to his place behind the defense table. The judge inhaled through her nose as she put the documents down and said, "Is that all, Ms. Scout?"

"It is."

"Mr. Shepard, would you like to address this Court, or do you stipulate to the imposition of a temporary protective order until an official hearing can be scheduled?"

"I would like to address this Court."

"Very well, please take a seat on the witness stand."

Solomon crossed the courtroom with his cane and sat down. When fresh out of law school, he would sometimes stick around the court after everybody left and practice his openings and closings, but he couldn't remember ever sitting in the witness chair.

He could see why witnesses were intimidated. Everyone in the courtroom who was there to have a hearing that afternoon looked directly at him. The bailiffs watched with disinterested glares. Lisa looked at him passively, and he knew she didn't believe what Alonso was saying but would still fight as hard as she could for him.

"What would you like to tell me, Mr. Shepard?"

"Your Honor, I understand that the bar for imposing a temporary emergency protective order is extremely low and that the evidence presented so far is enough to impose one, but I would ask the Court to issue a mutual protective order. Mr. Hafeez has a tendency for extreme violence and has been harassing me since he got out of prison. He blames me for the eleven years he spent incarcerated for nearly killing a man with a baseball bat. He showed up at my girlfriend's home and threatened to hurt her if—"

"Objection," Lisa said. "There's been no evidence presented as to any threats to any person outside of this hearing."

"Mr. Shepard, did you ask this witness for an affidavit or subpoena her to this hearing?"

"No, Your Honor. I don't want her involved."

"With no such corroborating evidence, I will have to disregard that last statement. Please continue."

Solomon took a second. Perhaps he should have asked Gesell for an affidavit, but the less she had to do with this, the better.

"I was simply stating that a mutual protective order would ensure that he couldn't, say, show up somewhere I happen to be and then call the police to say I've violated the order. If there's no mutual protective order, I would essentially have to lock myself in my apartment and not go anywhere to avoid such a scenario."

The judge listened passively, but a slight twitch of the corner of her mouth revealed a little anger at what Solomon had just said.

"Mr. Shepard, you're an officer of the court for the state of Utah. You know as well as anyone that mutual protective orders were prohibited in this state almost fifty years ago, and shame on you for suggesting such a thing. Do you have anything else to add, sir?"

"No."

"Then please have a seat."

When Solomon was seated, the judge said, "I am granting petitioner's request for an emergency protective order. The hearing will be scheduled sixty days hence. Until that time, Mr. Shepard, you are not to have any communication with Mr. Hafeez, including but not limited to text, telephone calls, social media, emails, or other such electronic or in-person communication. You are to stay at all times one hundred yards away from the person of Mr. Hafeez, and any third party, at your request, may not approach or communicate with him on your behalf. I am granting one exception to that order. If you choose to hire an attorney to represent you at the hearing, your attorney may have contact with Mr. Hafeez should his counsel wish to parley. Is that understood, sir?"

"Yes."

"Then we'll get the hearing on this scheduled. Thank you for your time. Next case, please."

25

Alonso sat on the outside patio of the burger joint and enjoyed the icy air that bombarded his skin.

After being locked up in a cell for twenty-three hours a day, he had spent as much time as possible outside since getting out. The most enjoyable time he'd had in the past eleven years was sitting outside a cabin and staring at a lake. Something his father would often do. A simple thing most people took for granted.

His father had been a peaceful man. Born in Kabul, Afghanistan, and having emigrated to the United States during the Soviet War, he'd seen enough slaughter and suffering to become a pacifist. He was a Sufi mystic who studied the Quran every day of his life and prayed so fervently he once pulled over on a busy freeway to get in his morning prayer. He tried to teach Alonso about the love Allah had for his children, and the respect that had to be shown nature as an extension of that love, but it had never stuck. The beauty of nature was lost on Alonso during his youth, and in some ways it still was.

Quiet was something different. Simply being somewhere with no other human beings around granted him a tranquility he couldn't get any other way.

The burger was juicy, and the sauce dribbled onto the table. He ate slowly and just enjoyed the flavors. Prison food was nearly inedible, and several times he had found worms or maggots festering in the meat. The prison got their beef at a discount from shady ranchers likely because it was already expired when bought.

A group of young men pulled up to the burger joint and got out of their car to go inside. One of the boys was massive. Not quite as tall as Alonso but easily six-five and wide. He wore a college football jersey and glanced at one of the tattoos Alonso had on his forearm. The tattoo was of Nemesis, the goddess of revenge, standing over a skeleton with her foot crushing its skull.

Alonso didn't need the wheelchair he was in. Still, just in case Solomon had hired a private investigator to follow him around, he used it to wheel over to the boys' car and looked at the license plate. His memory had been one of the strongest attributes he had since he was a child. Never, in the years he had been in the game, did he ever write anything down. He knew how much each borrower owed him down to the penny and never forgot.

"Whatchyu lookin' at?" one of the young men said. They were all near the entrance to the burger joint but not yet inside.

"Just admirin' your car," Alonso said.

"Yeah, what, you a cop?"

"Do I look like a cop to you?"

The taller boy looked to the one speaking and said, "Man, this fool ain't shit."

The boy who had been speaking lifted his shirt and revealed the handgun underneath. Alonso laughed, which was enough to give the boy pause.

Another one of the boys stepped in front of the boy with the gun and said, "Hey, man, chill. Chill! You wanna get locked up over this crippled fool?"

The calmer boy prevailed, and the other two relented. They'd turned to go back inside when Alonso said, "Hey, little man."

The boy turned to him.

Alonso took out the 9 mm handgun he'd tucked in a bag on the back of the wheelchair and clicked off the safety. He fired two rounds. Both rounds went into the vehicle's front right tire, and the car instantly lurched to the side.

The boys scattered, which made Alonso laugh even more.

He knew dangerous men. His entire life had been surrounded by dangerous men.

His mentor and employer growing up, Mr. Gerald, in addition to owning an oil refinery and several self-storage facilities, owned a bar, and Alonso was there as much as possible as a kid serving drinks for quarter tips. He liked the atmosphere of people with their inhibitions down, doing what they really wanted to do, acting how they wanted to act, defying society's expectations.

He'd seen drug deals, had his first sexual experience in the bathroom, and even witnessed a murder there. Some small-time hood had kicked a man to death in a bar fight. He remembered telling Mr. Gerald that he would call the police, and Mr. Gerald, in his croaky voice that sounded like he'd been smoking for decades, though he had never picked up a cigarette, calmly said, "We wash our own dirty laundry." The body was hauled away, and the episode was never spoken of again.

Growing up around Mr. Gerald and the thugs he always kept close had taught Alonso a valuable lesson: Truly dangerous men didn't threaten. They didn't lift their shirts to display weapons and put on a show. They smiled, nodded, and then struck when the victims least expected it. Those boys were little punks, and Alonso knew it instantly with just a glance. Still, he and the tall one were close to the same height, which was rare.

Alonso glanced at the license plate one more time, making sure he had it memorized.

26

The shooting range was outdoors on the top of a hill overlooking the city and mainly catered to recreational enthusiasts who wanted someplace scenic to shoot for an afternoon. Solomon and Gesell had spent time with the clerk finding the right gun for her and settled on a sleek black Smith & Wesson. They put on their goggles and ear protection and went out back to the range and found one other person there. A man with a buzz cut firing a massive semiautomatic rifle at a target at least fifty yards away and hitting the mark with each shot he took.

Solomon led her to the far lane and showed her the Weaver stance and how to breathe and let the kickback absorb into the body and out the feet to minimize the impact against the shoulder joints. He had taught himself how to shoot after becoming a prosecutor.

She held the gun, staring at the weapon like she didn't know what it was.

"I never thought I'd have to carry a gun. My parents were Woodstock hippies. They hated guns."

"I know," he said softly.

She exhaled loudly as though clearing her thoughts and said, "No use feeling bad for myself." She lifted the weapon. Solomon stood behind her to ensure she had the correct aim. He adjusted her stance a little, and then she fired. She fired again and again until the weapon clicked empty, and Solomon knew who she pictured as the target.

"That was good," he said, "but pick your shots. You don't want to empty the magazine and have the guy still coming at you. Two to the chest, two to the head, until the target goes down."

She nodded. "Two to the chest, two to the head. Got it."

Solomon had her reload the gun and then stood behind her as she took more shots. This time, it was better, spread out more evenly with the rounds going in the vicinity they needed to. But he could tell she was nervous. Her hands were trembling, and she chewed on her lower lip. If she panicked with someone as huge as Alonso running toward her, she could miss or hit only nonvital areas, and he would have the gun.

"Again," he said.

Gesell rubbed her wrists to alleviate the pain when they were done at the range. Then, as they sat at a diner and ordered lunch, she popped a couple of ibuprofen and stared at the bubbles in her Sprite, which would drift to the top of the glass and then pop in little explosions that made them disappear.

"You okay?" he asked.

She shook her head. "I just . . . you live this life in a bubble in small towns and think you're safe, that nothing will ever happen. So when something does happen, it feels like the entire world is falling apart."

"You have nothing to be scared of. I'm the target, not you. Everything we're doing is a precaution. Think of it as insurance. You always get the insurance."

"Yeah," she said with a forced grin, "guess you're right."

After lunch, Gesell dropped him off in front of his building and gave him a kiss. She tried to smile again, but it didn't contain any happiness or comfort, and he knew it. She was shaken, and it was his fault.

As he turned to go into his building, he saw something out of the corner of his eye. An enormous seated figure a couple dozen feet away. On the patio of the Vietnamese café a few buildings down, he could see

Alonso Hafeez staring at him. He smoked a cigar and blew the smoke out into the cold air, mixing it with his breath and making it look like he was breathing fire.

Neither of them moved. Solomon knew Alonso was thinking the same thing he was: that he was going to suffer, and the suffering had only just begun.

Solomon hadn't slept well the night before, so he tried to take a nap. It wasn't working, so he went to his bookshelf and searched for something to read. He settled on Sartre's *Being and Nothingness* and lay down on his couch.

He managed to read for an hour before his eyes drifted closed. He saw fields and sky and oddly knew he was dreaming inside the dream. The areas looked familiar, something from childhood he couldn't place. The sky was clear and blue, with a few white clouds drifting by. Screaming was somewhere behind him. High-pitched, bone-vibrating screaming that made his ears ring so loudly it hurt his face and jaw. But he didn't turn around; he didn't want to see where the screaming was coming from.

His phone woke him up with a start. The book was on his chest, and the phone vibrated on the glass coffee table. It was Billie.

"Hey," he said with a groan.

"You just waking up? It's like five in the afternoon."

"Yeah, well, I'm a night owl. What's up?"

"We found Ricardo Duran."

"Where was he?"

"In a lake."

27

The Great Salt Lake was the largest body of water in Utah, but the second largest was Chelsea Lake. A remnant of an ancient inland sea known as Lake Bonneville that had covered the state. The powerful waters of Lake Bonneville had carved the mountains in wide swooshes that made them look handcrafted rather than millions of pounds of rock thrown together randomly. Some were snowcapped all year, while others never had snow.

Solomon stood on the shore as Billie's team extracted the body from the water. Ricardo Duran had bloated to probably twice his size in life. The face was so deteriorated it was impossible to tell what he looked like. They could identify him only through dental records and tattoos, which were smeared on his loose skin like runny paint.

His flesh had been picked apart by something under the water, but Solomon couldn't think of anything that could survive the lake's salinity.

"Do you know the water here is the saltiest on the planet? Takes less than a cup to shut down your kidneys."

"It smells awful," Billie said. "Who would possibly drink it?"

"I'm sure back in the old West, people running from the law or something would be forced to stop here for a drink. I bet the bottom is littered with skeletons."

Solomon stared at Duran's body as the medical examiner's people worked it. The tire set ablaze around his neck had melted his face, revealing a charred skull underneath.

"That's a calling card if I've ever seen one," Billie said.

Solomon went to lean down closer to the body.

"Solomon, you shouldn't be close to any actual evidence," she said.

He understood Billie's reasoning, but it still bothered him, and he only reluctantly took a step back from the body.

The forensic techs were photographing and videoing the body, taking measurements and samples. The medical examiner himself, an older man with white hair named Jerry, was out here, which rarely happened. Most murders in Tooele County were drug deals gone bad, particularly methamphetamine, which seemed to be cooking in every trailer park in the county. A genuinely vicious murder that didn't involve drugs was a rarity and created curiosity hard for murder junkies to resist. After all, why else would someone become a medical examiner and constantly be with the dead if they didn't enjoy it?

As Jerry opened the mouth, gases inside the body were released and triggered the vocal cords, causing a heavy sigh from the corpse. The ME didn't flinch, but several deputies in uniform looked startled. Solomon could see where the myth of vampires came from: a medieval peasant with no scientific knowledge could easily conclude that the body was still alive. Staking it through the heart and cutting off its head would just seem like a logical move.

Jerry pulled several tiny organisms out of Duran's throat.

"What are they?" Billie asked.

"Brine shrimp," he said. "One of only a few species that can survive in the waters here. Looks like they made a nice little lunch out of him."

"What do you think you can get for me, Jerry?"

"Not much, Sheriff. I highly doubt any forensic evidence could survive this long with the salinity of the water being what it is."

"Even if you could only get the make and model of the tire, that would be huge."

"I'll see what I can do. No promises."

No promises.

The phrase ran through Solomon's mind as the putrid smell of the corpse mixed with the already disgusting rotten-egg smell of the hydrogen sulfide gas that the lake gave off. The algae took in the water's oxygen and then died, rotting in the thickly salted water, and the bacteria gave off the smell. It was strong enough to be gag inducing, and several deputies and forensic techs seemed to be hurrying through their jobs to leave as soon as possible.

Solomon didn't move. He needed to smell this, the smell of death.

No promises.

"Hello, hello," Jerry said. "What do we have here?"

He pulled out a crimson strip of cloth from Ricardo Duran's throat. It was shoved deep inside, probably to protect it from the flames of the tire that would melt the rest of his flesh.

"What is that?" Billie said.

Jerry shook his head. "No idea."

"It's for me," Solomon said. Everyone looked at him, and blood flushed his face as he felt their gazes on him like laser beams. "It's a Druid custom. Before a war with neighboring tribes, the Druids would kill the scouts and leave the bodies near the village with red cloth shoved in their mouths. A warning to the village."

"What does it mean?" Jerry asked.

"It means, *You're next.*"

28

Gesell finished her work early at the restaurant. When she had started the place, a small bistro that catered to more adventurous diners looking for exotic lunches, she did everything there, including being the head chef. Now, it was all hired out, and her manager ran everything. She could've worked from home had she chosen, but she liked the ritual of going someplace every morning. When it was her turn with David, she would make him breakfast, talk to him about the upcoming day, and then drop him off at school before driving to her restaurant, an old stucco-and-brick building in the middle of a residential neighborhood with a Laundromat as the only other business nearby. The neighborhood gave the place a particular niche feel that her diners enjoyed.

She had started with just herself and her best friend working part-time, growing the business to eighteen employees. It was a feat she was proud of, though she rarely spoke about her success since she found people bragging about themselves unflattering.

Amber, her manager, poked her head into the office and said, "I'm heading home, hon. You need anything?"

"I'm good, thanks."

"You okay?"

"Um, yeah. Yeah, I'm fine."

"You sure? I bet it's nothing a glass of wine at Oliver's can't fix."

"Rain check. I've got a lot of work left to do."

"Suit yourself. See you Monday."

When she was alone, Gesell went out into the dining room with the adjacent bar area and looked out the windows. Darkness had fallen outside, and she guessed she'd been there ten hours today. Normally she wouldn't spend that long there, but she didn't feel like going home to an empty house. She'd taken David back to his father to stay there until she arranged to stay with her parents at their ranch.

Her back ached, and she put her palms to her hips and pushed forward, tilting her head up to the ceiling, stretching her low back until she heard a soft crack. She unwound and stretched her neck from side to side.

The front door opened.

Alonso Hafeez pushed it wide with one hand from his wheelchair. He wore white linen pants with a white silk shirt and had a lit cigar in his mouth. His face appeared like it had gone through a plate glass window; lacerations everywhere with several wounds stitched together. Solomon had told her he had orchestrated being struck by a car and blamed it on Solomon, but she didn't realize he had hurt himself so badly.

Her gun was locked in the glove box of her car.

Fear instantly turned her cold. It seemed as if all the blood rushed from her limbs into her trunk, and it caused a slight shiver.

"Get out, or I'm calling the police."

"What're you gonna say? There's a hungry man at my restaurant?"

She took a step closer to her office as subtly as possible. The door was solid and thick, and she could get to it before him.

"Solomon didn't have anything to do with your injuries."

"Maybe. Or maybe you don't know him as well as you think."

She took another step toward her office. "What do you want?"

"To talk."

"I have nothing to say to you."

He shrugged. "How 'bout neutral ground, then? There's a coffee shop I saw up the street. Come meet me there." When she didn't move or say anything, he said, "I promise you, you have nothing to worry about from me, Gesell."

She swallowed. "Okay."

"I'll be waiting."

As soon as he was out of the restaurant, she called Solomon.

Solomon went into the coffee shop and stood at the entrance. He felt the handgun's weight in the holster underneath his brown leather jacket, and it gave him both a comforting feeling and one of utter fear. He had never fired a gun at anything other than targets at shooting ranges. Could he really look a man in the eyes and pull the trigger? He didn't know.

Alonso sat in his wheelchair at a table with two drinks in front of him. Solomon went up to him and noticed Alonso staring at his cane.

"I was wondering something," Alonso said. "That knob you got on your cane. It's a lion, right? Why a lion? You feel some bond with the king of the jungle?"

"Stay the hell away from her."

He smirked and held out an open palm. "Have a seat. I ordered you a tea. I know you don't like coffee."

Solomon sat without asking how he knew that.

"What do you want from me?"

"I wanna help you. I'm here to set you free."

"Enough of your bullshit," he nearly shouted, causing people at another table to look over.

"Easy now, Counselor. Remember, you're not even supposed to be within a hundred yards of me. I could have you arrested."

"Then do it."

He shook his head and lit his cigar. "Nah, that's not what I want. Where's the fun in that?"

"Fun? You think this is fun?"

"You gotta make everything fun. Otherwise, what's the point of even getting up in the morning?"

One of the baristas came up to their table and said, "Sir, you can't smoke in here."

"My bad," Alonso said, taking a giant puff before putting the cigar out. When the barista left, he said, "I went inside, and everybody smoked. I come out, and everybody's talkin' 'bout cancer. But we gotta sin, don't we? We gotta make life bearable."

"Just tell me what you want, Alonso. It has to be something. Money, revenge, overturning your conviction, what?"

"How 'bout my family back, Counselor? Can you give my son back, who's dying out on the streets somewhere? What 'bout my wife? Can you take her away from her new man and get her to fall in love with me again?"

Solomon said nothing as the two men sat in silence a moment.

Alonso leaned forward, his voice flat as he said, "When people say prison's like animals being locked in cages, they're not lying. You would not believe the things men do in there, the guards and the inmates. Closest thing there is in a civilized society to being back to the laws of the jungle. You're either vicious, or you have money. Only way to survive. Lotta ballers in there with people on the outside collecting for them, so they always had money. I didn't have money because the State, you, confiscated my assets as part of the case. I couldn't be vicious 'cause that meant I'd get infractions and not get early parole. So I was at the bottom of the food chain. You know what they do in prison when you're at the bottom of the food chain?"

Solomon saw this wasn't going anywhere.

"This is between me and you. You want me, you know where I am. Leave her out of it."

"I'm gonna help her, too, homie. I'm here to help all of you," Alonso said with a wide smile, holding out his hands in the posture of some traveling preacher.

"Like you helped Ricardo Duran?"

"I don't know who that is. But if I did, I would say he was like you. A betrayer. Hopefully, he got to confess his sins before he left this earth." He picked up his cigar and put it back into his mouth but didn't light it. "You look downright frightened, Counselor. You got something to confess? Confess it to me. Free yourself."

Solomon stood. "You believe in karma, Alonso?"

"I do indeed."

"She's the most innocent person I've ever met. Whatever you do to her, the universe is going to make sure you pay for it in ways you couldn't imagine."

He chuckled. "I believe you." Alonso rolled backward in his wheelchair away from the table. "Tea's on me. I heard you're currently unemployed." He began leaving. "Take care of yourself, Counselor. Dangerous world out there."

29

Billie was up early and went to Champion Chemical, a plant not far from Chelsea Lake. The medical examiner had deduced that Ricardo Duran was still alive when the tire was set on fire and thrown in the water while it was still burning. Which meant Alonso had killed Duran near the lake but probably far enough away that the smoke and screaming wouldn't attract attention. So it had to be close but not too close. Champion Chemical was the business farthest into Chelsea, where he would have likely been killed.

Champion Chemical looked like a warehouse and had the company's name on a tiny sign out front, as though it were trying to hide. The salt flats that surrounded it stretched for miles and appeared like soft white snow. Chelsea Lake was visible to the north, an offshoot of the Great Salt Lake, but the water was much darker and smelled worse.

The supervisor she'd spoken with was a pleasant man with scruff and a balding head with wisps of white hair on his temples. He greeted her with a smile in his cramped office and offered her coffee.

"I'm fine, thank you," she said, seated across from him.

"So you said something about fires near the plant."

"Yes, I believe a crime was committed near here and am following up."

"What crime?"

"A man was burned to death. His hands were cuffed behind his back, and a tire was placed around his neck and lit with gasoline."

"Good Lord! Who would do something like that?"

"No one you want around here. I'm hoping that one of your employees saw or heard something strange the past week. Maybe streams of smoke where there shouldn't have been any, or cars driving around they didn't recognize."

He paused for a moment. "I can't imagine anybody saw anything and didn't mention it. Anything important anyway. No one really comes out here except teenagers now and again. They come out to the salt flats to race dirt bikes. Sometimes they'll come out with some old car they wanna get rid of and get drunk and burn it for fun. Damn fools don't know to take the gas outa the tank, and you can hear the explosions a mile away."

"I would still appreciate some time with the employees to speak with them one on one."

"Yeah, of course, whatever you need. I'll get you an office."

The "office" was a janitor's closet where they brought in a desk and a couple of chairs. Billie canceled some meetings she had and began interviewing the twenty-nine employees. The men seemed pleasant enough and didn't appear to have much to hide. A couple of them were nervous and fidgety, and she figured they thought this meeting was about some perceived or actual crime in their own lives.

After two hours of interviews, she had nothing. The problem was that Chelsea was so massive people could go out twenty miles where nobody could see them. But there was no other way to *get* to Chelsea. Only one road led there, and it went past Champion Chemical.

She had ten more employees to interview and considered leaving instead. But she liked to finish things she started. Solomon could start a book, and if it didn't grab him immediately, he could put it down and never think about it again. She envied that. Deciding to read a book was a more significant decision for her because she knew she would have to finish it and would be filled with anxiety unless she did.

I'm already here, she thought.

The following employee who came in was a woman in jeans and a jean jacket. She smiled and spoke with a raspy smoker's voice, but there was erudition in her speech. She told Billie she was a chemical engineer.

"Wow. I'm impressed. Not a profession many people could do."

"My father and grandfather were both engineers. What about you? Was your father a police officer?"

"He was. In fact, he had my position before me."

"He still alive?"

"Yes. Yours?"

She shook her head. "Heart attack. Same as his father."

Billie nodded but said nothing, thinking about her mother, who had deteriorated to the point she no longer recognized her own family.

"So it's Cheyenne, right?"

"It is."

"I'll get right to the point, Cheyenne. A body was found in Chelsea Lake. I think the crime would have happened somewhere near here, and there's only one road that leads right past this property. I was hoping somebody saw something out of place over the past week that might help me find the man who did this."

"Oh, wow. We've never had anything like that here. We get kids coming up and getting drunk, but they're harmless."

"This man is definitely not harmless. My worry is that if he feels somebody saw something, he may consider it too much of a liability and come back to find them."

Her eyes went wide.

"What is it?" Billie asked.

"I wasn't going to say anything 'cause I didn't think anything of it. It didn't seem like a big deal."

"What?"

"I was here last Thursday and was leaving late because of a project me and Will were working on, and I saw a car driving past into Chelsea."

"Why did that stick out to you?"

She bit her lower lip. "I don't know if I should get involved . . ."

"Nobody ever wants to, but if you don't help me, and this man remembers that you saw him, he may be back. And he is *not* the type of man to offer polite conversation. He'll hurt you and anyone else he thinks might be a threat to him."

She nodded and began fidgeting. "I was coming out the back and saw him driving past, and I could see he was talking to somebody, which I thought was odd 'cause nobody else was in the car. Then I thought he must have Bluetooth, or I don't know, maybe he was crazy and liked talking to himself."

Billie waited patiently, but Cheyenne had a hard time going on.

"But you saw something that made this stick out to you. What was it?"

"I, um, saw someone in the back. His legs came up, and they looked . . . they could, maybe, have been tied together."

"Tied together?"

She nodded. "His feet were touching, like the ankles and toes were touching. I thought it must've been someone lying down in the back seat, but now that you tell me all this, it's pretty odd. I don't know. Maybe it was nothing. Just someone was tired and laid down."

"You were the only one who saw it. Do you think it was nothing?"

She folded her arms. "No. Something didn't feel right. My grandmother told me that our bodies know things right away that take our brains a long time to figure out. I felt I needed to make sure this man didn't see me. So I stayed perfectly still, and he drove by. I don't think he saw me because he didn't stop. Will came out a second after, and I told him about it, and he said it was nothing to worry about. Probably someone drunk or high going for target practice out in the salt flats. People come shooting here sometimes."

"Can you describe the driver to me?"

"I don't think so. That's really why I never told anybody. The car was black or blue, hard to tell, and he was a big man. Really wide. That's about it."

"How could you tell he was large?"

"He took up a lot of space in the car. I think he was bald, too, but I just got a glimpse of him. Maybe three seconds. Then I told myself it was in my head and left it alone. The person in the back seat wasn't struggling or kicking the windows, so I thought Will was right. Just some drunk idiots going out to shoot late at night."

"Did you see anything else that could help me find this man? Anything distinctive about the car, like damage you could see or unusual rims?"

"No, nothing like that. It was a really nice Cadillac. But nothing looked weird about it. And we don't have a camera on that side, or else I'd show you."

"Could you tell this man's race?"

"No."

"Did you see the person in the back seat?"

"No. Just his boots."

Ricardo Duran had been found with boots on. She pulled up some photos in the case file on her phone and showed her the boots.

"These boots?"

Cheyenne stared at them and then shook her head. "I really don't know. It was a few seconds late at night."

Billie, disappointed, put her phone away. "Is there anything else you remember that might help me find this man?"

Cheyenne blew out a breath. "Not really. I'm sorry, it was just too fast."

"I understand. I appreciate you talking with me."

"So, do you think that was the guy? The one that killed who you found?"

"I don't know. But so far, it's all I have to go on."

30

Solomon sat in an Uber outside the large home with the green Subaru in the driveway. A mailbox out front said *Donovan* in black lettering.

Michael Timothy Donovan was a lawyer specializing in wills and estates, though he could no longer practice. Forty-six years old with a family of three children and a wife who was a physician.

Outwardly, they had a perfect life. Three good kids, a tight-knit church community, good careers, and an extended family that came over for every holiday. But what was on the outside and shown to the rest of the world was rarely what was underneath.

Underneath, Michael had a severe gambling problem. In addition to being a partner at his law firm, he once had a successful nutrition business that operated out of the local mall. Unfortunately, the business had, out of nowhere, gone belly up. None of the creditors were paid, and the inventory seemingly disappeared.

People like Michael were Alonso's favorite victims.

Alonso had somehow worked his way into Michael's social circle, probably through charming him at local poker games. And Michael, at some point, borrowed money to get into a high-stakes game. Something he claimed he didn't even know existed until Alonso showed him.

The high-stakes game was far more high stakes than he realized. Within a few weeks of playing on Saturday nights, he had lost his entire life savings and owed Alonso over $100,000. But Alonso didn't care about that money: he wanted the business. That's why he hadn't offered to loan any money while Michael still had savings. But over the weeks of their supposed friendship, Alonso dropped hints that he would be willing to bankroll him for the high-stakes games.

The manipulation was subtle, taking patience. At any point, Michael could have called it quits and likely gotten a bank or family loan to pay Alonso back, but Alonso made sure it never got to that point. Telling Michael he had plenty of time to pay him back and Alonso wouldn't push it like a bank would. The debt built slowly.

Eventually, his nutrition business maxed out its line of credit, and all the inventory went to Alonso to fence. Solomon had spoken to Michael multiple times, and he guessed that he had ended up paying Alonso over half a million when all was said and done because of what was known as vig, or insanely high rates of interest that accelerated as time went on.

Michael confessed what had happened to his wife, who convinced him to go to the police. A mistake that almost cost him his life.

Alonso caught him one night as he walked out of a bar. He beat him with a baseball bat, fracturing his skull in several places. Breaking fingers, arms, kneecaps, and elbows and causing massive damage to his internal organs. No one was sure whether Alonso meant to kill him, but Michael ended up permanently disabled. The bat had sharpened nails thrust into the wood and tore Michael's body apart. The hospital photos looked like Michael had been attacked by a wild swarm of piranhas.

Alonso had claimed he wasn't the one who beat Michael and that Michael would be dead if he had been. But Solomon had something he'd never had before in a case against Alonso Hafeez: a witness. A young woman was in the parking lot of the bar and saw the beating. Someone Alonso hadn't planned on.

Solomon saw Michael and his family through the front room window sitting at a table near the kitchen. He still used a walker and had a limp on his left side. A portion of his head had caved in almost an inch from the vicious blows he took. The flesh on his face hadn't filled in completely, even after all the surgeries, and chunks appeared to be missing and scarred over.

Solomon wondered if he knew that Alonso was out now.

"You want me to wait here?" the Uber driver said.

"No, I don't know how long I'll be. I'll grab another car for the way back."

He got out into the cold, and a frosty wind caught him unprepared and caused him to shiver. He trudged across the fresh snow that was still drifting down and glanced back once to his tracks. Tracks consisting of two feet and then a hole from his cane. He didn't like seeing the contrast so clearly.

It took Michael's wife a bit to answer the door, and she was still smiling when she saw him. At first, she didn't recognize him, but she lost her smile as recognition hit. Solomon represented the worst time in her life, when her husband was on the verge of death and Solomon had to put her and her young children into protective custody.

"Solomon," she said with a sigh that sounded sad. She stepped out and gave him a hug, surprising him. He put one arm awkwardly around her and waited until she let go. "How are you?"

"I'm good. Got a new little accessory since I saw you last," he said, holding up his cane, which she'd already glanced at twice.

"I'm sorry to hear that. You okay?"

"I'm fine. I'm, um, actually here on some business. Mind if I talk to him for a minute?"

"Not at all. He'll be happy to see you."

Solomon was led inside and saw Michael's expression. He appeared shocked and then happy. He got up, using his walker, and gave Solomon a hug.

"You guys are some hard-core huggers," Solomon said.

Michael grinned and turned to his children, who were now teenagers. "You guys remember Solomon?"

Only the oldest one nodded.

"He's the one that helped me when I got hurt and put the man who did it in prison."

Solomon waved to the kids with a shy smile and said, "Mind if we chat somewhere for a bit?"

"Yeah, sure. Come to my office."

He followed Michael back to a room near the entrance. It was decorated with a grandfather clock, various framed photos on the wall, and a Swedish flag.

"Nice clock," Solomon said, approaching the clock and looking at the fine details on the hands.

"I inherited it from an aunt in England. It was my grandfather's. She didn't have any children, so the clock got passed down to me. The thing doesn't actually work, but I don't want to sell it." He paused a moment. "You wouldn't be here just to check up on me at this time of night."

Solomon faced him. "He's out, Michael. He got paroled early for good behavior."

"I know. The parole board sent me a letter and asked if I wanted to come to the hearing and speak."

"Did you?"

"No . . ."

Solomon glanced at the door to make sure it was closed. "Has he tried to contact you at all?"

"No. Not a peep." He paused again and looked down at his walker. "Is he going to come after me?"

"I don't know. He's been showing up places I'm at and threatening people close to me. I wanted to know if he was doing the same to you."

"After everything he did, I still have to worry about him . . . he's a monster."

"Monsters can be defended against. I don't know what security you have, but an alarm and a gun are probably the minimum you need."

He grinned. "Let me show you something."

Michael went to the closet in the office and opened the door. It had once been a closet but was now a gun-storage unit. Rifles, pistols, and shotguns on racks or leaning against the walls took every inch of free space. In the middle was a gun safe bolted to the ground.

"You expecting the zombie apocalypse?"

"Better safe than—" He paused again, and Solomon remembered that it was involuntary: he wanted to keep speaking but couldn't. A holdover from the severe brain injuries he'd sustained from Alonso.

"Do you think me not showing up to that hearing is why they let him out?"

"No. He didn't have a single infraction while he was locked up. He even volunteered for janitorial duties, which no inmates want to do. He was the model prisoner."

He nodded. "He's patient. It took him months to get close to me. He had dinner here with my family and played with my kids. We came from different sides of the tracks, but I thought we really bonded." He grinned remorsefully. "I thought I was helping him. He never had a stable family life, and I showed him some of that . . . I guess the joke was on me."

"Greater men than us have fallen for lesser scams. You have nothing to be ashamed of. Alonso is the crook."

"When I lost my kids' college fund in a poker game, it sure as hell didn't feel like he was the crook out of the two of us."

Solomon leaned on his cane, feeling the weight differential between his hands. If he gave it any thought, he knew he would feel off balance, so most of the time, he had to ignore the cane and treat it as a part of himself.

"Will he come after my family?"

"I don't know. But to be on the safe side . . ."

"No," Michael said with resolution in his voice. "I'm not running from him." He paused again. "Maybe we should consider something more extreme?"

"Like what?"

Michael didn't say anything but looked over to the gun closet.

"No," Solomon said. "You cross that line, and you can never go back. He's taken enough from you. Don't let him take the rest."

"Nobody would miss him."

"Maybe not, but there's people that'll miss you."

He shook his head, and Solomon saw tears in his eyes. "I don't know what to do. He destroyed my life, and if he wants to finish the job, maybe I should just let him."

"Hey, look at me . . . those kids need their father. That's not an option. Okay?"

"Yeah," he said, blinking tears away.

"I'll take care of this. I just wanted to warn you and see if he's tried anything."

Michael sighed. "Well, if he does, I'll give you a call right away." He moved over to the couch behind him and sat down with a groan. Even the effort of moving those few feet seemed to be gargantuan. "What about you? Are you going to be okay?"

"I don't know. If he wants to kill me, there's not much I can do other than carry around a gun and hope I get some shots off before he does."

"Gun's not his style. He wants people to suffer. A gun is fast."

Solomon leaned on his cane with both hands and glanced at a bookshelf. There were books about the tax code, law practice, court decisions . . . things from a previous life. Michael wasn't able to do much anymore. Solomon remembered the neurologist in the case saying that it was unlikely he would even be able to read again without inducing massive migraines.

"I better go and let you be with your family." Solomon took out a business card that said he was an assistant county attorney and wrote his cell number on the back. "If there's anything that doesn't feel right, you call me. I'll get the police over here fast."

Michael looked down at the card. "Is that all you want? To call the police? Or are you hoping I call you and Alonso's still here?" He put the card on the bookshelf. "It'd be a lot easier on the conscience if one of us had to shoot him in self-defense."

Solomon said nothing.

Michael led him to the door and said, "Is he coming after you?"

"I think so."

"To do what?"

"I don't know. But whatever it is, it's not good."

31

Solomon ate at the Vietnamese café but hardly had anything. A little soup and rice. His stomach was in knots, and he was worried he would vomit anything he got down. The waitress cleared some plates and left his bill.

Gesell texted him and asked if he wanted to meet, and he wasn't sure what to say. Solomon wanted nothing more than to be with her, but he also knew every second he spent with Gesell was another second he put her in danger. Or maybe she was safer with him around? He didn't know anymore and was angered that Alonso had his head spinning so much he couldn't think clearly.

He left a massive tip because he knew the waitress was a new mother and then went outside. The snow fell lightly, and he lifted his face to the moon. When he was a child and his father was in one of his alcoholic rages, he would go outside and stare at the night sky. He would imagine distant planets and ponder the wondrous alien civilizations that he was convinced thrived on them. Now, as an adult, he pondered whether aliens had figured out a secret to lasting or if they followed the same path as human civilizations: founding, aggression against weaker neighbors, ascendency, decline, and eventual fall. He could never decide where in that cycle current civilization was.

He kept a stone knife in his apartment that was crafted somewhere between sixty thousand and eighty thousand years ago. Something he'd picked up at an antique store at a Native American reservation. He'd taken it to the Utah State Crime Lab for analysis by a buddy who worked there. The dating was reasonably accurate, but the craftsmanship didn't match any known civilizations. After consulting a professor at the University of Utah, he concluded that the knife came from a yet-unknown tribe or culture, perhaps an entire people. A technologically advanced society that lived, loved, warred, discovered, struggled, and overcame, only to be taken down by time. And the only thing left of them was a stone knife on a bookshelf.

Solomon headed toward his building. Behind him, he heard the rumble of a car engine, and it sounded a little too close. He glanced back, expecting to see maybe a distracted teen or a mother yelling at her children in the back seat. Instead, he saw Alonso Hafeez in a Cadillac. Alonso had his cigar lit and his window open, letting out wafts of smoke. His eyes were glued to Solomon, and they held none of the fake delight that he had before. They held only venom. A predator looking at prey.

The car slowed and came to a stop in the lane. Someone behind the Cadillac started honking, but Alonso didn't notice. Unsure where this would lead, Solomon decided to ignore him and go to his apartment.

Well, if you're trying to creep me out, mission accomplished.

The apartment was cold, and he realized he'd left a window open. When he went to close it, he looked down at the street. No Cadillac. If Alonso hadn't taken out a protective order first, Solomon would have likely been able to get one. But now, because of Utah's law banning both parties from having one, he couldn't apply for a protective order for three years. Alonso had come up with the idea first and beaten him to it. Seemed like he'd thought of a lot of things first.

Solomon had asked an investigator at the County Attorney's Office to look into how Alonso had been following him so well, virtually unnoticed unless he wanted to be. The investigator spent a few days on it and concluded he had help—most likely whoever was driving the

Jeep that struck him. Probably some sketchy PI Alonso used before he went inside. Unless he could appear in two different places at once, he had to have help.

Gesell called.

"Hey, you," Solomon said, going into the bedroom to change.

"Hey," she said, sounding tired.

"You okay?"

"Just exhausted. It feels like my feet have been walking on hot coals all day."

"I did that once," he said, slipping off his pants and getting into basketball shorts. "The top coals aren't supposed to be hot, but the intern or whoever set it up screwed the pooch, and I got burned."

She chuckled. "I swear you're the only person I've ever heard of burned on one of those things."

"Wait until I tell you how I broke a leg playing chess."

She laughed now, and he forgot about everything else for a second. Some people might find her laugh odd, a seemingly impossible mixture of a squeal and deep belly laugh. On their first date, she hadn't wanted to show it to him, but he cracked a joke about how cats thought they were better than people but pigs knew they were humans' equals, and she tried to hold her laugh in. Instead, it burst out even louder, and she turned cherry red when the people at the table next to them turned and looked at her. She thought she'd screwed up the date and he wouldn't call again. Solomon had never told her that was the moment he knew he wanted to be with her. To him, it was one of those rare moments when someone's guard inadvertently dropped and a glimpse of their genuine self came through.

He put the phone on speaker and placed it on the bed as he took off his shirt. "How's David?"

"He doesn't understand," she said with a sigh. "His dad doesn't believe what's happening, either, and thinks I'm making up an excuse to spend more time alone with you. Speaking of which, how about I come over?"

Solomon hesitated.

"Solomon, we can't let him separate us. That's what he wants. Divide and conquer."

"If anything happened to you because of me . . ."

"I know," she said softly. "And I know you blame yourself for that girl's death in your building, that you could've helped her but instead turned her away. None of that matters. We have little control over what happens to us, and feeling guilty about it isn't going to do anything. Whether you're with me or not, he could still hurt me if he wanted to. If you really want to beat him, we have to show him we're not scared."

He let out a long breath. "I'll get some popcorn ready, and we can watch trash reality TV."

"Can't wait."

When he hung up, he checked his handgun. It felt silly somehow. Yes, Alonso was a threat, but he'd done nothing physical so far. It had all been carefully planned, so there was no physical attack. Maybe that wasn't his goal? Maybe it was to drive him to insanity by taking away his career and frightening anyone involved in a relationship with him? Solomon couldn't decide what was worse. He'd probably rather just take a beating.

He was in the pantry searching for popcorn when he heard something.

A door creaked. He couldn't tell if it was the front door, but it was loud enough that the sound was unmistakable. He turned off the light in the pantry as his heart started to thump and his breath quickened.

Slowly, he peeked out of his pantry door and saw the front door open. Solomon scanned from the door over his living room, the portion he could see, and the kitchen. Then, carefully so as not to make any noise, he stepped out from behind the door, making sure that his cane only lightly touched the floor.

From the entrance to the kitchen, he could see into his living room and didn't see anyone. The door wasn't open all the way, maybe a foot or so, and it was possible he had left it open, and it had drifted farther because one of his neighbors opened and closed their door and shifted the air in the hallway.

He went into the living room and to the door. He had to swallow out in the hallway because he didn't have any spit.

Looking one way and then the other, he was convinced the door had opened on its own. So he went back inside and locked it.

He turned to his bedroom, and his heart seemed to jump into his throat: Russ. Maybe the door had been left open a little and Russ had come back. The thought put a smile on his face, and he yelled out, "Russ? You here, buddy?"

A sound came from the bedroom, sheets or pillows moving on his bed. He wouldn't have even noticed that subtle, almost imperceptible sound had his senses not been heightened from fear. The door to the bedroom was open, and he rushed over.

Nothing looked out of place.

"Russ?"

"No, not Russ."

32

Billie lay in bed with her phone in front of her face. She had never tried online dating but gave Tinder a shot now. So far, three men had asked to see nude photos of her, and another sent naked pictures of himself. She responded with a picture of her gold shield in the black wallet that said she was sheriff, and the man's profile was deleted.

It was too soon to date again, she knew, but there was some sort of comfort in knowing she could if she wanted to. Since she had been a child, she had a heavy sense that she would live and die alone, and it never seemed to go away. She closed the app and lay in the dark, staring at the ceiling.

She had always been scared of the dark, more so than other kids. Growing up, she wouldn't even go to her room on the second floor of her house unless someone else was with her. It was never anything concrete she was scared of, but she did hear her brother talking to something in a corner one time.

She was maybe ten and stirred in bed because she heard her brother in the next room. Slowly, she got out of bed, went to his door, and looked in. He was sitting straight as a board and staring at a dark corner, speaking with whatever he was imagining was there.

Her phone vibrated and startled her. She let out a long breath before answering it.

"This is Billie."

"Billie, it's Gesell."

"Oh, hey. How are—"

"I was supposed to meet Solomon at his apartment," she said with panic. "I'm here right now, and he's not here, and he's not answering his phone. The bedroom's a disaster. His drawers are knocked over, and everything's a mess."

Ice slithered its way down her belly, and Billie pushed herself up in bed. "When was the last time you talked to him?"

"Like seriously, half an hour ago."

"Do you have a key?"

"No, his door was unlocked."

"I'll be right over."

Billie quickly got dressed and checked the magazine in her gun before putting it in a holster and slinging it over her shoulder. She wore a leather jacket over it, a black one that was difficult to notice any bulges through, and went to her truck. She texted one of her deputies to meet her at the apartment and stay with Gesell.

The drive to Solomon's took longer than usual because of an accident that blocked all the lanes of traffic. A semi had tipped over on the icy roads, and the inability of the plows to get through meant all the roads for miles would be more dangerous.

When she finally got there, she parked in front and ran inside. Gesell was standing in the hallway on the ground floor near the elevators, speaking with the deputy.

"Sorry to call you," Gesell said. "This just isn't like him. And with that guy following him . . ."

"I'm glad you called. Deputy, stay with her. I'm going to take a look."

She went up the elevators and got off on his floor. The hallway was warm; many elderly people lived here and liked the heat on at all times. As she got to his door, she drew her weapon.

The apartment had the lights on. She stood at the entryway and listened, but she could hear only her own breath.

Nothing looked out of place. Solomon was a neat freak, and everything had to be just right at all times, so if there were any disturbance, she likely would have noticed. Walking along the wall to make sure no one could surprise her from behind, she slid over to the bedroom door and glanced in. It was a mess.

With one hand, she pushed the door farther open, ensuring no one was behind it, and then came into the bedroom. She bent down and checked under the bed, and there was nothing. Not even dust bunnies. The space was as spotless as everywhere else in the apartment.

We need to get you a hobby, Solomon.

The closet had double doors. One of them was off its hinges. She opened the other one and lifted her sidearm, swinging it left to right before using one hand to split apart Solomon's clothes. Nothing behind them. She lowered her weapon. The only other place to hide was the laundry room. But before she could go there, she noticed something near the corner of the bedroom. It was hidden by the way the bed was angled when she came in, and standing at the door, which was probably what Gesell did, she wouldn't have been able to see it.

It was Solomon's cane.

33

Billie had a forensic team over to Solomon's apartment in less than twenty minutes. She'd woken up the supervisor and given him the address and, to prevent any argument, just said, "Get down here now. Don't even stop for coffee."

She told Gesell to go home and wait there in case Solomon showed up.

The techs were working the apartment to see if they could find anything, and their movements weren't particularly slow, more like the usual speed they worked a scene, but Billie told them to move things along as fast as possible. That all other cases they were working were officially on hold. She wasn't technically their boss, but people did what the sheriff said.

Billie knew Alonso's parole officer and called him at home.

Instead of a greeting and idle chitchat, she just said, "I need everything you have on Alonso Hafeez."

Billie got the text message with Alonso's information linked to a Dropbox file. She scanned it quickly and then decided to check his motel before anywhere else.

The Buena Vista Inn was in an industrial section with a few sandwich and burger places between the ugly square buildings. The motel was two stories of dilapidated stucco and chipping paint, looking even worse at night than it had during the day. She parked in front of the office and got out.

The man behind the counter, tall with wild hair like he just woke up and a flannel shirt, angrily said, "You can't park there."

She showed him her badge and didn't let him get out any other questions as she said, "I need you to open a motel room for me."

"I can't do that without a warrant," he said, folding his arms.

"A county attorney is missing, and the man in that room may have taken him. If you don't help, I can only assume you have something to hide, and maybe I do get a warrant, but not just for that room. For your entire motel, your car, and your home."

No judge in their right mind would give such a broad blanket warrant on so little evidence, but she wasn't sure he knew that.

"I known cops like you my whole life. Think you can boss around the little man. Well, the little man's gonna fight back one day."

"One day. But not today."

A beat of silence passed between them; then he sighed and said, "Lemme get my keys."

She followed him up to the room. The bitter cold stung her exposed skin, but the man didn't seem to notice the frigid temperature.

"The guy in that room ain't here much."

"During the day?"

"Nah, at night, too. Mostly at night. I don't think I ever seen him sleep here. Most of the people here use it as an address to give their parole officers and stay wherever the hell they gonna stay."

They got up to the room, and he knocked first, waited a bit, and then unlocked it. He didn't go inside but motioned that she was free to enter.

Billie brushed past him. She hadn't expected to find Alonso here, but she had expected to find his things. Maybe even something indicating where he would have taken Solomon if he did take him. But there was nothing. No clothes, no bags, no suitcases. The only thing that indicated someone had stayed there was a used-up cigar in an ashtray on the nightstand.

"Did he check out?" she asked without turning around.

"Nah, he was on a week-to-week, and the week's only half over."

She took out a card and gave it to him. "If he comes back, don't mention anything about the police looking for him. This man is extremely dangerous, and if he views you as any sort of threat, he may harm you. So just call me and tell me that he's here."

The man glanced down at the card and then back up to Billie. "Who is this guy?"

She took one last look at the room and then turned away. Brushing past him again, she said, "A monster."

34

Billie sat in her truck outside an apartment complex in West Valley City, about a half hour from Salt Lake and an hour from Tooele. She was outside her usual jurisdiction, but few people knew that. They saw the badge and treated her the same as any other police officer. Although technically, under Utah law, the entire state was her jurisdiction for investigating crimes, she had to admit she liked telling people she was the sheriff of the county they lived in. Her declaration certainly didn't have the same ring when she told them she was the sheriff of some county an hour away.

The criminalist with the state crime lab had texted and said they didn't have anything at Solomon's apartment yet except some boot prints leading from the front door into the living room and past that into the bedroom. The prints were size eighteens. She didn't know Solomon's shoe size but guessed it wasn't eighteen.

"I'll get you a make on the boot," the criminalist had said, "but that's about it over here. Prints will take a few hours to find matches."

She tried Solomon's cell phone again. It went to voice mail.

Billie got out of her truck. The walkway into the complex wasn't cleared, and she had to step carefully, as it was packed with snow and ice underneath.

The apartment she was looking for was on the ground floor, and when she got there, she could smell something cooking from inside.

She knocked and waited.

Alonso's younger sister, Caroline, answered. She was almost as tall as he was, with her hair pulled back and ruby lipstick on a beautifully symmetrical face. She had large brown eyes and white teeth that gave her a model-like appearance.

"Caroline?"

"Yes."

"Sorry to bother you. I'm Sheriff Billie Gray. I'm a police officer from Tooele. I'm looking for your brother Alonso."

"He's not here."

"I know. We don't actually know where he is. I was hoping maybe you could shed some light on where he would've gone?"

She thought it over a moment and then opened the door. "Come in. I'll get my mom."

The home was clean and decorated well, with lots of family photos. Alonso had five siblings, and all five were successful without any criminal records. They all had a background of intense poverty and poor schools surrounded by violence and drugs. And yet, according to the parole officer's notes, all his siblings had pulled themselves out and become successful and productive. She wondered what would make five siblings turn out normal and one into an Alonso Hafeez.

Several Islamic decorations were up. Billie spotted plates trimmed with golden verses in Arabic, a painting of flowers near a mosque, and a large, intricately woven prayer rug consisting of grays and blues.

"You can sit down. I'll get her," Caroline said.

Billie sat on the couch. On the coffee table was candy in a glass bowl. It reminded her of trips to her grandmother's house, where she left out little candies and almonds for Billie and her brother, the condition being that they had to eat three almonds for every piece of candy.

An elderly Latina woman in a blue dress with a metal cane came out of the bedroom. She put on glasses she had around her neck and smiled warmly at Billie.

"I'm so sorry to disturb you," Billie said.

"No disturbance. I was only watching my shows."

Caroline helped her mother into the love seat, and the older woman said, "I'm Judy."

"Billie."

She sighed as she adjusted her position on the love seat. "That's a cute name for a girl."

"Well, it's Elizabeth, but I always hated that name."

"It's a beautiful name, too." She took a small candy out of the glass bowl and unwrapped it before putting it into her mouth. Her hands were leathery, probably from a lifetime of hard work, and her face had wrinkles like folds, but she had happiness and confidence that shone through her age.

"What can I do for you?"

"I'm looking for your son, Ms. Hafeez. I'm sure you know he's on parole, but he's left his motel, and his cell phone no longer works. So his parole officer doesn't know his whereabouts."

"Um-hm," she said, crumpling the wrapper and putting it down on the coffee table. "So why isn't the parole officer here talking to me?"

Billie wasn't about to tell Alonso's mother what she needed to find him for. Families were always less inclined to help the police when they knew their loved one was facing more incarceration.

"There's a connection to something I'm working on. Either way, I would like to speak with Alonso, and so would his parole officer."

"I don't know where he is."

"He hasn't been here to see you?"

She shook her head.

"You two aren't close?"

"I loved the boy, but he was off on his own at nine years old. Always working at that refinery and hanging on corners with troublemakers. He liked the streets. I think he understood the streets and didn't understand all this, this world here. The streets made sense to him."

"Did he contact you while he was in prison?"

"No. I got a phone call the day he got out, and that's it. He's not one for family. Except for his older sister. She's the only one he speaks with."

Caroline had been in the kitchen but came out with two cups of tea and put them on coasters on the glass coffee table. Judy said, "Thank you, sweetie," and picked up the cup. A little bit sloshed over the rim because of trembling hands.

"Arthritis," she said, noticing Billie looking at the spilled drops.

Caroline helped clean it up and then disappeared into the kitchen again.

"Worked in a garment factory my entire life, and it gave me the gift of arthritis. Nobody warned me about that. We didn't have protections as workers back then." She took a sip of her tea. "He's in real trouble, isn't he?"

Billie hadn't wanted to bring it up, but she couldn't stomach lying to someone's mother either. "Yes. I think so, anyway. I won't know until I speak with him."

"Hm," she said as though it was something she was used to hearing. "That boy's been in trouble his whole life. His father and I tried to instill religion and a fear of God in the boy, but it never stuck. His father would say he listened too much to the jinn on his shoulder. Mischievous creatures that live beside us in this world. Ahmad was always superstitious that way." She was lost in thought a moment. "When he passed, I didn't know what to do with Alonso. I tried to get him into a sport where he could hit people, like boxing and football. But the boy didn't stick to it. He didn't want to work hard. Or at least not in that way."

"I'm sorry to hear that. My brother was the same way. Some people need to walk their own path."

"I suppose." She took another sip of tea, this time more slowly so as not to spill the liquid. "You can tell me what he's in trouble for. I'm still gonna help you."

"You will?"

She nodded. "His grandfather, my father, was a police officer in Havana before the revolution. My husband's father was a judge in Afghanistan. We follow the law in this house."

She took another candy and slowly unwrapped it.

"My father was a police officer for thirty-two years. It's what killed him. Fell over at the sink while getting a glass of water one day and never got back up. It's the stress. It eats you. Even while you're sleeping. But you know that, don't you, Sheriff? My father was strong, but he kept all that bottled up and let it eat him so it wouldn't hurt us. Never talked about his job a day with my mother or me. He didn't want me to know the things he saw. And it killed him." She teared up a second and then regained her composure. "You don't stay in it too long now. The stress'll eat you up, too."

Billie thought of her own father. He didn't keep the stress bottled up. Every night, her entire family would share their day at the dinner table, including him. Of course, he kept out the inappropriate details, but it seemed like her father wanted her and her brother to know that the world wasn't always a kind and welcoming place and that the actual danger wasn't monsters under the bed or aliens in the sky but other people.

"He hurt somebody?" Judy asked.

"I hope not. Someone Alonso had been harassing is missing now. I'm worried Alonso may have done something drastic."

She didn't ask who it was. Instead, she yelled for Caroline to get the box above her shoes in the closet. Caroline did and brought it out. Judy held the box on her lap and then opened it. It contained various trinkets ranging from papers written in crayon to a photograph of Alonso in a football uniform. At the bottom was a series of old Polaroid photos and Alonso's trinkets. Judy didn't keep them with the rest of her kids' things, but it was clear she couldn't bring herself to throw them away either. No matter what he was now, he was still her son.

"I kept these for . . . I'm not sure why. Maybe to remind me what he was, what part of him was anyway. He's broke my heart more times than I can tell you, so I gotta remember that, too."

She handed the Polaroids to her. Billie flipped through a few. They were of animals, primarily cats and dogs, a few bunnies and birds, dead and mutilated.

"You're saying Alonso did this?"

She nodded, looking as if she might burst into tears right there. "Boy liked to hurt things. Started with fights at school, and we just thought he was a hothead. But I found these pictures in his room. He said he would find dead animals and take pictures, but some of the dogs and cats in the neighborhood here started disappearing, and I knew it was him."

Billie could only stomach a handful of photos as the image of Solomon's cat came to her, and she handed them back to Judy, who put them in the box.

"Judy, do you have any idea where he could be?"

"Only thing I can think of is if you talk to his wife and his older sister. They knew him better than I did. As well as anyone could know a man like that."

35

Waves of light distorted the field. Solomon stood in the middle, surrounded by tall golden grass. The sun was out, but somehow it didn't light up the sky. Instead the sky was gray, dark. Pulsating.

Solomon saw his mother in the sundress she wore on the day of her suicide. White with yellow flowers and a wide-brimmed sun hat. She smiled at him, and it broke his heart because now he knew the smile hid the agonizing pain underneath, but at the time, he hadn't even known it was there, and he blamed himself. Even as a child, he had an abnormal perception of other people's feelings and motivations, but when it counted, he was as blind as everybody else.

"You awake, Counselor?"

Solomon tried to open his eyes. His left opened quickly, but his right felt stuck, and he knew it was sticky with dried blood.

"It's morning. You should get your ass up. Too much sleep weakens the body."

The first pain he felt was in his wrists. They were bound behind him so tightly that the backs of his hands were touching. Then the throbbing in his head got his attention, and he tried to remember what Alonso had hit him with but couldn't. The last thing he recalled was walking into his bedroom.

He was in a chair in a vast open space in what looked like a factory. The rafters were metal and probably thirty feet above him. The floor was cement, and the windows were large, up high on the walls. A building constructed in the '40s or '50s, when factories like this were needed before technology overtook most jobs. Off to the side were gasoline canisters and a fire lit in a metal garbage can. Acrid smoke filled the space. All the windows were closed.

Across from him, he saw another man bound to a chair. The man was older and thin with salt-and-pepper hair. He looked familiar, but it wasn't until Alonso's voice boomed, "You remember Judge Elrod, don't you?" that Solomon knew who he was.

Judge Elrod had been Alonso's trial judge.

Blood had crusted from a wound on his head. The judge was barely conscious, his eyes glued to the floor as he sucked in deep breaths and tried to stay awake.

Alonso came around to Solomon. He wore an orange shirt with the same color pants, and the shirt had stains of darkened blood. Not just Solomon's but Alonso's too. Now Solomon remembered: He had managed to get in a few good whacks with the silver knob of his cane before Alonso overpowered him. The cane had opened up Alonso's wounds on his face. He wasn't in a sling or neck brace anymore, but he couldn't fake the injuries on his face he'd gotten from the accident; those were real.

The wounds had ripped open and blood oozed from them, over his face and down his chin. Alonso paced between the judge and Solomon. In his right hand, he held a chrome handgun.

"All rise, the Honorable Judge Elrod presiding." He looked to Solomon, and in a movement faster than someone his size should be able to make, he swung and slapped Solomon in the face. Pain exploded in his jaw and radiated up his skull to the middle of his head, making him feel like he wanted to vomit. Alonso slapped harder than most men punched.

"Stand your ass up, Counselor." Alonso stared at him, his eyes wide, and then laughed. "Oh, my bad. Forgot you can't stand up."

Something had changed. His countenance, his posture, his energy. Maybe everything had changed. Solomon now understood what he'd seen in Alonso was a mask he held in place. And now that they were isolated, the mask had slipped off. Underneath the mask, he was insane, and he didn't care.

"Judge Elrod, would you please call the case?"

Alonso waited a beat, and when the judge didn't say anything, he pressed the gun against the back of the judge's head. "I said call the case, Your Honor."

The judge took two breaths and managed to get out, "The Court calls the matter of *State of Utah v. Alonso . . . Alonso . . .*"

"Hafeez, you wormy piece a' shit."

"Alonso Hafeez," he gasped, out of breath.

"Thank you." He took a step back and raised his arms as though he were the ringmaster in a circus. "Your Honor, we're here today to prove my innocence. The Constitution creates a presumption of innocence, but that doesn't work. 'Cause not a damn person on a jury don't think someone's guilty just by sitting in that chair. So we're *not* gonna do it that way. We're gonna prove with overwhelming evidence that I did not commit the crime of attempted murder. We will show to this Court that the State's witness was coerced into giving false testimony, Joy Rio, who testified that she saw me commit this crime. We will provide evidence," he said, his voice rising to a shout, "that the State's witness was coerced by Mr. Solomon Shepard, and such information was never provided to the defense."

Alonso came up to Solomon now, and the two men stared at each other.

His voice calmed, and he said, "We will prove to this Court that Mr. Shepard committed an unlawful act by abusing the discretion of his office to commit malicious prosecution of an innocent defendant." He leaned down so that their faces were inches apart. "We will prove to this Court that Mr. Shepard is a so-called *expert* in criminal psychology and that his status as an *expert* has so clouded his thinking that he is bound to confuse himself of even simple truths having to do with justice. We will prove to this Court that Mr. Shepard betrayed his oath to uphold the Constitution so he could get a conviction."

His nostrils flared as he inhaled deeply and rose to his full height.

"The defense has read your book, Mr. Shepard. We read it many times. We know you are a man of intellect and see the world as it really is, and we know this burden you carry of convicting an innocent man must weigh heavy on you. That's why the gods put me in your life, Mr. Shepard. For you to learn the lesson of humility and be freed of your sins."

Alonso was out of breath, sweat running down in long streaks over his face. The droplets slipped down onto his collar and chest. He didn't look well.

"You rudely ran out when I told you I loved your book, and how my favorite chapter was on the Druids," he said. "Aren't you curious, Counselor, why the Druids? I'll tell you. It's the custom you described." On the floor next to a jacket was a large cardboard box. Alonso took out a copy of Solomon's book from the box and opened it to a page about halfway in.

He read loudly from the book to the judge.

"And the sacrificial custom of the bifurcation of the physical body to manifest itself as the spiritual body contained a process that required the help of a male high priest. The ritual took only one form and deviated little from its genesis in the ninth century BCE, even across centuries.

"The ritual involved those deemed guilty of any crime punishable by death. Such custom may seem alien to the modern ear, but penalties were neither simple nor easily understandable by the mostly illiterate population. This put the high priest in a unique position of power in that he spoke for the gods and was, therefore, the only interpreter of the laws.

"The condemned were bound before a great fire, and the male high priest would send an exceptional advocate on their behalf: the grave singer. This particular post involved a process of brutality upon initiation that is hardly imaginable today. First, young men were skewered by the pectoral muscles and left in the sun for three days. Those who survived, and survived any subsequent infections, were then put through a rigorous set of challenges involving such things as drinking snake venom to induce hallucinations and burning by fire swaths of flesh across the limbs and torso. The point of these rituals was to cleanse the grave singer for their sacred duty.

"When the grave singer was blessed by the high priest, they then drank a concentrated dose of snake venom to put them in the netherworld between life and death. It was only then," Alonso began to shout, "that the grave singer offered the condemned absolution. The condemned were to confess their deepest sins if they wanted to reach the Land of the Winter Sun, and once the burden of these sins was removed, the grave singer would release the newly cleansed soul from the body with one slice across the throat. From earlobe to earlobe."

He took a large hunting knife from his waistband and pressed it into Solomon's neck.

"Earlobe to earlobe," Alonso said, blood from his wounds dripping onto Solomon. "I *am* your grave singer, Counselor. And I will cleanse your soul."

36

After a long night working with several deputies going door to door in Solomon's building, Billie realized she hadn't slept only when the sun came up.

The calendar on her phone dinged with a reminder: she had court this morning.

Billie had to testify in a case from last year, a drug case involving a thirteen-year-old boy. She tried to get out of it, but the prosecutor said they had used all their continuances and needed her there. She called the judge's clerk and explained to her what she was working on and that there was a missing assistant county attorney that was feared kidnapped, but the judge said she had to come in. That the case had been continued too many times. Judges were isolated from criticism, so their sense of importance became skewed.

"Sheriff," the prosecutor, a younger man named Paul with an egg-shaped head, said when she was sworn in and on the stand, "do you recall the events of October fourteenth of last year?"

"I do," she said.

"Will you please share them with the Court?"

"Certainly. The respondent in this case, Mr. Stephen Williams, was involved in an altercation with a Mr. Yazzi, who I believe testified yesterday. This occurred on 300 West here in Tooele. During the alter-cation, a witness telephoned the police. The nearest responding officer was twenty minutes away at the scene of a major crash on I-15, and I happened to be in that neighborhood on an unrelated matter. I notified dispatch that I would respond."

"And will you please share with us the events that transpired?"

Billie spoke for long stretches, and the defense attorney didn't object. He appeared to be taking notes, but she suspected he was doodling.

Billie testified that she'd been arresting the defendant, and a baggie containing a white powder fell out of his pocket. He subsequently confessed, and a field test came back positive for methamphetamine. The defense attorney didn't provide a single objection.

"That's all I have for this witness," Paul said.

"Mr. Adams?" the judge said. "Any cross?"

"Not at this time, Judge."

"Very well. Next witness then."

On her way out, Billie leaned over to the defense attorney and whispered, "You didn't ask me a single question or file a single motion, Tommy. Maybe it's time to retire from criminal law."

She left the courtroom and got a Diet Coke from a vending machine before going out to her truck. The anger of what had just happened stuck to her like syrup on her skin and made her feel like she needed a shower. The defense attorney was the lowest bidder on the public defender contract and wanted to churn out cases quickly. The faster he took care of the cases and the less effort he put in, the more the contract was worth since he could spend time on his firm's own cases.

Juveniles, especially, bore the brunt because they either didn't have the confidence to speak up if their attorney did nothing or didn't know their attorney was doing nothing. The defense-attorney lobbying group objected to public defender bidding contracts in the state, instead asking for permanent public defender offices where there wouldn't be an incentive to quickly get through the cases. So far, they had been unsuccessful.

She took in a deep breath and let it out slowly through her nose, her eyes closing for a moment. When she opened them, she put the address for Heather Jackson into her phone.

The home was an hour away from Tooele in the opposite direction of Salt Lake, going into Nevada and a town called Wendover. The city attempted to be a close gambling hub to Salt Lake City and was packed with cheap casinos and two-dollar buffets. Boxing matches were held here every Friday and bet on by locals and tourists alike. A scandal had recently erupted when a group of people had banned together and paid one of the fighters to take a dive. She didn't understand why people would be shocked at that and it would be a news story. Little anyone did shocked her anymore.

The home was on the bluffs overlooking the city, where business owners and politicians who ran the town lived. It was one long street and sat like a king overlooking its kingdom below.

She parked in front of a large house with an expansive driveway and a fountain in the front yard. Considering they were in the middle of the desert, having a water fountain in front of your house was the ultimate sign of wealth. Anybody could buy gold, but when you could waste water in a desert, well, then you knew you'd really made it.

The large wooden double doors had brass decorations, and a camera was on the side, a device about the size of a wallet. She rang the doorbell, expecting someone to answer, and a voice said, "Yes?" through the camera speakers.

The voice was female, and Billie said, "Yes, I'm looking for Mrs. Heather Jackson?"

"And who may I say is calling on her?"

The way she phrased her words, *calling on her* rather than just asking Billie why she was there, bothered her. But Billie didn't know if she was bothered because of what was actually said or because of the type of house in the kind of neighborhood that it was said from.

Billie hadn't had much as a kid growing up on her father's salary as a cop with a mother who was too ill to work. Just a lot of secondhand clothes and peanut-butter-and-pickle sandwiches for dinner. The fact that her upbringing still stuck with her and caused feelings of envy surprised her, and she had to consciously try to ignore it.

"I'm Sheriff Elizabeth Gray. I need to speak to her about her ex-husband."

A long silence.

"I know the sheriff, and you're not him."

The hint of erudition and education left her voice after Billie had mentioned her ex-husband.

"I'm the sheriff for Tooele County, Heather. I think he's hurt someone I care about, and I could really use your help."

Another silence, and then the door opened a minute later.

Heather was tall and white with strawberry-blonde hair. She wore a blue jumpsuit with clean white sneakers that looked new.

"What's he done now?"

"I think he kidnapped the prosecutor who put him away."

"I told that man to make sure Alonso never got out."

Billie nodded but said nothing for a second. "Can we talk?"

"I was about to go to the gym. You can talk to me on the way to the car."

They hiked a gravel walkway to a five-car garage. There were three cars, and Heather went to the blue BMW on the far side. She leaned against it and folded her arms as she looked down at the clean floors.

"This is a beautiful home," Billie said.

"We built it ourselves. John, he's my husband, he's done everything he could to make sure I'm happy. He's a good man."

"Does he know much about Alonso?"

"I've told him most everything. Not all of it, though. There's nothing he can do to change the past, so I didn't think he needed some of those things in his head. Alonso raping me and leaving me bloody on the floor, or throwing me off a balcony and then asking me why I'm crying, like he didn't know."

She tightened the fold in her arms, and her eyes glazed over.

"I went through hell, lost my son, and not a single person lifted a finger to help me. Not a cop, not a lawyer, none of my family or friends. Alonso was smart, and he had money. When you got money, you can get away with a lot. And now you're asking me to help *you*. Why should I?"

Billie felt guilty about the bout of jealousy she'd had at the intercom.

"I'm sorry I have to bring all this up again, but I don't have a choice. Alonso knows you don't kidnap a prosecutor if you plan on returning him. It's a federal crime and a life sentence. Alonso's going to kill him, and he's a good man, like your husband, who doesn't deserve to die like this."

Heather shook her head, and Billie let her take as much time as she needed.

Heather finally looked at Billie and asked, "What do you want to know?"

37

Solomon kept his eyes low as Alonso disappeared somewhere behind him. He pushed against whatever was holding his wrists in place and figured it was some sort of industrial tape wrapped over and over, creating an extremely tight seal.

After taking some deep breaths to calm himself so he could focus on his surroundings, he didn't hear any other source of breathing besides himself and the judge. Alonso had left the room.

"Judge, can you hear me?"

Judge Elrod opened his eyes. "Yes," he whispered.

"He took my phone. Did you see where he put it?"

The judge had to take a couple of breaths before responding. "It's in his jacket on the floor."

Solomon looked over to the jacket and guessed it was ten feet away. He wasn't sure he could make it even that far. Everything hurt.

Some of the memories were coming back to him now, of walking into the bedroom and feeling a tremendous power lift him off his feet, as though he were struck by a wave while swimming in the ocean.

Solomon had swung his cane with everything he had, hoping to see Alonso flop on the ground with buckets of blood coming out of his head. Trespassing in his home with an intent to harm: it would've been justifiable homicide if Solomon had killed him. Solomon just hadn't been strong enough. For the second time in his life, he felt subject to overpowering forces he didn't understand.

"Do you know where we are?" Solomon said.

"Shh. Keep your voice down. He's in a room back there. And no, I don't know where we are."

"What's the last thing you remember?"

The judge took two short pants before answering and, even then, was still out of breath. "I was walking out to my garage . . . I think he hit me from behind when I got to my car. He must've been waiting for me."

"Can you get your hands loose at all?"

"No."

Solomon looked out the windows to see if there were any landmarks he could use to figure out where he was. He discerned nothing but sunlight.

A door behind them opened, and Alonso's heavy footfalls echoed in the space.

"Sorry about that, Counselor," Alonso said as he came into view. He had a hand towel that looked old and dirty, but he used it to wipe the blood off his face. A good chunk of the skin on his forehead was missing, and Solomon remembered it was the impact point of the first swing.

The sweat was coming out of him in streams, and his eyes were too red, as though blood were ready to burst from them. He looked sick, like he was holding back vomit . . . he looked like he was dying. Solomon glanced at the fire in the bin and realized why.

"Alonso, tell me you didn't drink snake venom for this."

He kept wiping the blood off his face and didn't respond.

"This won't go how you want it to," Solomon said.

"Oh, I think it'll go exactly like I want."

"If you cut us loose now, you'll have several hours' head start to take off. You could be in Mexico before the cops even know where to look."

"Mexico? You think I wanna run, Counselor? Do I look like a man that's run from *anything* in his life?"

He stepped close to Solomon.

"I did eleven years in a pit of vipers and didn't complain once. I didn't bitch, didn't go to the warden, didn't plead my case to some bleeding-heart types lookin' to help inmates. I did my time like a man. And now I'm getting my justice like a man. Are you a man, Counselor? Or are you a cockroach? You got the look of a cockroach, but there's something else there, isn't it? Something darker than that."

Solomon looked down to the floor. He didn't know how much blood he'd lost, but it must've been substantial, because his light-headedness wouldn't go away, and he was fatigued from talking. The smoke choked him and gave everything the smell of burning plastic.

"Do what you have to do," Solomon said.

"That's what I like to hear! Enthusiasm. You hear that, Judge? You're sitting over there like a dead fish, and Solomon here's ready to get this going. So why don't we begin? The defense'll go first since I gotta prove my innocence like I did in my trial instead of the prosecutor proving my guilt. Isn't that right, Judge?"

Judge Elrod glanced up. "I suppose."

Alonso struck him on the side of the head with the back of his hand. "You suppose, or yes, I'm right?"

"Yes," the judge gasped, "you're right."

"Damn right I am. Then let's get this trial going. Judge, if you would?"

Judge Elrod glanced at Solomon. With a voice seeming too exhausted to speak, he said, "The defense may call its first witness."

"Thank you, Judge. The defense would call Lieutenant Randall Beard to the stand."

Alonso disappeared again, and Solomon heard wheels rolling along the floor a minute later.

Lieutenant Beard was pushed in between Solomon and the judge. He was darkly tanned with black hair and scruff, dried blood crusted in long threads down his face. A dark-purple ring around his throat said that he'd been choked out, and he wore boxers and a T-shirt. He was bound to a chair, but Solomon could see the deep bruising along his arms and knew that he had put up a helluva fight.

"Lieutenant Beard, please state your name and relation to this case."

Solomon knew Beard. He'd been a marine and was an avid hunter and outdoorsman. Not the type of man who rattled easy. Whereas in Judge Elrod's eyes he saw terror, he saw nothing but rage in Beard's.

"Go fu—"

Alonso smacked the lieutenant's mouth before he managed to get the words out. His arm was meaty and thick as a stone club. It whacked Beard across the jaw so hard he looked dizzy. Blood instantly came from his mouth from whatever teeth had been knocked loose.

"Objection," Alonso shouted. "Nonresponsive."

No one said anything, and Alonso looked to the judge.

"I objected, Your Honor."

The judge took a breath and looked at the lieutenant. "The witness will respond to the question asked."

Alonso nodded, as if there were any other expected outcome from that request, and then turned back to Beard. "State your name and relation to this case, Lieutenant."

Beard spit a glob of blood onto the floor by Alonso's feet. A moment passed when none of the four men said or did anything. The smoke from the fire in the garbage can grew thicker, and Solomon began to cough.

"Your Honor," Alonso said, "will the Court please direct the witness to answer?"

Judge Elrod didn't say anything, and Alonso rushed over and grabbed the man's head with both hands. One palm underneath the jaw and the other on the judge's head. He pressed in like a vise, and the judge groaned in pain.

"I asked you a question: Can you direct the witness to answer?"

The judge squeezed his eyes shut from the pain, a moan escaping his lips. Solomon had no doubt Alonso could crush the judge's head like a plump grape if he wanted to.

"Lieutenant Beard," the judge managed to get out as he strained against the pressure. "Please answer Counsel's question."

"Thank you," Alonso said, letting go. He turned to Beard and said, "The Court has directed you to answer, Lieutenant. Would you please be so kind as to state your name and relation to this case?"

Beard looked at the judge. He spit blood again and said, "Lieutenant Randall Beard. Eleven years ago, I was a patrol officer for Tooele City."

"You were the arresting officer in my case, correct?"

"Yes."

"And the lead detective you worked with was a Mr. Kevin Doyle, who passed away a few years ago, correct?"

"Correct."

"I'd like to bring your attention to your record as a patrol officer, if I may." Alonso reached into the box next to his jacket. He took out a file folder and threw it at Beard's feet. "I have there your entire record for the six years you worked patrol at the Tooele City Police Department before moving to the Sheriff's Office and accepting a post as a junior detective. Can you tell us your duties as a patrol officer?"

Beard took a breath and wouldn't look Alonso in the eyes. Alonso moved slowly toward him, and in a whisper so low Solomon had a hard time hearing it, he said something about Beard's wife and daughter.

"I was tasked with traffic duty in the area of Highland Drive," Beard said, his eyes to the floor.

"As part of your traffic duty, you were expected to pull people over for traffic violations, right?"

"Yes."

"And you pulled over exactly one thousand three hundred and seventy-six motorists in those six years. Is that right?"

"You tell me."

"I went through and made a list, Lieutenant. When you're locked in a cage twenty-three hours a day, you got nothing but time, and so anything that will take up a little of that time gives you an edge. It saves a little of your sanity."

"How the hell did you even get those?"

"The Freedom of Information Act. Not that government tyrants give a shit that citizens can learn about their misdeeds, isn't that right, Lieutenant?"

"Go to hell. You were a piece a' shit then, and you're a piece a' shit now."

"I disagree. Prison opened my eyes." He reached down and picked up Solomon's book and held it high like it was the Bible. "I read Counsel's book. I read it twice, then I read it another time and another, until I knew it like you know your wife's . . . well, now never mind that. We gotta keep decorum in a court a' law, don't we? We wouldn't want people to get the wrong idea that salacious and scandalous things happened in our courts."

The sweat had drenched Alonso's collar and was streaming into his eyes.

"I'm not playing this game anymore," Beard said. "You wanna shoot me, shoot me."

"Come on now, Lieutenant. Don't be like that. Here we are, two old friends back together. So much has changed in eleven years. I heard K-pop the other day. Never in a million years could I have guessed Korean boy bands would be popular in the States. Seemed like we had enough of our own."

Beard spit again, the glob of blood going across Alonso's boot. "I'm done."

"You're done when I say you done. Or that pretty little wife of yours is gonna get a visit from me tonight. But you do your part, and it might be in my best interest to take off early. What you think?"

Beard didn't answer. Solomon could feel the man's fight. He wanted nothing more than to show Alonso he couldn't be broken, but he had a weak spot. Diamonds had shatter points, a place where a tap that would do nothing anywhere else on the diamond could cause the entire thing to crack and crumble to dust. Family was Beard's shatter point.

Beard fought against his restraints, using the strength of his legs to lift the chair off the floor. But he fell back with the awkward weight of his seat and his inability to stand straight. Alonso laughed.

"Woo! That's a bucking bronco right there. Heart of a lion, son. I like you, Beard. But I'm afraid this Court is on a tight schedule, and I'm gonna need you to answer the question. Did you pull over exactly one thousand three hundred and seventy-six motorists in six years or not?"

Beard didn't respond. Alonso shook his head. "You're not being rational, and I don't like people who don't like being rational."

He took out what Solomon thought would be his handgun but instead was his phone. Alonso pulled something up, and a second later, he could hear breathing and cars passing by on a road. He only glanced at the phone as Alonso turned it toward Beard, but it was enough to see it was a video of a house. Solomon guessed it was Beard's home.

"Leave them outa this!" Beard said.

Alonso inhaled and looked at the screen on his phone. "One more chance."

Beard's eyes filled with uncontrollable fury, and he fought against the restraints, but as he fought, his eyes welled with tears, and his head lowered. His nose watered. Something was breaking inside of him.

"Yes," Beard finally said. "That's how many people I pulled over."

Alonso grinned and put his phone away.

38

Heather decided to skip the gym but said she'd feel better talking if they also walked. So they took the sidewalk down the hill and into the town's main street, where all the restaurants, casinos, and grocery stores were. She kept her arms folded as she talked, and the way she'd initially spoken, with erudition and a hint of sophistication, was completely gone. In addition to moving physically away from Alonso, she'd had to move psychologically away from him and even changed the way she spoke so she could do it. But now, the memories all came flooding back, and Billie guessed it was excruciating to go back to the role of victim.

"He was so charming at first," Heather said with a suggestion of a grin. "He was scary because of how big he was, but I was working at a tanning salon, and he'd come by my work and bring me flowers or teddy bears. You should've seen how my mom treated him. She was in love with him. He could be so . . ."

"Likable?"

"Yeah, likable."

"Men like him excel at superficial charm. They let you see what they want you to see, usually hiding something much worse underneath."

"I don't know . . . I felt like such a fool for so long that I pushed it all out. I got to a place I don't think about him every second of the day. Whether or not he's going to come through my door and hurt John or our baby daughter."

Billie looked at her. "You think he would hurt a child?"

"I don't know. He was drunk one night, and this guy came up to us at a club. We had a booth in the corner, and Alonso wanted to be alone and watch the show, some rapper he really liked, but the guy kept talking to Alonso, and Alonso finally said something like, 'I've killed everything that's ever walked or crawled on this earth, and killing a cockroach like you won't mean nothin'.' That's when I knew I had to get out."

They stopped at an intersection, and a McDonald's was on the corner. Billie watched some children roughhousing in the outdoor play area. One of the little boys looked like Solomon, and she imagined him as a child, his face buried in books as he tried to ignore all the heartache around him.

"I have to find him, Heather."

"I'm sorry. I wish I could help. But I don't have any idea where he is."

"There's got to be something you know about him that nobody else does. Somewhere he goes to relax or feel safe when he's stressed, maybe. He hasn't been sleeping at the motel that's his registered place of residence, so he's got to be sleeping somewhere."

Heather paused. "I guess there is one place."

"Where?"

"It's past the salt flats. Chelsea. You heard of it?"

A slight chill went through Billie's body. "I have."

"He would go up by the lake there and shoot bottles and birds and things to relax. I'm sure he kept things there too. Things he didn't want me to see."

"Like what?"

She shrugged. "I knew he was dirty, and what he did for a living and all, I couldn't help that, but I told him to never bring it around me. Never put me in a spot where I had to get arrested because of something he did. He said he wouldn't, and he never did. So he had to keep things somewhere. It's probably in one of the cabins on the north side. He would always talk about how peaceful it is because no one ever goes to Chelsea anymore. That's the only place I can think of."

The light turned, and Billie sighed and said, "I better get up there if I'm going to search the entire north side."

"By yourself? You know meth heads and devil worshippers are the only ones up there."

"I don't have much of a choice."

Heather hesitated a second before saying, "Don't let him charm you. If you get the chance, you shoot."

39

Alonso paced back and forth like an attorney scanning his memories for any statute or case law he could use to more effectively prove his innocence, though Judge Elrod didn't appear to be listening. Solomon was worried the old man was going to hemorrhage.

"Alonso," he said, interrupting his questioning of the lieutenant, "the judge is hurt bad. He had nothing to do with this. Let him go to the hospital."

"We need an impartial adjudicator, don't we, Counsel? How can we reach the truth without someone to adjudicate? Unless you'd like to skip the trial and go right to sentencing?"

Solomon most certainly did *not* want to go right to sentencing, but he also knew Elrod was in bad shape. The wound on his head had matted his hair with blood, which was dribbling down onto his clothes and the floor. Alonso had hit him too hard, and soon the man would be dead.

"Do you know the penalty for murdering a judge, Alonso? It's death. Not lockup, man. Death. You wanna die over this?"

He laughed. "I'm already dead, Counselor. I died eleven years ago in that courtroom when everything I had in my life was taken from me. Now, if you'll excuse me, I have to finish my cross-examination of the good lieutenant." He turned to Beard, who stared at him with eyes that could light on fire, filled with so much anger. "Lieutenant, of the one thousand three hundred and seventy-six people you pulled over in your six years as a patrol officer, do you know how many were white?"

"White?"

"Yes, Lieutenant. How many people did you pull over that were white?"

"I don't know. I didn't care about that."

"Would it surprise you if I told you that eight hundred and fifty-six were white? A percentage of about sixty-two percent?"

Beard didn't answer, but Solomon could see the muscles in his forearms flex as he pushed against the tape on his wrists.

"Lieutenant, I asked you a question."

"No, that wouldn't surprise me."

"Why not?"

"Why should it? I was working an area that was mostly white."

"*Mostly*, not all. You pulled over five hundred and twenty non-whites. Is that right?"

"I don't know."

"Would it surprise you if that was the number?"

"No, it wouldn't."

"Now, here's the interesting part." Alonso flipped through a file folder and took a printout that he showed to Beard. "Of the eight hundred and fifty-six whites you pulled over, five hundred and sixty-six of those led to convictions. You see that?"

Beard glanced at the paper and then up at Alonso. "What the hell's the point of all this?"

"You got five hundred and sixty-six convictions, right?"

"Yeah, right. Whatever."

"And of the five hundred and twenty nonwhites you pulled over, you got four hundred and ninety-three convictions, correct?"

"I guess."

"Okay, so that's about sixty-six percent conviction rate for whites and almost ninety-five percent for nonwhites. Do you agree those are the numbers?"

"I don't know. Why don't you cut me loose and lemme take a closer look at that paper?"

Alonso grinned. "Lieutenant, we are in a court of law, and I will remind you that the crime of perjury is a federal offense. Perhaps one of the worst offenses there is." He looked at Solomon. "Wouldn't you agree, Counselor? Is there anything lower than lying in a court of law where we seek the truth?"

Solomon managed to straighten up. "Alonso, let them go. None of them have anything to do with this."

"Then you need to pay closer attention, Counselor." He turned back to Beard. "I got another paper here . . . this here, Lieutenant, is a list of convictions grouped by crimes. Do you see the numbers there? Would you please read the plea bargain rate for whites that were subsequently arrested for more than a traffic violation?"

Beard spit blood onto the sheet.

Alonso punched him so hard the crack of fist on jawbone echoed in the room. Even with such a display of power, Solomon knew he was holding back.

"I'll ask again. Would you please read—"

"It's eighty-six percent."

"That's right. Of those cases, eighty-six percent ended in plea bargains, about seven percent were dismissed, and seven percent went to trial. Now, look at this line here. It's the list for nonwhites. What's the plea bargain rate for nonwhites you pulled over that were subsequently arrested for more than a traffic violation?"

Beard didn't say anything, and Alonso didn't move. Solomon tried to speak again, and in a flash of movement, Alonso took out the handgun tucked in his waistband.

"It is not your turn to talk, Counselor!"

He put the gun to Beard's head. "What is it?"

Beard took a breath. "It's twenty-four percent."

"Yes! That's right, Lieutenant, twenty-four percent. I thought that was odd that the whites you pulled over settled their cases at three times the rates of nonwhites, so I looked into it a little more. Do you wanna know what the deciding factor was? *Law enforcement recommendation.* In your reports, you wrote more favorably about white defendants than you did about defendants of color."

"What the hell do you want!" Beard said, fighting against his restraints.

"I want the truth. You wrote the reports to look worse for nonwhite defendants, and when the prosecutor asked your opinion, you told them to give inferior plea deals to nonwhites."

"I never said anything like that."

"You did. And I bet you didn't even know you were doing it, did you? I can see in your eyes you didn't know. You know what that's called, Lieutenant? Undiscovered inherent bias, which means that you're completely unaware that you treat whites and folks of color differently."

He chuckled. "My wife is Hispanic. I'm not a racist."

"I know. That's the shit nature of inherent bias, Lieutenant. The person has no idea they're displaying prejudice. How you supposed to fix a system where people don't even know why it's broken?"

He shook his head and stopped struggling. A gash was across the side of his skull that slowly oozed blood.

"Alonso, he's bleeding out."

"I don't remember asking you a damn thing!"

Alonso rushed Solomon and pressed the muzzle against his forehead. Solomon closed his eyes. Someone had once said you don't hear the shot that kills you, and he wondered if it was true.

"He's going to die, Alonso," he said calmly.

"I coulda died. Every second I was locked up in that pit. Everybody in there is a shark, 'cause all the fish get eaten when they come in. You get eaten, or you turn into one of the sharks."

"Don't kid yourself. You were a shark long before you went in there."

He chuckled. "You're right, I can't blame you for that." He turned to Beard. "Getting back to it, Lieutenant, on the night in question, you got a call from dispatch saying a witness saw a man beating another man and then driving away in a black car. I had a black Chrysler 300. But this was later. First, you pulled me over for speeding, right?"

"I don't remember."

Alonso grabbed a file out of the box and threw it at Beard's face. The file slapped his cheek, and its contents spilled onto the floor.

"Speeding?" Alonso said.

Beard slowly looked up at him, their eyes meeting. "Yeah," he said.

"But you didn't have a lidar or radar gun, did you?"

"No."

"No. You did something called pacing." Alonso glanced at the judge and took a step back. "Explain to this Court what pacing is, Lieutenant."

Beard swallowed and said, "It's where the law enforcement officer follows a speeding car and clocks his own speed once he's traveling at the same speed."

"How close do you have to follow to pace somebody?"

"One car length for every ten miles per hour."

"And how far behind me were you?"

"I don't know."

"You don't know, or you don't wanna say?"

"I don't know. I don't remember how fast you were going."

"Are you aware, Lieutenant, that I have never gotten a speeding ticket? Not once. Not even when I was a teenager. Are you aware of that?"

"No."

"Are you aware, Lieutenant, that I studied the traffic code so that I would never get pulled over? That I have not only never received a speeding ticket but any kind of ticket?"

He looked down to the floor, energy slowly seeping out of him. "No."

"No. I'm a pretty damn cautious driver, don't you think?"

"Whatever you say."

"Now, I'd like to show you something." He reached down to the file he'd thrown at him and found a color photo of a speed limit sign. "You pulled me over at 1250 North, and here's the nearest speed limit sign. What's it say?"

Beard glanced up. "Forty."

"Forty. You paced me at forty-seven, right?"

"I don't know."

Alonso grabbed his report from the floor and shoved it in Beard's face, grabbing his hair. "What's it say, Lieutenant?"

Beard managed to spit out, "Forty-seven," before fighting against the tape again.

He let go of Beard's hair.

"Forty-seven. And you were going forty-seven?"

"Yeah."

"Do you realize, Lieutenant, that some patrol officers purposely follow close to drivers they want to pull over so that the driver thinks they might get rear-ended and go faster? And when they go faster, they get paced and then pulled over?"

Beard said nothing.

"Are you aware, Lieutenant, that of the nonwhite motorists you pulled over for speeding, over ninety percent were because of pacing and not a lidar or radar gun?"

Beard didn't do anything and kept his eyes on the floor.

"I asked you a question, Lieutenant."

"No, I wasn't aware of that."

"So it's possible you caused the crime you pulled me over for, isn't it? That's called entrapment. What's entrapment, Lieutenant?"

He took a breath, and Solomon saw the blood dripping faster from his head. "It's where law enforcement causes the crime they arrest the perpetrator for."

"And if a court finds that entrapment occurred, the case is dismissed, isn't that right?"

"Yes."

"My incompetent lawyer didn't file an entrapment motion. Would you say that's ineffective assistance of counsel?"

"I don't know."

"If your daughter was on trial, and her lawyer didn't file an entrapment motion when he could have, would you say that's a good lawyer or a shitty lawyer?"

Beard inhaled deeply; his blinking had slowed.

"Alonso," Solomon said softly, "let him go to the hospital."

"Be patient, Counselor."

Alonso leaned down so the two men were at eye level. "Lieutenant, what other suspects did you investigate for the beating of Michael Donovan?"

"I don't remember."

"Well, let me refresh your recollection. Zero. Not one. There was not one other person you investigated for this crime, was there?"

"We had a positive ID on you."

"Oh, right, the positive ID of a junkie who got a deal on some drug charges for testifying against me. Joy Rio, that was her, correct?"

"Yes."

"Ms. Rio had a long history of drug charges, didn't she? Eight cases were filed with six convictions. One more conviction, and she could've been looking at serious time, couldn't she?"

"I don't know."

"You knew then, didn't you? Or did you not look into her at all?" He used the gun to lift Beard's head by the chin. "She became your confidential informant after my case, didn't she?"

"Just briefly. Not even a month."

"Funny," he said, looking at Solomon. "You didn't remember anything about the case before, but now you remember how long she was your CI?"

Beard didn't respond.

"Isn't it true that you told her the felony case she had pending could be dropped if she testified against me and then made a few buys for you and Doyle when you asked?"

Beard didn't respond.

"Lieutenant, isn't it true—"

"Yes, it's true. She was a good person. Just messed up. She deserved another chance."

"But I didn't? You didn't look for another suspect, and the only witness against me is a junkie who has a motive to lie. And you didn't even think maybe you should find some other suspects just in case she was wrong?"

"No one else was there."

"There was a convenience store near the bar. Did you talk to the clerk who was working that night?"

"Yeah, he didn't see anything."

"Did you ask him if anybody else saw anything?"

"Nobody else was in the store."

"Did you watch the video?"

"The video?"

"From inside the store. The surveillance video behind the register."

"Yes."

"You're lying, Lieutenant. You put in an order for the video but didn't think it'd show anything, so when the cashier forgot to send it, you never followed up." He pulled out some grainy photos. "This is from the video, Lieutenant. Look at the time. What does it say?"

Beard looked at the photo. "Eleven thirty-seven."

"Right at the time Mr. Donovan was assaulted, right?"

"Yeah."

"How many people you see in this picture?"

Solomon couldn't see the photo right in front of Beard's face, but Beard had something in his eyes he didn't have before: shock.

"Tell the Court how many people you see in this photo?"

"Two," he said quietly.

"Two. That girl right there, that's the cashier's girlfriend, who was hanging out with him at work, and he didn't want her involved. You didn't know that, though, 'cause you never checked the video."

"There was no reason to," he said half-heartedly.

"No reason," Alonso scoffed. "I was on trial for my life. My *life*, Lieutenant! And there was *no reason* to check the video to see if another witness could confirm what your junkie said?"

Beard didn't know what to say. He glanced at Alonso and Solomon before looking back down to the floor, his eyes drifting closed as he breathed deep.

"Innocent until proven guilty, right, Lieutenant?"

Alonso took a cigar out of his jacket and lit it with a gold lighter.

"No further questions, Your Honor. I tender the witness to the State."

40

Chelsea was a pan of thick salt that looked like open sand dunes of pure white. A lake was in the center, and many people mistook it for a mirage since Chelsea didn't look like the kind of place that would have water. Billie came here once in high school with a boy she was dating. He and his friends would race their cars, as law enforcement never came out this far.

Chelsea was a bastardization of what the place west of the salt flats was actually called: *Dead Sea*. Some of the pioneers who passed by here to establish the first settlements in Utah were suffering from an epidemic at the time, probably an outbreak of cholera. Over half their party died in a matter of days.

Not wanting to waste good fuel for fires or take the time to bury the bodies—since the survivors wouldn't get through the winter if they didn't get somewhere warm—they dumped the corpses in the closest body of water, which happened to be Chelsea Lake.

Ever since, people coming here reported seeing things that weren't there and hearing voices when nobody else was around. Chelsea became a place of cold, dead air, but no one would find it on any "Haunted Places in America" maps. Some places were considered haunted and fun and would draw tourists, but the truly dark places, the places where even the land didn't feel right, they were never talked about.

That night more than a decade ago, when the boy showed her Chelsea and they sat near the shore and listened to the crackle of the waves, Billie heard something. A single word. It sounded like . . . *Leave.* The word was whispered in her ear as though by someone only inches away. She turned her head, and nothing was there.

Now, with time, she had concluded she was already scared that night from hearing the stories, and her mind filled in the gap on a gust of wind making an odd noise. But occasionally she would think back on the voice and wonder if it really was a trick of the wind.

After parking near the shore of Chelsea Lake, she sat in her truck and left the engine running. The water looked inky black, as the sky was a deep gray, the sun hidden behind clouds. She turned the truck off and got out.

A cold wind gave her shivers, and she zipped up her coat. The briny scent of the Great Salt Lake wasn't as prevalent here. Instead, there was more of a rotting smell.

On the shore closest to her were several cabins. The homes were set up as a development project decades ago since the land was the cheapest in the entire state. She had heard people had lived here for months, but everyone slowly left, down to the last family. The cabins had since been abandoned, and no one had tried developing here again.

The first cabin was two stories with a steepled roof. A padlock was on the door. It looked like a strong wind could've blown it over. She went to the next cabin and the next. Down a long row. She walked briskly and occasionally glanced at ripples along the water's surface. Her boots crunched the snow and made her think of walking on gravel.

All the cabins appeared the same: a cookie-cutter community, one that should've been filled with children and families and instead held nothing but empty salt-whipped structures.

She came to a cabin that looked oddly different from the two flanking its sides. The windows of the cabin were covered with something black, perhaps a blanket or sheet, while the other windows were either broken or open. She looked at the door: no lock.

She withdrew her firearm.

The interior of the cabin was covered in sand and salt. The floors had a thin layer over most of the space. No graffiti or garbage like she usually saw in abandoned buildings: vagrants stayed away from here.

She left the door open behind her. When the wind whipped debris against the exterior walls, it startled her. And she didn't startle easy.

There was a crash behind her.

She spun around, her firearm in front of her as she spotted motion in the shadows. She pulled the trigger twice, the kickback causing an ache in her wrists because she hadn't braced appropriately. Her chest tightened as she held her breath.

The wind had swung the door open, and it hit the wall. Two holes were prominent in the door at the exact spot someone's chest would have been if they were standing there.

If Solomon were here, she imagined he would say something like, *Well, if I'm ever attacked by a door, I'm glad I have you on my side.* The thought of his humor gave her some relief.

She inhaled deeply and lowered the gun.

The upstairs was connected to the kitchen by solid wood stairs that looked as dilapidated as the rest of the cabin. She took the first step cautiously, and it creaked so loudly that she debated whether to go up there at all.

After a few seconds, she put her shoulder against the wall and held her weapon low, her finger over the trigger guard. Then she slid up the wall slowly, testing each step before putting her full weight on it.

While downstairs had been emptied, upstairs still retained something of a livable space. It was cleaner, and there was a bed with blankets and pillows. In the corner, she noticed a garbage can. A few white plastic bags were tied off and filled with refuse, including empty food containers and bottles of Jim Beam, from what she could see through the bags. A space heater was near the bed.

She swung the flashlight left and right methodically, getting every inch of the floor. What, exactly, was she hoping to find? A slip of paper with an address where Alonso had taken Solomon? Even if he did have a place up here, he didn't leave any clothes, so clearly he knew he wasn't coming back. He wouldn't be dumb enough to leave a note behind.

On a table against the wall, she saw an ashtray. She picked it up and smelled the remnants of ash. It had the distinct smell of high-end tobacco and marijuana.

Parolees were required to maintain an address their parole officers could visit, and that's what the motel was, but this was where Alonso came to rest. Something about this place was comforting to him.

A garbage bag on the floor was separate from the rest, thrown against the wall far away from the bed. The bag seemed to contain coiled black wires. As she went to pick it up, it moved and hissed. She jumped back and held her firearm in front of her, nearly pulling the trigger again.

The snake slithered inside the bag and made it crinkle. A slow hiss escaped that sounded like air from a tire.

What the hell was he doing with a snake?

41

Solomon stared at Alonso. He looked worse: Sweat wouldn't stop pouring out of him, and his lips were taking on a bluish hue. His eyes were severely bloodshot, and his wounds' bleeding wasn't stopping.

As he smoked his cigar, he leaned against a table and motioned with his head toward the lieutenant.

"Go ahead, Counselor."

"I'm not playing this game, Alonso."

"Not a game. We're in a court of law. And it sounds like you're saying you don't have any questions for this witness. Is that right? Because I gotta tell you, his testimony was devastating for the State. Ain't that right, Judge?"

Elrod didn't say anything but gave a slight nod. Lieutenant Beard looked between both of them and then lowered his head. He was losing energy and would bleed out if he didn't get to a hospital soon.

"If I cross him, will you cut him loose before you take off?"

He blew out smoke. "When the witness is finished, he may be excused."

Solomon looked at Beard again. "Lieutenant, during your time on patrol, what was your assigned area?"

He took a couple of breaths. "From 100 West past the high school to the east and up to the granary to the north."

"That's a mixed-use area, correct? Lots of different apartment build-ings, condos, and businesses?"

"Yes."

"You have office space over there for high-end businesses like wealth-management firms and factories right next to them?"

"Yes."

"Because it's economically diverse, it's also racially diverse, is it not?"

"It is."

"Would you say a higher concentration of Blacks, Asians, and Latinos live in that area?"

"In my experience," he said, his breath slow, "yes. It's predomi-nantly white but more racially diverse than other areas."

"Did you ever consciously pull over anyone specifically because of their race?"

"Never. Not once. I didn't care what anybody's race was."

"Do you remember pacing the defendant's car?"

"Vaguely. It was a long time ago."

They were getting into a rhythm, and the lieutenant was answering as he would on the stand. But the blood had soaked Beard's entire left side of his shirt and seeped down his arm, painting it crimson black. He was losing blood far too fast, and Solomon feared there might be no saving him now no matter what they did.

"When you pace a car, you have to maintain a certain car-length distance so that you don't cause the suspect to speed, hence causing entrapment like the defendant said. Were you at the appropriate car distance?"

"I never got too close. If I did, it was accidental."

"What did your dashcam video of the incident show?"

"Objection," Alonso said. "Stating facts not in evidence."

The judge nodded and said, "Sustained."

Solomon rephrased. "Is there a video of this incident?"

"No," Beard slurred. "My dashcam wasn't working properly at the time."

"Was that common?"

"Yes. They were old. Electronics wear out over time and need to be replaced, and police equipment is used until it breaks to get the last penny of use because our budgets are so tight."

"In your career, how many other entrapment motions were filed against you for pacing too closely?"

"None."

"How many complaints have you had for excessive force?"

"None."

"Racial or gender discrimination?"

"None."

"Had you met the defendant before the night you pulled him over?"

"No. Never."

"So you had no reason to have any animosity toward him?"

"None whatsoever. I wasn't even going to cite him for speeding. I was just going to give him a warning. Then the call came in while I had him pulled over to be on the lookout for a black sedan with a possibly Hispanic male traveling alone."

Alonso scoffed and shook his head.

"What made you think he could've been the suspect a BOLO call was put out for?" Solomon said.

"When I came to the window, I remember he was acting strange."

"Strange how?"

"He wasn't moving his right arm, and it was tucked lower than his thigh, so I couldn't see his hand. In my experience, that usually means someone is holding a weapon."

"So what did you do?"

"I called for backup and withdrew my weapon and told him to get out of the car."

"And then what happened?"

"I don't totally recall, but I remember he started arguing with me. I didn't want the situation to escalate, so I kept him talking until backup could get there so he couldn't escape."

"Objection," Alonso said. "Speculation."

The judge nodded. "Sustained."

Solomon didn't try to argue: the judge was in no position to do anything.

"What happened when the other patrol cars arrived, Lieutenant?"

"They parked in front of the defendant's vehicle, and the other officers withdrew their weapons and approached. I was on the driver's side, and the other officers were in front and on the passenger side." Beard's tongue sounded heavy in his mouth.

Solomon tried to finish up his line of questioning. "What did you do then?"

"We asked the defendant to put his hands on the steering wheel."

"Did he comply?"

"Not at first. I remember that because I really thought I might have to use force." Beard had to take a moment and not speak, the blood loss and fatigue draining his face of any color. "He talked about us getting a warrant, and I told him we didn't need one to get him out of the car and secure him for our safety."

"What was his demeanor like?"

"Agitated. Aggressive."

"Did you apply for a warrant at some point?"

"To search the vehicle, we did. But we had to get him out of the car first for our safety."

"Did you get him out?"

"When the other patrol cars arrived and he got scared, he did get out."

"Objection. Speculation. I've never been scared of another man in my life."

"Sustained," the judge said.

Solomon was relatively confident the judge hadn't fully understood what the objection was.

"What did you do when he got out, Lieutenant?"

"We had him get on his knees, and I guided him to the ground, where we effectuated an arrest. We had to use two pairs of cuffs and lock them together so they would fit on him."

"Did you notice any injuries on him?"

He shook his head. "I don't remember."

Solomon looked at Alonso. "We ask the Court to allow the lieutenant to refresh his recollection under rule 612 of the URE."

"Don't ask me. Ask the judge."

Solomon looked at Elrod, who nodded. He then looked at Alonso and said, "Would you mind showing him his report?"

Alonso inhaled a puff and kept his eyes glued to Solomon. Then he set the cigar down and picked up some of the papers that had struck Beard in the face and showed them to him. It took a minute, but Beard finally said, "Yes, we did notice injuries."

"What were they?" Solomon asked.

"His hands. The knuckles on both hands were cut and bleeding."

"What did this tell you?"

"It told me that—"

"Objection, Judge," Alonso said. "The lieutenant isn't qualified as a medical expert and shouldn't be allowed to conjecture where injuries came from."

The judge responded, "Sustained," quickly enough that Solomon knew that was the actual ruling he would've made in court.

"How long have you been a law enforcement officer, Lieutenant Beard?" Solomon continued.

"Twenty-two years."

"And in twenty-two years, did you arrest many people for assault?"

"Yes."

"When someone assaulted someone else with their fists, were there injuries to their fists?"

"Same objection, Judge," Alonso said.

Before the judge could say anything, Solomon said, "He's allowed to testify as to his experience without making medical inferences."

Elrod said, "Overruled," and Alonso gave the judge a look that made Solomon think he wouldn't be getting many rulings in his favor.

"You can answer," Solomon said. "Were there injuries to people's fists when they got into a fight?"

"If they struck the other person in the mouth where the teeth can cut skin on the hands, yes, there were usually injuries."

"Were the injuries on the defendant's hands consistent with what you've seen after someone assaulted someone else with their fists?"

"Yes. I thought they were caused by him striking somebody in the mouth multiple times."

"Did you ask him?"

"I did."

"What did he say?"

"He told me to go self-fornicate."

"So you arrested him?"

"Yes. The BOLO call was for a large Hispanic or possibly Middle Eastern male, extremely tall, with a bald head. The defendant matched the witness's description, and with the injuries on his hands, it seemed we had enough probable cause that he was a suspect in the assault."

"During the defendant's preliminary hearing, the judge reviewed the evidence in the case, and you testified, correct?"

"Yes."

"What was the judge's ruling?"

"He found sufficient probable cause to justify the arrest and the bringing of charges."

"So all your actions were reviewed by a court and determined to be within the bounds of the law, correct?"

"Correct."

Alonso chuckled. "Within the bounds of the law . . . what if what's allowed within the bounds of the law is the problem?"

"That's enough," Solomon said. "End this, Alonso. Let him go."

Alonso smoked and said nothing.

"Let him go, damn it! He's dying."

"No, he's already dead."

Alonso pulled the handgun and turned to Beard. Solomon heard ringing in his ears and the tiny clinks of spent rounds hitting the bare floor. The smoke from the fire had overwhelmed his scent, but he knew he was close enough that he should've smelled the gunpowder.

Beard had three points the size of golf balls on his shirt that turned wet and dark. They broadened as the blood left him. He took only two more breaths, straining against his own collapsed lungs, and then his head dropped, and he didn't move again.

Solomon was about to shout when Alonso turned. He charged at him, his cigar hitting the floor and sending tiny ash embers off the tip. The hot muzzle of the gun tasted like salt in Solomon's mouth.

Alonso grabbed his collar with one hand and said, "Maybe you're right. Maybe we just end it now."

Using his thumb, he cocked the gun.

Solomon closed his eyes.

42

There was only one more place Billie could think of to go. But if the location turned out to be a bust, she wasn't sure what she would do next to find Solomon before Alonso killed him.

She had called the forensic team up to the cabin in Chelsea and told them there was a live snake in a bag on the second floor. They thought she was joking until one of them texted her, Holy shit, you meant a real snake!!!

She texted back, I have no idea what this man was doing with a snake, but I can only imagine. Please get some antivenom made as soon as possible.

Alonso's older sister lived in town as well, out in a subproject near a farm. The rail tracks that carried the resources miners in the mountains sent down to the city for processing cut across the land and around the homes.

Before it was officially founded as a city, Tooele had been a mining town. Several accidents at the mines sent the miners away. Being a superstitious group, they had decided as a collective that the mines in the Tooele Mountains were cursed and unminable. A few, the more desperate, had stuck around, and their descendants became the city's founders. Even without a single remnant of mining, the place still felt like an old mining town.

Billie pulled her truck to a stop, listening to a country song she liked.

She got out. Blackened snow piled up from plows that got too close to the curbs. Cars spattered muddy-gray water as they drove by.

She got to a wooden door with a list of residents on the wall next to it, written on paper tabs in pen and pushed into transparent plastic sheaths. Alonso's sister had changed her name, but Billie had been able to pull it up after a bit of effort. It required more than just a name search to find, which meant she must've taken some pains to completely erase her old identity.

The condo was on the fourth floor. There was no elevator, and she took the stairs as quietly as she could, listening to the sounds around her. People speaking loudly on cell phones, a television blaring, food cooking, a couple arguing.

Some vending machines looked broken down, and a few teenagers were smoking near them. They ignored her as she walked past.

She knocked on the condo door. No one answered. She knocked again and waited. Blowing out frustration through pressed lips, she turned away to head back to the truck but stopped.

Damn it, Solomon.

She glanced down both directions of the hallway and then took out her key chain. Attached was a set of what looked like black keys but was actually a universal lockpick. Her father had always carried around a set and never spoken about it.

It took three attempts to find the right fit, but she got one of the black keys in and opened the lock.

The condo had pale carpets and a couch with a glass coffee table. On the other side of the room was a chair upholstered to match the sofa. Live plants were up in the corners and spread their branches across the wall. The home smelled like it had recently been cleaned.

Billie made sure the door was locked behind her before she looked around. The kitchen was spotless and didn't have a single dish in the sink. A wooden plaque with a homey saying was up on the fridge.

Magazines were under the coffee table, and a sliding glass door led to a balcony. The bedrooms and bathrooms were down a hallway. The bedroom was large and had one massive bed. There were pictures on the nightstand but none of children. Just Alonso's sister and her boyfriend. The closet held no men's clothing.

As she was about to leave the bedroom, Billie heard a sound. She froze. A voice. Female, and coming down the hallway. Billie stared at the carpet as she hoped the person was walking by, but then she heard the jingle of keys near the lock. Making the decision quickly, she went out to the living room and waited.

The door opened, and a tall woman in yoga clothes came in with a phone to her ear. Her face had no makeup, but her beauty still came through, her black hair with strawberry highlights pulled back with an elastic. Billie could see the resemblance to her sister and mother.

"I'm sorry for the intrusion," Billie quickly said. "My name is Elizabeth Gray. I'm a police officer."

"What the hell are you doing in my house!"

"I just need your help," she said, raising a hand in a calming gesture. "I'm looking for Alonso, and you weren't home. I don't have much time and thought maybe I would find something here telling me where he was."

The woman said, "I'mma call you back," before hanging up and telling Billie, "I'm calling 911."

"He's going to kill someone I care about."

She stopped dialing and looked at her.

"The prosecutor that convicted him. Alonso kidnapped him last night. He's going to kill him and run. And when the police find him, they won't give him a chance to surrender. Not after murdering a law enforcement official."

Billie lowered her hand. "Your name's Camila, right? Camila, I'm desperate, and I need your help."

The woman lowered the phone and glared at her awhile. Then she sat on the chair across from the love seat Billie sat on and folded one leg over the other.

"First, you need to tell me how you got into my house."

Billie showed her the lockpick. "It opens nine out of ten locks in the world," she said, her words slightly tinged with shame. "I had no right to do it, and I'm sorry, but I didn't know what else to do."

Camila folded her arms. "You don't look like a cop."

"I get that a lot."

She glanced out the sliding glass doors. "So? What do you wanna ask me?"

"Have you and Alonso always been close?" Billie asked.

She nodded. "He didn't have anybody else. My mom loved him but didn't know how to raise him. When our daddy died, my mom wouldn't get remarried. She's old school and believes in one soul mate for life. So Alonso had to learn how to be a man on his own, and the only teacher he had was the streets. I've traveled all over the world for work. You wouldn't think Utah of all places would have ghettos, but ghettos are the same everywhere and teach the same lessons."

"Your mother showed me some disturbing photos. I'm not sure those were lessons the street taught him. Something deeper is wrong with him, isn't it?"

Camila looked away, out the balcony sliding glass doors to the empty fields cut across with train tracks.

"When he was four, I caught him cutting the heads off my dolls. I didn't think anything of it. I had three other brothers, and little boys are crazy. But it started to get worse the older he got."

"Worse how?"

"He told me once that he dreamed about hurting people. He was maybe ten. I was the only one he told because I was his protector, and he knew it."

Billie saw the pain in her eyes and knew she loved Alonso, but also knew that her love would end only in tragedy.

"You had to protect him from himself his entire life, didn't you? That must've been exhausting."

She stayed quiet for a while. "It's not his fault he's different."

"Was he ever diagnosed with anything?"

"Depression, bipolar, ADD, schizophrenia, you name it, they said he had it. But they don't even have any tests to tell you if any of that's true. Not like you can test someone's blood and say they're mentally ill." She paused and bit her lower lip. "I found out later that none of it was real. Alonso knew what the psychologists were looking for in their tests and would play with them. Sometimes being normal and sometimes shocking them with the things he said."

"He suffers from something they can't test for." Billie leaned forward, her elbows on her knees as she interlaced her fingers. "Camila, do you know where he is?"

The woman said nothing but stared at Billie with a combination of curiosity and hate. Curiosity probably because she wanted to know how Billie could help Alonso, and hate because she likely knew he was beyond help.

"I'm not telling the police where my brother is so you can put him down like a dog."

"If there's any way I can save him, I will. But we both know he can't be free." She paused as a train rumbled by just outside the building. "I know you love him, but the man he's going to hurt . . . has people who love him, too."

Camila looked her up and down. "You didn't threaten me."

"Why would I threaten you?"

"Because whenever the police need anything, they threaten you with obstruction of justice. Seems like that's just a law to force people to cooperate with cops."

"That's probably true, but that's not why I'm in this job." Billie held out her open palms in a pleading gesture. "I have nowhere else to go. If you turn me down, I have to wait until I get notification that they've found Alonso. And if he kills this man, they won't take him alive. I can guarantee you that."

Camila didn't speak for a while and then uncrossed her legs and leaned forward. She put her face in her hands, and Billie thought she heard her whisper something to herself. "Then you have to promise me something. You can't kill him. You have to arrest him and get him back in prison where he can't hurt anyone else."

"I'll do everything I can."

"Not good enough. I don't know if you're religious, but whatever you believe in, you have to swear to me that you will *not* kill him. You'll arrest him, get him back inside, but you won't kill him. I have no reason to trust you other than you don't act like other cops. You act like someone trying to save a person they care about, which is what I'm doing. Swear it to me."

She nodded. "I swear, he will not die by a police officer unless he tries to kill them first."

Camila's phone dinged, and she silenced it and put it on the coffee table. "He's in a cabin in Chelsea. He's been going there since he could drive."

Billie's heart sank. "I've already been to the cabin. It's cleared out."

"Then I don't know where he is. Last I spoke to him, he was in the cabin."

Billie leaned back on the couch. The train had passed, but another one was coming from the same direction and gave the condo a slight rumble in the floors that she was surprised she didn't notice before.

"Is there anywhere else he could have taken him? Somewhere secluded but not too far?"

Camila shook her head. "No. Home never meant much to him, so he always went back to places he felt comfortable. The cabin was what was there for him. And the refinery, I guess."

"Refinery?"

She nodded. "It's owned by Champion Chemical. Or was. He'd be gone for days, and I'd have to go find him there. He'd sleep on a mattress in the back so he could work early in the morning before going to school."

"They let a child work there?"

"The owner did. A man named Reginald Gerald. They were close. He had a son Alonso's age who died of leukemia, so him and Alonso bonded. He taught Alonso all about the business and had him work in some of the places he owned. Alonso loved it there. That and the cabin were the only places he was happy."

She said *happy* in such a way that her voice pierced Billie. It was the only time Alonso would be happy ever again.

"It's worth looking into. People are creatures of habit. I really appreciate you talking to me, Camila."

"You just do right by me and keep your promise."

43

The gun tasted like sucking on a mouthful of salty, hot pennies. Solomon felt the muzzle against his tongue as Alonso pushed it farther into his mouth. Then, after a moment, he opened his eyes, and the two men stared at each other. Alonso pulled the gun out.

"Don't worry, Counselor. I'm here to cleanse your soul before sending it back to the Maker. You haven't been cleansed yet."

Alonso's hands trembled violently, and he was drooling. He'd wipe his meaty palm down his face, come away with drool and blood, and wipe his face again, forgetting he already had. He was sucking breath like he couldn't get enough. The fire eating up the oxygen in the room and replacing it with bitter smoke wasn't helping.

"You don't look well, Alonso. The grave singers would ingest a little venom every day over months to build up immunity. You drank too much, too fast. You're going to die."

"No, Counselor, we're all going to die." He took out a fresh cigar and lit it, exhaling the puffs of smoke in gray rings. "The defense calls Joy Rio to the stand."

Alonso disappeared again, and this time there were footsteps on the bare floors instead of wheels. He appeared behind Solomon a minute later with a woman stumbling along in front of him. Her hands were bound with industrial tape as well, which also covered her mouth. Her hair was messy, and her makeup ran down her face. Her eyes were bloodshot, and she looked exhausted. Creases on her skin told Solomon she'd been shoved somewhere that was a tight fit, and he wondered how long she'd been held by Alonso.

Alonso cut loose Beard's body and let it slump to the floor. Joy started quietly sobbing.

"Will the witness take a seat, please?" Alonso said.

Joy was trembling and staring at the blood pooled around the chair. The corpse lay on its side, Beard's lifeless eyes staring off at nothing. Alonso kicked his head away so Joy couldn't see his face. Then he used his hand to wipe the blood off the seat, leaving smears of dark red on the chair.

"Take a seat," he said flatly.

She did as she was told.

Tears flowed, and the muffled sound of sobbing accompanied it. Alonso lifted the gun. Joy screamed through the tape. He grabbed her by the hair and held her in place as he brought the gun up to her face. She got deathly still, holding her breath.

"Don't do this," Solomon begged.

Alonso ripped the tape off her mouth in a quick motion that was little more than flicking his wrist. Then he let her go and went back to pacing.

Joy kept her eyes low and stared at the floor. Alonso inhaled deeply and said, "Please state your name and affiliation with this case."

"What?" she said, her voice cracking.

"We're in trial, and you are in a court of law," he bellowed. "State your name and your affiliation with this case."

"I don't understand," she cried. "Please let me go. I don't know anything."

"You know a lot. Now state your damn name."

She looked at Solomon and the judge. Then, seeing that no one was able to help her, she said gently, "Joy Rio."

"And what's your affiliation with this case, Ms. Rio? The case of the *State v. Alonso Hafeez.*"

"I don't understand. What do you want?"

"You testified against me once, but that trial was a fraud. Now we got the real trial." He stood in front of her and then bent down, looking into her eyes. "So testify."

"I don't remember anything."

"Really? You lock away a lot of innocent men with your testimony, then? Enough so you get them confused and don't remember?"

She calmed herself enough to make sure the words came out succinctly. "I don't know where I am. I don't know who you are. Just let me go, and I won't say anything. I promise. You'll never hear from me again."

Alonso stood straight and exhaled loudly through his nose. "Don't remember, huh? Well, let's refresh your recollection." He flipped through papers he picked up off the floor and lifted one in front of her face. "What does it say across the top of this form?"

"Please, I just wanna go—"

"What does it say!"

She yelped and jumped. His voice boomed like a cannon as it bounced off the walls.

"It says, 'Witness Statement.'"

"That's right. And whose name is under that?"

"Mine."

"And the date is from a little over eleven years ago, isn't it?"

She read the date. "Yes."

"Is that your handwriting?"

"Yes."

"Your Honor, the defense would move to introduce defense exhibit one into the record."

Judge Elrod watched him and then looked at Joy and then away. Shame was on his face as he said, "So granted."

"Thank you." Alonso turned back to Joy. "Read it to yourself."

She read. Time slowed, and Solomon knew he had a few minutes to do nothing but think of a way out.

He began by searching to his right along the column of large windows. There were six panes on each window with the tops curved, and the windows were close enough that they appeared to be one large window rather than separate smaller ones. They were probably six feet off the ground. It'd be difficult for someone to see inside if they were standing right out there, never mind on the road leading past the warehouse. Help wasn't going to come from the outside.

He looked to his left and saw a locked sliding metal door, the type often contained in self-storage facilities. Another similar door near the back was open, and a light was on above it. Dirt and dust swirled in the beams.

Above them was a crane, probably used to lift the heavy oil drums lined up against the far wall. The crane was thick metal; if it could somehow fall, it would crush anyone underneath.

Alonso had dropped the knife. Solomon knew he could get up, at least to his feet, while still strapped to the chair, but then what? He had no hands to grab the knife. The harsh realization weighed on him that nothing would get done unless he cut his hands free. But they were pressed together so tightly they were numb. And there was nothing sharp on the chair to rub them against.

"You done?" Alonso said.

Joy nodded, sniffling as tears continued to roll down her cheeks.

"Where were you on the night in question?"

She swallowed. "At a bar."

"Any bar? Please be specific."

"It's a place called A Bar Named Sue in Midvale."

"What were you doing there?"

"It was my friend's birthday. We were there celebrating."

"You snorted methamphetamine in the bar bathroom with this friend, correct?"

She didn't answer.

Alonso took a step toward her. "Answer the question," he said flatly.

She nodded.

"At around midnight, you then left the bar?"

She nodded.

"Please answer affirmatively for the record."

"Yes, I left."

"What happened when you left?"

"Please, I just want to go home. Please!"

She wept now, begging God to not let her die there. Solomon lurched against his restraints. "Let her go, damn it!"

Alonso laughed. "You got some fire in you, Counselor. That's the Solomon Shepard I remember. You stood up in front of that jury like you were a preacher speaking the truth. It was downright inspiring. But I'm afraid you're gonna have to keep it down. We can't let Ms. Rio get distracted." He turned to her. "Now, Ms. Rio, please don't upset the Court and make us hold you in contempt. You wouldn't like that. So answer the questions asked. What happened when you left?"

She hesitated a second, still sobbing, and Alonso let her. When she stopped, she looked at him, his eyes fixed on the woman.

"I went to my car," she said quietly.

"Something happened on the way to your car. What was it?"

"I . . . heard people fighting."

"People?"

"It was one person shouting and another one crying."

"What happened then?"

She looked at Solomon with desperate eyes but knew he couldn't do anything. Solomon had never felt so helpless in his life.

"I went over there and looked around a big truck."

"You hid?"

"Yeah, I hid behind the truck and looked out so I could see."

"What'd you see?"

"I saw . . . a man beating someone with something."

"*Something?* Like a wet fish or a loaf of bread? What the hell does *something* mean?"

"It was a baseball bat, I think. It looked like it had nails in it, on the end where he was hitting the man. And he was swinging the bat over his head." She paused and looked down at the floor. "I could hear the man's skull crack."

"And you could see all this clearly?"

"No. There was almost no lights back there. I only saw the bat because the man lifted it over his head, and it got into the light."

"Did you see the man swinging the bat at all?"

She nodded.

"What'd he look like?"

"He was big."

"How big?"

"I don't remember, but really big. Much bigger than the man on the ground."

"You see his face?"

She didn't do anything but close her eyes.

"Oh, you remember something now, don't you? What do you remember?"

"It was you," she said softly. "You were beating that man."

He pointed the gun at her face. Joy screamed and lurched backward. Fury was in his eyes, but Alonso managed to calm himself and say, "You saw me there?"

She nodded, tears running down her cheeks. "You moved into the light where I could see better."

"And what did you see? Describe this man that you say was me."

"He was darker skinned and really big. Fat but also really muscly."

"Did you see his eyes?"

She shook her head.

"So big and dark is what you got?"

"Yes. Please, I just want to go home. I just want to go home!"

"You saw this man for maybe half a second when he moved into the light. Was he wearing sunglasses?"

"What?"

"Sunglasses. Was he wearing sunglasses?"

"No, it was nighttime."

"Are you aware that I have light sensitivity and wear sunglasses even at night?"

"No. I've never met you before."

"Alonso, you've proven your point," Solomon said. "Let her go."

"I haven't proved a damn thing. And we still got us another surprise witness." He turned back to her. "You picked me out of a lineup. You remember that?"

She glanced at Solomon and then nodded.

"Did you tell the prosecutor, that man over there, that you only saw this man for a fraction of a second before he took you to that lineup?"

She nodded.

"What did he say?"

She looked at Solomon again and then away. "He said that you were really dangerous."

"That all he said?"

"He said . . . he said you hurt that man and you'll hurt other people. I didn't want to testify against you, but he said I had to."

"You didn't want to testify against me?"

"No."

"But he *forced* you, didn't he?"

"Yes. I didn't do anything."

"But you did. You got up on that stand in front of the jury, pointed your finger at me, and said, 'That's him.' You remember doing that?"

She sobbed again. "Please. I just wanna go home. I have a daughter."

"I had a son. What about my boy? Did you think about him before you got up there and pointed your crooked-ass finger at me?"

He was shouting at her from less than a few feet away, and she trembled so badly the uneven chair legs rattled against the floor. Solomon saw a wet spot on her jeans and knew she had urinated on herself.

"Objection," Solomon said. Alonso looked at him. "She's under duress. I would move to strike her entire testimony."

Judge Elrod glanced at Solomon but said nothing.

Alonso turned to the judge now. "Well, you got an objection, Judge. Make your ruling." The judge said nothing a moment, and then Alonso turned to Joy. "Ms. Rio, am I forcing you to say what I want you to say, or are you speaking the truth?"

"It's the truth."

"It doesn't matter because we can't know the truth right now," Solomon said. "She's worried you're going to kill her. Her testimony's unreliable and shouldn't be allowed in this proceeding."

The judge took a breath and said, "The objection is sustained. Accordingly, the witness's testimony will be disregarded."

Alonso flipped over the table as though tossing a toy. He strode up to the judge and grabbed him by the collar.

"You set the rules down," Solomon shouted. "You can't be pissed now that they don't cut in your favor every time. Is this a trial or not?"

Alonso gripped the judge a little tighter and then let him go. "You're right." He turned back to Joy and picked up the knife. He cut her hands loose. She rubbed her wrists, which had bruises on them.

"Ms. Rio, I'mma let you go. But first, I need you to testify in this trial of your own free will and choice. Do you understand?"

She nodded, still rubbing her wrists. "Yes."

"So, do you understand you do not have to testify today, and I am in no way forcing you to?"

"Yes," she said, her voice barely audible.

Alonso turned to the judge. "Good enough, Judge?"

Elrod said nothing. He was pale, his breathing shallow.

"Alonso, he's injured bad. He's going to die."

"Freedom ain't free, is it? You gotta make sacrifices if you live in a free society. That's what we live in, right, Counselor? Land of the free?"

He turned back to Joy. "You were interviewed by a detective that night with Officer Beard there, correct?"

"Yes."

"And you told them you didn't get a good look at the man that did this?"

She nodded. "Yes."

"What did they say to you?"

"The detective said not to worry about it. Just tell him what I saw, and they would work it out."

"That's not all he said, though, was it? He told you they knew the man was big with brown skin and then asked if he had a beard, right?"

"I think so."

"And you said yes?"

She nodded.

"Then he asked you if he was bald?"

"I . . . I think so."

"Are you aware, Ms. Rio, that such questioning methods are called *planting*? What he should have asked you is, 'Did the man have any noticeable features?' But what he said was, 'What color was his beard?' You see the difference? He's already planted in your head that the man had a beard, so the only question is what color it was. Then your brain fills in the rest. Ain't that right, Counselor?"

Solomon breathed a moment. "Alonso—"

"Ain't that right, Counselor!"

Solomon watched him a second and then glanced at Joy. "Yes, that's right."

"And planting is coercive witness interrogation, considered unreliable in a court of law, isn't that right?"

"That's right."

He kicked Beard's corpse. "But the detective and this piece a' shit right here, they knew this was a chance to lock me up." He turned back to Joy. "Ain't it true that you didn't say anything about the suspect having a beard until the detective asked you what color it was?"

"Yes."

"Objection. Counsel is testifying."

The judge said nothing but looked at Alonso, who stared him down.

"Overruled," Elrod said.

Alonso straightened up and paced in front of the witness as though addressing a board of directors as CEO. "Ms. Rio, when you identified me in the lineup, what traits were you looking for?"

"What?"

"What was it you were looking for when Mr. Shepard and the detective asked you if you saw the man that committed the crime that night?"

"I . . . don't know."

"If he was bald?"

"Yeah, I guess."

"If he had a beard?"

She nodded. "Yes."

"So the ID you made was based on the planting that the detective had performed earlier, correct?"

"Yes," she said, though Solomon could tell she didn't totally understand what had just been said.

"Your Honor, the defense would move to exclude the lineup identification of Mr. Alonso Hafeez as tainted. It was based on an earlier constitutional violation of the Fourth, Fifth, and Sixth Amendments and is therefore subject to fruit of the poisonous tree."

Weakly, the judge said, "So granted."

"So all we got from Ms. Rio without the identification is big and dark, holding a baseball bat. Is that right, Judge?"

"It is."

"Ms. Rio, are you aware they didn't find a baseball bat in my possession?"

"No."

"Are you aware they didn't find any blood on me?"

"No."

"If someone took a beating that bad, wouldn't you think there'd be blood on the person doing the beating?"

"Unless he changed his clothes," Solomon muttered.

Alonso glared at him.

"Finish this, Alonso," Solomon said, all the strength leaving him. "I don't have any fight left. Just let them go and do whatever you want to me."

He grinned. "We still gotta finish the trial. But I'm done with her for now. Your witness, Counselor."

44

Before going to the refinery, Billie headed to the sheriff's station. She checked in with a couple of detectives about the search for Solomon and gave them instructions like where to wait in front of his building in case he came back. The instructions felt empty, and she knew it was busywork, but at least it was something. Some forward motion.

She suddenly pictured Solomon burned to death with a tire around his neck, making her physically ill. She had to excuse herself and go to the bathroom in case she threw up.

On her way out of the building, she saw a car parked at the curb. Dax sat in the driver's seat. He got out and looked concerned. He came up to her and widened his arms to hug her, and she stopped him by putting her palm on his chest.

"What the hell are you doing?" she said.

"I heard Solomon's missing. I'm so sorry. I know he's your friend."

"You can't be here."

"I just came by to check on you. Sorry that someone cares about you."

"Dax," she said, a small trickle of anxiety in her gut letting her know that it might not matter what she said. "You need to leave me alone. We're done. I'm moving on, and you need to as well."

"This has nothing to do with us. I thought you might need a shoulder right now."

She put her hands in her jacket pockets and walked back toward her truck. "Don't come here again."

As she walked to her truck, Dax followed after her and shouted, "It's Solomon, isn't it? I see the way you look at him. You love him. But guess what? He doesn't love you. So think about that before you walk away from me."

She didn't respond and instead got into her truck and drove away.

The sky was the color of gray paint, and the stars seemed to be hiding. No moon and few streetlights as she left the confines of the city. *You love him.*

The words kept running through her mind, and she knew they couldn't right now. What was it Solomon always said? *Thoughts are just energy, and you only have a finite amount of energy, so be careful what thoughts you spend it on.*

All she wanted to do as she drove down a long stretch of empty highway was talk to him. Feeling this type of stress without him around was difficult because he was the one she called when she needed advice or to vent.

The oil refinery and plant were in a stretch of desert that held nothing but industrial businesses that poured pillars of black smoke into the air. The sands swallowed her as she raced down the dirt road, feeling the icy wind hit her face from the open window. A thought came to her now that she had been pushing away: What if they never found Solomon?

She'd known Solomon awhile through her father, but it wasn't until the last year that they'd begun to spend most of their free time together. He was easy to talk to and didn't judge anybody for anything. His intellect was staggering, and she found herself enthralled by his stories of humanity and its customs and how they could be explained through evolutionary psychology. She had always found him physically attractive. That was never the issue, but he seemed aloof until she got to know him, living in his own head. Now she knew he lived there for a reason.

He seemed like a man who didn't belong in any point in history. Out of place no matter when or where he was born.

What would she do without him?

The first refinery was still operational. She could see a flame burning on top of a black tower. Trucks loaded with oil were lined up in a row in front of the hexagonal building. Even this late, people were running around with hard hats on. The refinery never turned off, never rested. There was always a fire billowing out smoke.

She looped off the freeway and went around the refinery farther into the desert. The smaller companies and refineries were up the next few miles, along with some far-out-of-the-way office space. The three surrounding counties had split the area, and thus sections of it were under her jurisdiction as sheriff of Tooele County.

Many people who wanted to cook meth and didn't want prying eyes came out here, past the businesses, to Chelsea. Privacy was assured. There were no mountains to climb, no lakes for people to swim in, and a dull landscape that didn't conjure up any notions of beauty or awe. Someone would need to have a really good reason to come out here.

Google Maps didn't work, and cell phone service was nonexistent. The desert itself was barren and hostile to life.

The address she had gotten online for the refinery didn't make sense, a result of three different counties with three different address systems staking their claims out here.

She parked at a warehouse in a row of buildings and got out. The air was cold; a vicious wind was blowing. The icy particles stung the skin on her face as she trudged into the building.

The wind howled out here in a way it didn't do in cities. A lonely sound. A groan of pain, almost like a human voice.

She went inside the first building. The front office door was locked, but some of the delivery entrances were open. She went through one wide and high enough for a semi to pull into. Two men were on a ramp off to the side.

"Excuse me, I'm looking for the old refinery."

One man in a hard hat and thick coat with grease stains said, "Why you wanna go out there?"

"Call it curiosity."

The two men glanced at each other. "Little lady, I really do not recommend goin' out there on your own. Lotta dangerous people come out here to do what they do."

"I can hold my own. But I would appreciate your help so I don't drive around for the next several hours."

"Well, don't say I didn't warn ya. It's up the road a ways. Head straight west, and you'll come to a fork. Stick to the right and go all the way down, you can't miss it."

"Thank you."

She turned to leave, and he said, "Hope you brought a gun."

Billie opened her jacket, revealing the holster and firearm, and grinned at the look on the man's face.

Once back in the truck, she drove a solid half hour before coming to the fork the man had mentioned. It was only a few miles from there to the next complex of buildings.

A powerful gust of wind rocked her truck, and she had to strain her arms to keep the truck from swerving into a ditch.

She saw several trailers huddled together off the path, vehicles that were probably used for cooking meth. She didn't know precisely when meth had become so popular, but in recent years the practice had overtaken marijuana as the drug of choice for producers and pushers. It cost less to make and could be sold for more but also came with stiffer penalties if caught, not to mention the enormous danger involved in the actual manufacturing. Most producers used household chemicals they could buy in bulk, like antifreeze, battery acid, or drain cleaner, to save money on ingredients, all of which potentially made each batch a highly explosive bomb. She'd been called out to more than one trailer that had burst into flames with people still inside.

A quarter of a mile after the turn was a large hill with a burnt-out car abandoned near the base. She took another turn and drove in between tall patches of wild grass. Past those, on the other side of the hill, was what looked like a factory. One building of three stories, but wide. It was made of red brick with large windows and looked like a storehouse from a hundred years ago, when industrialism was still taking over the world and seemed novel.

A gate with a guard station was in front, but the gate had long since collapsed. The guard shack was run down, with broken windows and covered in salt and sand.

She drove past the shack to the building. Some of the parking spaces were littered with metal parts, and the ground surrounding the structure looked uneven; sections of the lot had come apart and been replaced by sand. Some of the windows were boarded up, but not all. She stopped by the front entrance.

She took a deep breath, checked her firearm, and opened her door.

45

Solomon felt strength drain out of him like sweat. A head wound throbbed from the back of his skull that he was surprised he hadn't noticed earlier, probably because of the adrenaline and a concussion. Solomon thought he might've blacked out for a minute, when Alonso was in a different position after he blinked. He didn't know how much longer he had, but he had to do something. Playing along wasn't working; fighting might not, either, but there were only two choices, and neither of them seemed to lead to him living through this.

"I'm not playing this game anymore," Solomon said weakly.

"It's not a game, Counselor. You got your witness right here. Ready to speak the Lord's honest truth for us today. She admitted on the stand that she was illegally coerced by the detective and that you unduly influenced her in the lineup. Her ID is invalid, and without the ID, you can't place me at the scene. Don't you want to address that? Seems downright damning if you leave that out there."

"Alonso, listen to me—"

"No! You listen to me. You locked me up once on this shit evidence, and no one said a damn thing, but now I'mma make you see. You're gonna see exactly what you locked me up on. Now you wanna cross-examine her, or do you stipulate that her testimony should be disregarded?"

He looked at her. "Joy, you're going to be okay. I need you to just relax."

"Objection, Counsel is testifying."

"Overruled."

Solomon looked at Alonso and then back to Joy. "Ms. Rio, had you ever seen a violent crime before that night?"

She shook her head. "No."

"Did you ever see anyone get beaten with a baseball bat?"

"No."

"Other than drug charges because of your addiction, you've never been arrested for anything, have you?"

"No."

"But the drug charges had you on probation, right?"

"Yes."

"And drinking and doing drugs at a bar would have violated your probation, correct?"

"Yes."

"So you were scared?"

"Yes."

"So scared that you didn't call the police, did you? The victim still had his phone in his pocket and managed to dial 911 before losing consciousness, correct?"

She nodded. "Yes."

"And when the police arrived, you were sitting in your car?"

"Yes."

"What were you doing?"

"I . . . I didn't know if I should talk to the police and tell them what I saw."

"Because of your probation?"

"Not just that. I was so scared. The man was huge, and he was . . . he was laughing while trying to kill that other man. I didn't know what he would do to me if he found out I helped the police."

"So when the detective and Lieutenant Beard were interviewing you, you weren't very talkative, were you? What I mean is you weren't really answering their questions?"

"I don't remember. I was just, like, in shock. I could barely talk. I told him I could come back tomorrow, but I remember he said it would be better if I talked to them then because my memory would be better."

"So he did express concern that your memory would fade with time, and he wanted you to be as accurate as possible in what you saw, correct?"

"I guess, yeah."

"Did he ever threaten you?"

"No. He was really nice. He got another police officer to drive my car home, and he drove me because I was so shaken up. And he called and checked up on me a few times to make sure I was okay."

"When he first brought up a beard on the suspect, what he actually said was, 'What type of facial hair did the suspect have,' correct?"

"I don't remember."

"Your Honor, we would ask that the witness be allowed to refresh her recollection."

"I'll allow it."

The judge said it before Alonso glanced at him, and the judge turned away. Alonso lifted the table he had thrown and found his cigar. He lit it again and put it between his lips without sucking.

"Unless you'd like to cut me loose so I can do it, could you please show her the reports and her statement?"

Alonso stared at him and then lifted the reports and handed them to her. Joy's hands were trembling, causing the papers to shake, but her eyes searched the sheets frantically, hoping to find something that would make Alonso happy.

Joy said, "The detective's words were, 'Did the person you saw have any facial hair?'"

"That's a yes-or-no question, right?" Solomon asked.

"Yes."

"You didn't know what facial hair he was referring to, right? It could've been a mustache, a goatee, lamb-chop sideburns, or even no facial hair."

"Yes."

"You were, in fact, the first one to mention a beard, were you not?"

"I don't remember."

"Well, what does your witness statement say?"

She looked through the statement again. "I don't see anything about it."

"Look at the police reports. There should be a transcript of your interview with the detective."

Joy flipped through sheets of paper and then found what she was looking for. She took a second to read it. Solomon searched the rest of the room as subtly as possible in the silence. The only exit he could see was the door on the far side . . . maybe twenty yards away. Without his cane, Solomon moved one step at a time in a slow walk. Anything quicker, and he would fall over. There was no way he could make it to the door if Alonso was still breathing. But the way he looked, Solomon guessed that might not be that long. He just had to survive long enough for the snake venom to kill Alonso.

"Did you find it?" Solomon said.

"Yeah. I guess I did say it."

"Read it."

"I said, 'I thought he had a beard, but it was dark, so I don't know for sure.'"

"So the detective never mentioned a beard to you, did he?"

"I guess not."

"What about the bald head? How did he ask you about that?"

Joy read another moment. "He said, 'What type of hair did he have?'"

"What type of *hair*. He never said anything about being bald?"

"It's not on this paper. He said what type of hair, and I didn't see any hair."

Solomon glanced at Alonso, who was staring at his shoes, lost in thought. If he was having any reaction to what was being said, he kept it to himself.

The fire had died down the past few minutes but still smoldered, giving off the pungent odor of burning chemicals. The garbage can holding the flames had blackened on the outside, and the smoke was no longer gray but jet black.

Joy kept stealing glances at Alonso, but he was a million miles away. His eyes were unfocused, the cigar burning him several times without him noticing. The whites of his eyes were splotchy with deep-purple rings, places where the blood vessels had burst. He took out his sunglasses and put them on.

Solomon asked, "Did Lieutenant Beard make you a confidential informant?"

"Kind of. He said if I testified and helped him with some things, he could get my new case dropped. Like going into bars and making buys while wearing a microphone. He got me in touch with some narcotics detectives who made me do some buys, and then they got my probation terminated and my new drug case dropped. I went into recovery after and have been clean for eight years now."

She looked at Alonso.

"I've answered everything," she said. "Can I go?"

He inhaled through his nose and seemed to notice the cigar for the first time. He looked at the tip. He blew on it lightly, causing the already red-hot end to glow even brighter, then took another puff before lowering the cigar.

"I think we're going to need you to testify again. Judge, I'd like to keep Ms. Rio as a rebuttal witness on deck."

Elrod still didn't move. Solomon had only seen his front side, but he was now leaning so far down from a lack of strength that Solomon saw the blood that had soaked his back. His face was ghostly white, lips blue and quivering.

"He's dying, Alonso."

"Judge," Alonso roared, ignoring Solomon. "I asked you something."

The judge nodded but didn't speak.

"Thank you. Ms. Rio, you will be on deck as a rebuttal witness. I'll take you back to the waiting room."

"No!" She jumped up now and backed away. "No, I don't want to."

Alonso pushed off the table and charged toward her. "You'll do what I tell you to do."

"No, please, not again. Please."

Alonso grabbed the back of her neck. "Get back there."

Sobbing, barely able to even walk, she trudged past Solomon. The two exchanged a glance that held nothing but a recognition that neither wanted to admit: they were going to die here, and there was nothing they could do about it.

46

Billie tried to look for any sort of insignia or labels on empty junk left over in the refinery. She didn't see much except barrels and buckets stained black. Everything else had been moved or scavenged.

The front door was thick steel. It was unlocked, and she pulled it open. The hinges creaked like rusted metal scraping along cement. The interior was completely dark, and she took out her flashlight from her jacket pocket. Holding it in front of her, she stepped inside.

The dust was thick in the air, making her sneeze. The place smelled like wet dirt, the floors filthy. An office was off to the side. She cautiously went to the entrance and found a light switch. She flipped it up and down. Nothing happened.

The office had a large brown desk with garbage thrown everywhere. She shone her light around, hoping to see some papers that had a letterhead stating the company's name, but there were only invoices or ledgers, faded with time. They were written in pen with an illegible handwriting style.

She scanned around the office one more time.

A noise made her jump. It was so loud it filled the entire building.

Her heart thumped against her ribs, and she quickly slid behind the door. She'd dropped the flashlight, which rolled a few feet away, illuminating the desk. Her breathing was labored, and she had to consciously work to slow it down so she could hear.

When her breathing was under control, she listened. The noise had sounded like metal on metal. Her first thought was that it was gunfire. But now, with a bit of time and a little less fear, the most likely culprit was something dropping. Opening the door and letting the wind inside might have pushed something loose that was ready to fall. The thought calmed her, but there was still a pinching feeling in her gut that said it was something else. Something waiting behind a dark corner for her to pass by.

She went to the center of the room and picked up her flashlight. The beam swinging left to right created moving shadows in the corners.

She lifted the flashlight and gun, the firing arm's wrist resting on her other forearm. Stepping outside the room, she turned a corner to get to the work floor. There were several different rooms, but they had thick, semitransparent sheets hanging from them rather than doors. Something she thought she'd seen in a butcher's shop.

The plastic was heavier than it looked, and she had to use both arms to move it aside. It was storage space. A few empty shelves and gray buckets. Not much else. She moved on.

The next room was as empty as the first, but she had arrived at the end of the hall and the entrance to the work floor.

Old, dilapidated machines were lined up to one side, and she realized this used to be a power plant. She was in the wrong building.

"Damn it," she mumbled.

Before she could turn to leave, there was another noise. A voice. It whispered in a tone that made her skin crawl. She took two giant steps back and swung the beam of light and the gun left to right. The light was unsteady in her shaking hands. She took a deep breath, steadying herself, and said, "This is the police. Answer if you're there."

A small voice from somewhere on the work floor said, "I'm here."

Slowly, trying to minimize the sound of her boots, she went around one of the machines and saw someone leaning against the wall on top of a sleeping bag. Old food containers were spread around the man, along with empty bottles.

He flinched and covered his eyes from the flashlight. His clothes were worn, and his hair was gray and tangled. The dirt under his nails was pure black, as though they'd been painted, and his black sneakers had massive holes. Amber pill bottles were lined up against the wall.

"Who are you?" she said.

"This is my house. You're in my house."

She scanned around to make sure someone else wasn't hiding. "There's a shelter in Tooele," she said. "I could have someone drive you there if you would like."

"No. This is my house."

"This is far from anywhere. How do you even get food here?"

"You can find food. You can't find cigarettes. You got any cigarettes?"

"I don't smoke." She holstered the weapon. "Stay here."

She went outside and got a twenty-dollar bill, the biggest she had, and went back inside, rounding the corners cautiously in case the man had decided he wanted more than chitchat.

He was still leaning against the wall and had a look on his red and swollen face as though he'd forgotten who she was. She held out the twenty for him, and he took it.

She took out her card and placed it down near him. "If you change your mind, call the number on there and tell them you would like someone to come pick you up and take you to the shelter. We have a program where a shuttle will come get you wherever you are. Do you have access to a phone?"

The man nodded and looked at the twenty but didn't say anything. She sighed and watched him a moment. Men like him were why she'd begged the county council for money to start the program. So many homeless in the city were severely mentally ill, and there was only one shelter that could help them. But some of them were too far gone to read addresses or use phones. It was a problem that didn't seem to have a solution. How could you help people who didn't know where they were or, many times, who they were?

"Do you know where you are?"

He nodded. "I worked here, but it's my house now," he said proudly. "I worked the lines for forty-two years. Then they closed the plant down like none of us ever meant nothin'."

"Do you have any family that could help you? Anybody you'd like me to contact?"

He shook his head as he opened a jar with some liquid and took a sip. "No family. Don't have anywhere else to go."

Perhaps she could make a call to the social worker she'd assigned to the Sheriff's Office to do evaluations? She could send him out with the paramedics to at least check on him and make sure he wasn't in any physical danger.

Before she turned away, she thought of something and said, "I'm looking for a place. Champion Chemical. Do you know where it is?"

He nodded. "Yeah, it's around the bend."

"This bend leading past the building and farther west?"

"Yup."

"I didn't know there were any buildings farther than this."

"That's where it is. But you don't wanna go there."

"Why not?"

He grinned. "Lotta bad stuff happens there."

47

Alonso paced a little and then sat down in the bloody chair as he lit his cigar again. He looked exhausted. His face was pale, more blood vessels in his eyes and nose bursting every minute, his hands starting to shake. The sweat had stopped, but Solomon guessed it was because he didn't have any more fluid in his body.

His voice was calm, almost contrite, as he said, "When I worked out here, we'd go to lunch at a sandwich joint next door. The workers were the only customers. The boss man, Mr. Gerald, he owned that, too. He was already old as dirt when I met him. His grandfather had been a slave in Georgia, and his mother was the first person in his family that wasn't born a slave. The war ended, and Lincoln had said Black folks were free, but nobody told all the white folks. Mr. Gerald told me the war took away the whip but didn't break the chains. His father was killed one day because he wouldn't sell his house to a white man."

Alonso puffed out rings of smoke.

"You know what that crazy old man did? Snuck into the bedroom of the fool that killed his father and stuck an axe in that man's head while he slept. Then Mr. Gerald left the state, left everything he had, and moved out here. Where the law couldn't reach him. The man grew up in the gutter not much better than a slave, but he was a millionaire by forty. And he wanted all of us to be millionaires, too. That's how you know someone is a true hustler: when they want other people to be rich, too."

He looked at the judge but somehow past him, as though the judge weren't there and Alonso were looking out at the deserts surrounding the building.

"Utah has lower alcohol limits than other states, so he had us sell kegs of homemade beer that was so strong it'd make your eyes water. Then he gave us a piece of whatever we sold. When I was fifteen, I made ten thousand dollars in one day, and he gave it to me in cash. I thought that was the best feeling in the world. That it was worth doing anything to keep that feeling."

Solomon breathed deeply in the silence and watched Alonso as he was off somewhere else, in memories from a time he didn't want to leave.

"What happened if you got busted?" Solomon asked, genuinely curious.

"If some fool was crazy enough to rat Mr. Gerald to the police, he would send a new Mercedes to the sheriff, the chief of police, and the county judge. He said you had to have all three. If you only sent one of them a car, the other two would get jealous and get you arrested. So it had to be all three. And they left him the hell alone, until they needed a new car anyhow."

As though not remembering he had one already lit, Alonso dropped his cigar and took out a fresh one. He tried to light it without remembering to cut off the tip.

"He would loan money to the men with their paychecks as collateral. Payday loans before anybody knew what that was. But you default on your loans to Mr. Gerald, he didn't just take your paycheck. He broke you. He'd start with a finger, and then if you were late on paying vig again, he broke another one. Then a hand, then a foot. He'd tell me, 'Youngblood, you never hurt 'em so bad they can't work. They can't work, they can't pay you. But you gotta let 'em know your money gets paid first. Before their rent, their food, and gifts to their woman.'" Alonso inhaled and blew out the smoke from his nose. "Mr. Gerald taught me how to make something from nothing . . . I loved that old fool."

He moved his thumb against his pointer finger in a stroking motion, and Solomon knew he hadn't realized he'd dropped his lighter.

"Mr. Gerald died four years ago. I tried to get permission to visit him at the hospital, but they denied me. Wouldn't let me go to the funeral neither. You took even that from me."

"Alonso, listen to me: I didn't do anything to you. Nobody did. You made a choice to hurt somebody and got busted. It happens. You paid the price, and it's over now. There's no need for all this."

"You still haven't learned, have you, Counselor? Maybe I'm not doing so good as your grave singer? I better step it up."

He left again, and a moment later, Solomon heard a voice. It felt like he'd been punched when he heard it. Though it was muffled with something over her mouth, Solomon would recognize Gesell's voice anywhere.

"Let her go!" he shouted without the ability to see behind him. "Alonso, don't do this. Let her go!"

She was dressed in a shirt and jeans but had no shoes on, blindfolded with her hands bound in front of her. Alonso led Gesell to the chair and forced her to sit down. She had tape over her mouth and eyes. He ripped it off, and she winced.

"No point in screaming. No one's gonna hear you out here."

Alonso went back to the table he used as a judge's bench and leaned against it, the cigar coming to his lips again.

"We got us a bona fide character witness, Counselor."

"I'm not on trial, Alonso. This is in your head."

"You are on trial. The most important trial of your life, and you don't even recognize it."

"Let her go."

"You didn't let me go."

"You disabled that man for life! What was I supposed to do? Give you a cookie and Valentine's card?"

He paced a moment, sucking on his cigar with his eyes on the floor.

"You know when the first time was I seen a man die? Ten. Some boys hollered at this fool's woman, and she told him how he gonna let some boys disrespect her like that, so he stepped up to 'em." He went to Gesell and stared at her. "One of them boys took out a Glock and blew that fool's face clean off. His head looked like a canoe. The body fell, and his woman walked away like nothing happened. Didn't say a damn thing. Didn't even look down at the body. Just walked."

He sucked in a few deep breaths.

"Don't nobody give a shit about nobody."

"I am so sick of your bullshit," Solomon shouted. "Michael's family gives a shit about him, and you beat him so bad he almost died. He was in a coma for weeks. They talked to his wife about letting him die because they didn't think he would wake up, and if he did, he would be nothing but a vegetable. You put that family through pain they'll never recover from. You deserved to be in prison. If he would've died, I would've gone for the death penalty. I would've been there, too, Alonso. I'd watch you strapped in that chair, closing your eyes for the last time." He glanced at the lieutenant's corpse. "And now I'm going to get to. My face is the last thing you're ever gonna see."

Alonso chuckled, but for the first time, Solomon knew he'd actually surprised him. A small window of seconds was open when he wouldn't be thinking clearly.

"Let us go and walk away. I won't look for you. Clean break, Alonso. I hear Canada's cold as shit, but the people are really nice."

"Solomon Shepard," he said with a grin, "always wheeling and dealing."

The thunderous bang of the gun firing crackled the air.

48

Billie ran through different scenarios as she drove. Maybe the man had a point? Sure, she was armed but entirely by herself with no cell service. If she emptied her magazine and Alonso still came at her, no one would be coming to help.

She didn't know what Alonso had planned, but whatever it was probably wouldn't take a lot of time. He wouldn't stick around to torture Solomon for long.

Torture.

The thought of Solomon being tortured revolted her, and she decided backup or no, she was going in.

Night was falling now. The storm had stopped, and she could see the stars in large swaths of the sky where clouds had parted. One thing she had to admit about Chelsea was that nowhere in the world had more stars on a clear night. If circumstances had been different, she would have stopped and looked at them. Her father had said to never waste a clear night. Always stop and look at the stars, with someone you love if possible.

She wished she could talk to her father now.

The road opened up with a patch of cactus fields. The large tubes of green had needles so fine they couldn't be seen from anywhere but up close. With her headlights bouncing off them in the dark, they looked like people holding their arms at unnatural angles.

Some buildings came into view, and she slowed down.

The first was an office building. No windows were left, but they hadn't been broken out. She wondered if the owner had taken the windows to sell. He'd probably lost so much money on the property a few pennies was better than nothing.

The following two buildings looked like factories surrounded by tall barbed wire fences. The two buildings looked identical and had no signage. A deli stood in between them.

There was a guard post that had a collapsed-in roof. A wooden barrier arm was stuck upright, and old garbage fluttered on the ground.

A long driveway connected the guard post to the main buildings. She took it and parked.

The larger building was dark and had circular windows about six feet up, giving the place an unusual shape that caused her a twinge of discomfort. It seemed about the most remote location someone could choose to put a business, and Billie wondered what they really used to do out here.

As she got out of her truck and approached, she could see the windows were actually higher than six feet off the ground. She was only five-six, so she couldn't peer inside without jumping up and catching only a glimpse of the interior. She found a thick board and leaned it against the wall. She climbed up the board slowly until she could grab the window ledge and look inside.

The space was dark except for one section: a metal door was open, and light came through into the hallway.

The world spun.

Her stomach heaved up into her chest as the board slipped out from under her. She crashed to the ground. The sand and snow stuck to her face, and the palms of her hands burned.

"Shit," she said, spitting out salty, wet sand.

She sat up, wiping the sand off her face. The light was likely left on by someone, maybe a security guard who occasionally came out to check the property. But she had nowhere else to check. If Solomon wasn't here, he might be in the next building, but after that, it was back to the station to wait for a phone call from someone who came across a body in some isolated location.

The entrance was around a corner. The wind whipped sand and salt against the steel doors and created a strange echo, something like whispering. A cold feeling slithered up her spine.

The doors were unlocked.

She withdrew her firearm and went inside.

49

Alonso had shot Judge Elrod twice in the chest. Gesell screamed, and Solomon fought against his restraints.

"You'll fry, Alonso. I swear it."

He laughed. "Don't worry, Counselor. You'll see him again real soon." He puffed on his cigar. "But first, I'm taking a little break. Me and your woman are gonna go spend some quality time in the office back there."

"No," she gasped, "please don't."

"You'll like it more than being with a cripple. I can guarantee you that."

He moved toward her, then roughly took her arm and lifted her off her feet. She screamed and fought, but it looked like a child hitting an adult, with each blow doing no more than tapping his massive chest. He began to drag her to the office in the back.

"No, Alonso, stop! Stop!" Solomon shouted. He strained against his restraints, against the chair, against anything that would give him resistance. He heard his shoulders pop as he tried to twist his arms in different directions to get the tape loose.

"Fight me then, coward!"

Alonso stopped and looked back at him.

"What do you even think you could do to me, Counselor? You really think you can hang?"

"Untie me and see."

A moment passed, and it seemed like the world had stopped. The dry itchiness of Solomon's throat irritated him.

Alonso tossed his cigar. He threw Gesell to the floor and then laid his gun on the table. He cracked his knuckles like some cartoon bad guy and strolled toward Solomon.

"Please," Gesell said. There was emotion in her voice, but it was held in check, and her words were clear. "Don't do this. I'll do whatever you want. He's a good man."

"Now that's relative, ain't it?"

He cut Solomon's wrists free. The blood that rushed back into his hands felt like cold water. It stung as his hands, which had turned a shade of purple, returned to normal.

"You're free, Counselor. There's the gun. What you gonna do now?"

Solomon used the chair to stand. He rose straight, his legs feeling like needles were thrust into his skin. They had fallen asleep, and he stayed still to allow the feeling to rush back into them.

Now that he was on his feet, he understood the distance between himself and the door. Alonso would catch him long before he could get there. There was no choice: he would have to fight.

"Oh"—Alonso chuckled—"you seriously wanna do this? You ever even been in a fight, Counselor?"

Solomon thought back to his youth. He had never been in a fight while his parents were alive. But after their deaths and his stints in foster homes, he felt he had become an expert.

At first, he didn't defend himself because it felt like an aberration. But once he saw that bullies wouldn't stop until he fought back, he learned that fighting, at least for someone without parents, was necessary. One man, an old drunk and former boxer who took in foster kids with his wife, taught him some boxing, and Solomon used the skill almost from day one. But that was before—before his injury and before he relied on a cane. Even at his best, Alonso would've been able to break his back. Now, there was no challenge. But maybe he could get to the gun or knife or at least give Gesell time to run.

"Win or lose, you let her go."

Alonso shrugged and watched Solomon as he began to move away from the chair he was using for balance. "Can you walk without a cane?"

"Worry about yourself."

He smirked. "You ready?"

Solomon stood in the center of the floor and brought up his fists, a posture he hadn't taken since he was a teenager. It felt awkward, and with his leg only partly responsive from his spinal cord injury, he couldn't get into a good orthodox stance.

"Tell you what, Counselor, you take the first hit. Free of charge."

"I won't say no."

Alonso sauntered up to him and lifted his chin. "Give it your best, 'cause then it's my turn."

Solomon grabbed the chair and swung it with everything he had without a second thought. It smashed into Alonso's head with a loud metallic clang. The chair legs bent, and the hinge broke. Alonso lost his balance with the momentum.

Solomon tried to make it to the gun. He got three steps before his leg gave out, and he hit the floor. Alonso's head was bleeding, blood pouring out of the wound above his right eye. It stained half his face red, like some ancient warrior painted for battle.

"Gesell, run!"

Alonso grabbed him by the collar of his shirt. He lifted him like a doll and cocked back his fist. He swung once, and the knuckles bashed against the side of Solomon's head. The blow felt like getting hit by a boulder. He became dizzy, colors drifting in his vision. Alonso swung again as Solomon heard Gesell scream from where she lay.

"Run. Now!"

She scrambled to her feet.

Alonso's fist might as well have been made of cement, rocking him so hard he felt pieces of teeth against his tongue. Blood gushed from his mouth, but because his head was tilted, it ran down his throat and choked him. He coughed up blood as Alonso lifted him again. He cocked back his fist but saw that it was already over. He dropped Solomon back to the ground.

"Two hits," Alonso said, strolling over to where he'd left the knife. "I've had bitches able to take more than that."

He came back over and stood like a giant. "You ready to confess your sins? You'll be freed after, Counselor. Think of that. Your soul is gonna fly. You're gonna learn something nobody on this planet knows: what happens when we go to those pearly-white gates."

A noise echoed through the space. Alonso looked back to Gesell, who had gotten to her feet and was near the door. The sound had come from outside. A crash against the building. Wood or thick plastic. Solomon heard it as well. It sounded louder than the wind blowing debris against the exterior.

Solomon spit out blood so he could talk. "You expecting someone, Alonso?"

Alonso's brow furrowed, and he turned away. Gesell backed off, but Alonso didn't acknowledge her. Even if she got out, there wasn't anybody else for ten miles in every direction. No one could get away.

Gesell ran to Solomon when Alonso had left the space through the open door. She had to hold up his head because he barely had any strength left.

He spit blood again. "So in terms of relationships," he said, out of breath, "I'd say it's going pretty well."

She laughed through tears as she wiped the blood away from his mouth with her fingers.

"You need to run," he said.

"*We* need to run. Get up."

"I wouldn't make it out the door, and you can't carry me. You need to run. Go directly east and walk only in the dark. When it's daylight, find somewhere to hide. He'll be looking for you."

"I'm not leaving you."

"You have to."

"No," she said, sobbing. "I'm not doing it. I can't."

"You can. Your son needs his mom. Go."

She inhaled, building up her courage, and kissed his forehead. "I'm going to get help as fast as I can."

"I know," Solomon said with a grin. He didn't want his last moments with her to be a goodbye. He hated goodbyes.

She kissed him again and then ran out the door.

"I'll be back. Just hang on."

A second later, she was gone, and he was alone.

The pain radiated from his head like a slow pounding on a drum, pulsing waves of fire. It hurt his neck, and his spine felt like it had twisted too far from Alonso's blows. He inhaled deeply into his chest and lifted his heart, feeling his back leave the floor's surface, and then he relaxed. Letting everything go. Giving up. It didn't sound so bad anymore, just like closing his eyes and going to sleep and not waking again.

Every night when he was a kid, he imagined himself not waking up again and didn't know what prevented him from dying. Why didn't his heart just stop? What kept him alive every night? Eventually, he just had to accept that he could die in his sleep and never know it, and there was nothing he could do about it.

It felt like that now. Release.

50

The interior of the building was filled with so much dirt and sand it made Billie sneeze several times. The sound was unnatural here. It didn't seem like someplace that people should be in, and she pictured the rusted, decrepit roof collapsing in on her in a heap of debris.

A long hallway led to the doors she had seen through the window where the light was coming from; between where she entered and the doors were dirt-covered floors with abandoned junk. She took out her flashlight and held it up with her firearm. The place looked even worse in the light.

Creaks and crackles like voices came from everywhere in the building. She slowed her breathing to listen but heard nothing except the building responding to the wind outside. She glanced out the windows and saw snow falling against the moonlight. If there was anywhere she could imagine not wanting to be during a storm, it was out in the middle of nowhere in an abandoned building that looked like it was about to fall over.

She tried her phone again and got nothing, so she slipped the device back into her pocket.

The doors were maybe thirty feet away. Pictures of creeping vampires waiting against the walls in shadow filled her head. Images from movies she'd seen as a child that she hadn't thought about for decades.

It made her wonder if everything someone saw and heard was stored somewhere.

A streak of faded paint was on the wall, but when she got closer, she could see it wasn't paint but blood.

Her chest tightened like a fist. A loud knock behind her made her spin around, her eyes wide, her breathing heavy. Nothing was there. She scanned the light up and down the halls and then wondered why she checked the ceiling.

She closed her eyes for a second and then turned again toward the door with the light streaming through. She could see now that it was metal, the kind that had to be rolled up by hand, as if she was in a storage facility.

Hurrying now, she scanned in short, staccato movements from left to right, making sure no one could get close to her without her seeing them.

The metal door was in front of her, and she glanced inside the massive room, making sure to keep her body shielded.

Inside was an open space with machines spread near the walls. Canisters of some type of gas used in the refinery were stacked against the walls.

She saw an older man slumped over. He was strapped to the arms of a chair. After letting her eyes adjust to the light, she saw the two holes in his chest. His face was white, with blue veins slithering up from blood loss. Another body was on the floor, and she recognized it as one of her men. Randall Beard. She thought of his wife and children, and her heart sank.

Solomon lay on his back.

A jolt of pain went into her heart like a needle.

No.

She ran to him, and only when she was almost directly over him did he open his eyes.

Relief washed over her, tingling like electricity. She put her gun and flashlight down and began checking him for wounds.

"At least buy me dinner first," he groaned.

"Where's the blood from?"

"My mouth. I think. I can't really feel my legs."

She ran her hands over his legs, looking for gunshot wounds.

"How'd you find me?"

"We can talk about that later. Your legs are fine." She ran her fingers through his hair, checking for any head injuries. He grinned through the pain and blood and said, "Just couldn't imagine your life without me, huh?"

"Something like that."

The first round barely missed Billie. The bullet went between them and ricocheted off the machine behind her, being flung somewhere in the room.

She felt a sting on her left ear and knew she'd been hit. Whether it was in her head or just grazed her, she couldn't tell and didn't have time to think about it.

Alonso stood at the door, holding a semiauto pistol in front of him. He fired again, and she jumped to the floor, over Solomon.

He fired for the third time, and she lurched and slid behind one of the giant machines a few feet behind her. Bullets hitting steel deafened her and made her jar with each shot. The machine was thick steel and could take the hits, but she noticed the angle changing. Alonso was coming around.

She saw Solomon and her gun and flashlight next to him. Alonso took a few paces but kept steadily staring in her direction. Then, while his eyes lingered on her, he aimed the gun down at Solomon without even turning his head and fired.

"No!" she screamed.

She couldn't see if Alonso had shot the floor or actually hit him. Solomon wasn't moving.

"That you, Sheriff? Damn, you are good to find us all the way out here, aren't you? Your daddy taught you some shit."

He fired at her, and the bullet hit maybe a foot from where she was. She ducked back as far as she could against the wall.

"Sheriff, why don't you come out now and save us the trouble?"

"There're twenty officers outside, Alonso. Don't go out in a blaze of glory. There's no honor in that. Lay down your weapon and surrender."

He laughed and then laughed some more. Until he began to cough.

"Damn, that was good. You deserve an Oscar for that shit."

He fired at her again, and the round missed her leg by inches. She curled up in a ball to keep her legs out of sight and looked over in the other direction. The machine was near the wall, but there was a small passage. A few feet of space. She crawled behind it. The slickness of cobwebs and dust covered her hands as she squeezed through the opening.

51

Solomon couldn't move. His chest felt like a car had backed up onto it. The blood didn't look real because of the lighting. Solomon had seen a lot of his blood, been coated in it, and felt it dry on him as the paramedics told each other he wouldn't live long enough to make it to the hospital. But in this lighting, his blood looked different. Darker.

He listened as Alonso fired two rounds, and they both hit something hard and loud like steel or tin. He could see Billie crawling behind the massive machine and over to the next one. Alonso wasn't far behind. He was only feet away from being able to take a good shot at close range. Billie wouldn't survive. Gesell might have, but she would never live a normal life, never see anything the same way again. Severe trauma could do that: taint everything.

The pain of rolling over made him feel like he wanted to vomit, but he swallowed it down and grabbed Billie's gun.

Alonso was almost to Billie. The machine was giant, and Solomon could see only legs. He tried to suck air but got no more than a partial breath.

Screw it.

He held his breath, steadied his hand, and fired. The first round missed, but the second connected.

Alonso hit the ground and looked over, his face contorted in rage.

The two men glared at each other for a moment.

Then they both fired.

Solomon would've pulled the trigger until he heard dry clicks, except he couldn't hear. The loud boom of both guns firing simultaneously had created a piercing ring in his ears. All he could see was Alonso's body, partially covered in darkness, lying on its stomach. It took a second for him to see that his eyes were closed. The sunglasses crushed underneath him.

He heard Billie pick up Alonso's gun.

"Solomon! Are you hit?"

The gun felt like it weighed a hundred pounds, and he dropped it and rolled to his back. "That or this is one helluva beesting."

She ran up to him, took off her jacket, and pressed it to the wound. The round had gone through his shoulder at the trapezius muscle and wasn't near his heart. She rolled his shoulder forward to look at his back.

The pain increased so quickly that he thought he might vomit again but decided that probably was a good sign.

"I'm so glad I have government-employee health insurance right now." He grimaced.

His words made Billie grin as she looked at the wound underneath his shirt. "Looks like it went through the muscle. You're lucky he was trying to intimidate me and shot you without looking."

"No. I think it was a final *Up yours, Counselor.* That I'm so beneath him he won't even look at me when he shoots me."

"Here," she said, taking his hand and pressing it to her jacket over his wound. "Hold this down. The bullet didn't hit anything vital, but you can still bleed out." When he'd pressed his hand to his wound, she said, "I can't get reception here. I'm going to try my cell phone on the roof. Stay here."

"Don't think that'll be a problem."

He stopped her with a "Billie?"

"Yeah."

"That was stupid coming here by yourself . . . thanks."

She took a breath before she said, "What are friends for?"

When Solomon was alone, he heard something. Movement. He looked over to Alonso, and the body wasn't there.

He reached for the gun, and Alonso kicked it away. He looked insane with rage. A bullet wound on his leg bled out in a stream that made his boot glisten. An injury in his upper chest bled, but it didn't stream. It spread in a circle over his chest.

Alonso held a container of gasoline. A green canister with warning labels worn away over time. The room was filled with them.

"She is something, isn't she, Counselor? She's the one."

Solomon tried to roll over onto his stomach and crawl away to hide behind a machine. Alonso didn't even try to stop him. Instead, he chuckled as he went over to some of the other canisters and popped the lids off. They hissed as he opened them and spilled out the gasoline.

The empty barrels had remnants of oil and sprays that they likely used to clean the machines. With whatever amount of gas was in those canisters, the entire place was a tinderbox. This spot was chosen very purposely.

Billie came rushing back into the room. Alonso picked up his lighter. He held it close to a canister as he opened the last one. She took aim at him with his own gun.

"This isn't gasoline, though it smells like it. It's grease remover. Much more flammable," he said. "I was thirteen years old and handling this shit all day. One slipup, and you'd catch your ass on fire. That's life, though, ain't it? You get up in the morning and take your chances all day." He had to stop and take a breath. "You ever," he stuttered, "listened to the cry of a baby being born, Counselor? It's the same cry an old man makes when he dies. Now you tell me something that begins and ends that way is meant for anything but pain."

He was out of breath and on the point of collapse.

"You'll kill yourself, too," Solomon said.

"I'm already dead, Counselor. Didn't you know that?"

"Drop it and put your hands on your head," Billie shouted.

He grinned. "Gladly."

He struck the lighter and dropped it.

52

The explosion was like a fireball on one side of the room. The flash-over, where every combustible surface ignites, didn't happen right away. Solomon guessed that was the only reason he was still alive.

The fumes ignited first, the liquid caught fire, and then the oil barrels with whatever chemicals were inside went up in fiery booms. Solomon covered his head with his arms as another explosion shook the building.

He felt hands on him and fought at first, thinking Alonso was here to finish the job, but looked up to see Billie pulling him to his feet. The room around them was in a flurry of blazes and small explosions filled with so much bitter smoke he couldn't see or even suck in a breath.

"This way," he croaked, the smoke burning his throat.

They hurried in the direction of the open door. He glanced back once but didn't see Alonso.

As they approached the door, Gesell and another man came rushing in. The man wore jeans and a camo vest, and his eyes went so wide Solomon thought they could've popped out of his head. The man ran to them and grabbed Solomon's other arm.

They got outside, and a semi was parked in front of the building. They'd gotten to the truck when the building went up entirely in flames. Fire released carbon monoxide in lethal amounts, and more people died inhaling smoke than from flames. If Alonso had been alive, he wouldn't be now.

Solomon watched the flames as he leaned against the truck. Gesell held him, and Billie stood staring at the building. No one said anything as sirens grew louder in the distance.

The fire crew put out the blaze slowly, letting it burn itself out first. Solomon could see sections of the roof inside collapsing under the weight of water. The water had likely gone into the walls and floors, and as old and dilapidated as the building was, it wouldn't last now. There would be nothing left but a charred husk.

Paramedics checked Solomon in the back of an ambulance. He had first-degree burns over his hands and neck, and his throat and nostrils were raw from the flames and smoke. A patch of hair on the left side of his head had been singed. The bullet wound continued to bleed and had soaked the gauze and bandages around his shoulder and upper bicep.

Billie came up to him and watched the paramedics treating his gunshot wound and stabilizing him on a backboard. Gesell sat next to him and held his hand. She'd cried so much her eyes were bloodshot and dry. She stared off into space. Billie turned away and watched the building smolder.

"Sheriff," a deputy said, "we got another body. Three of them now."

"Alonso Hafeez?"

He nodded. "He's dead. Burned up bad. Completely burned the skin off his face and hands, burned out his eyes . . . it's worse than I ever saw."

"Billie . . . make sure," Solomon said.

She nodded and left with the deputy.

Gesell touched a bandage that was taped to the back of his hand. She ran a finger over it and then held his hand again. They were quiet while the paramedic put a gel over his wound and a fresh set of bandages.

"Does it hurt a lot?" she asked.

"I'm sure it will, but morphine's a crazy drug." He grimaced as the paramedic pushed on his gunshot wound to tighten the bandages. "At least I know what a hot dog on a grill feels like now."

She leaned one elbow on a leg that was folded over the other. The ambulance didn't have much room, and her hair brushed against Solomon's face.

"I thought I lost you," she whispered.

"You didn't. I'm right here."

The trucker Gesell had stopped on the road came up and exchanged a few words. Solomon thanked him profusely, and the man went off. A detective said he would need to speak with Solomon when he was ready, and Solomon replied, "Tomorrow."

By the time the paramedics were done and ready to go to the hospital, Billie had returned.

"He wasn't exaggerating. It's bad. He must've been knocked unconscious by the blast and then burned up. You probably only survived because you were down on the floor."

"What about Joy Rio?"

"We found her locked up in another room like you said. She's hurt, but she'll survive." Billie glanced back to the building. "What was he doing in there, Solomon? Trying to get justice?"

He shook his head. "Whatever the hell he was doing in there had nothing to do with justice."

"We're ready to go," the paramedic said.

"I'll see you at the hospital," Billie said to Solomon.

They held each other's gaze as the doors closed, and the ambulance began to move.

53

The hospital had been a flurry of people fussing over him. Solomon hated people fussing over him and hated hospitals even more, but he was too tired to do anything. Gesell stayed with him, and Billie came by and checked on him. She'd been at the door when the blast had gone off, and other than soot smeared over her and a few singed hairs, she was unharmed. She brought him his cane, and there was still some of Alonso's dried blood on the lion's head handle. Billie said she would check on him tomorrow and nodded goodbye to Gesell.

The round had gone clean through, and the wound was non-life-threatening. The doctor had said he was lucky, but Solomon wondered if Alonso had purposely not gone for the headshot. Maybe he really had believed he would release his soul only after it was cleansed?

Solomon got out of the hospital as fast as they would let him, and Gesell drove him home and parked at the curb.

"You're staying with me," she said.

"No need. I'm okay. Really."

"My house is huge. You're not being a burden. You've been through a massive shock, Solomon. You need someone with you."

Solomon didn't point it out but thought that she had also been through a massive shock. The trauma would catch up later, in nightmares and bouts of depression and panic attacks. He hated that she would have to go through all that because of him.

"I don't have the energy to act tough right now, so I'm going to say yes."

"You don't ever have to act tough with me."

She kissed him, and it stung, as his lips felt like they had intense sunburns.

"I'll help you get your stuff," she said.

"No. I just need a second to myself. Be right down. Promise."

He went up to his apartment, leaned his cane against the couch, and sat down. His nostrils burned, his throat was tight, and his lungs ached from smoke inhalation. Every muscle felt tense, like someone had grabbed them and tied them in knots. He breathed deeply for a minute and wondered how long it would take to process everything. He knew himself and knew he would pretend it wasn't a big deal for as long as he could. Then things—images, sounds, fragments of conversation—would pop up over time and send shocks of anxiety through him, and he would blame something else as the cause.

He tossed his phone on the cushion next to him, leaned his head back, and closed his eyes, taking a moment to himself. Staying with Gesell would be nice, but a strength came from isolation that nothing else could give a person. He wouldn't stay at her house long.

His phone vibrated. He ignored it and reached over with his eyes closed and sent it to voice mail. It rang again. He sent it to voice mail again. Then texts started coming through. A sigh escaped his lips because this moment of potential peace had been stolen from him, and he opened his eyes and checked his phone.

There were two missed calls from Billie and then text messages in all caps:

THIRD BODY FOUND NOT ALONSO'S. GET OUT OF YOUR APARTMENT NOW

A creak sounded behind him. Weight on the floor. Solomon's eyes drifted up from the phone to a dream catcher he had up on the wall. Something a Navajo shaman had given him as a gift when Solomon prosecuted the man who had sexually assaulted his daughter and locked him away for life.

He jumped forward to get off the couch, and a force unlike anything he'd ever felt wrapped around his neck. It held him like an iron vise and squeezed, air unable to move in his throat. He felt his eyes bulge from the pressure and wouldn't have been shocked if his neck had been crushed.

Solomon was lifted off the couch by his neck and flung across the room like a wet towel. He hit the wall and slid down, slamming into the floor on his side. His gunshot wound ripped open, and warm blood flowed down his arm.

Alonso glared at him with wild eyes. The side of his head had been charred black, with slight remnants of red underneath where his skin had peeled away from flames. The cuts over his face from his stitches bled uncontrollably now. His hands were black with soot, and patches of his beard had been singed down to cracking skin.

He grabbed Solomon by the waist and neck and lifted him high into the air without a word. He turned and tossed Solomon to the other side of the room, his body crashing into a large painting encased in glass that shattered into pieces. Solomon felt one of the pieces impale him, thrusting into his hip and causing him to groan through clenched teeth.

All the memories came flooding back. His face to the jury, the arguments coming out of him effortlessly from the hours of practice as he paced in his apartment. Then the first stab and a shudder of pain as it hit a nerve. The shock on the jury's faces as the defendant grabbed Solomon's collar to prevent him from running, continuing to stab him. Getting in five more thrusts before he was tackled by a bailiff.

Solomon had been left the same way, lying on his back on the floor and staring up at a ceiling. Wondering if it was true that your life flashed before your eyes as you died and questioning why it wasn't happening.

Alonso grunted like an animal, and Solomon doubted he could speak if he wanted to. He wasn't human anymore. No reason, no sympathy . . . nothing but fury and hatred.

He rushed at Solomon and came to where his head was lying. He lifted his tree-trunk leg to smash the boot onto Solomon's head. The one advantage Solomon had against his size and power was speed. Alonso was fast, but not as fast as him.

Solomon ripped out the jagged piece of glass from his flesh and thrust it up as hard as he could. As he held it with both hands, the glass cut Solomon's palms and fingers as it impaled Alonso's flesh. The leg came down, and Alonso hollered in pain as he lost his balance.

Alonso stumbled back, the glass embedded deep into his inner thigh. He ripped it out with a growl as blood poured from the wound.

Solomon felt his breathing slow. His vision began to haze at the edges, almost like a dream. The pain in his hip faded, everything faded, and he felt numb and suddenly warm. The type of warmth someone would feel in a sauna. Relaxing his muscles, soothing his heart and his mind. Everything softened, and his head tilted back to the floor.

Alonso ripped Solomon's large television off the wall, lifted it over his head, and limped over. The blood from his thigh ran down his leg and pooled on the floor.

Solomon weakly held up his hand as though he could stop the force of the television slamming down into his face. Then he let his hand lower as Alonso inhaled and lifted the television as high as possible.

The gunshots sounded like bookshelves falling to the floor. Loud bangs that had bass. In an apartment with all the windows closed, the sound had nowhere to go and hurt Solomon's ears. It snapped him out of his warmth, and he was cold and on his back.

Alonso stumbled forward, dropping the television and missing Solomon by inches. Round after round plunged into Alonso's body. The apartment smelled like spent gunpowder.

Alonso slumped against the wall as Solomon heard Gesell's sobbing. He managed to tilt his head back enough to see her at the door, her trembling hands holding her gun for only a few seconds before it slipped out of her hands and to the floor. She made no motion to pick it up.

Solomon tilted his head the other way and watched Alonso. He didn't know how many of the rounds had caught him, but he saw blood everywhere on his chest and stomach. One round had cut through the side of his neck. The wound was deep, and blood spurted out as if someone were blowing it through a straw.

His eyes filled with every ounce of hatred he had left as he stared at Solomon. His gargantuan arm lifted, reaching for him, and then fell. He sank forward and his neck became loose, letting his head dangle with his eyes open and glassy.

Solomon's head fell back, too, and he lost consciousness.

54

The first thing Solomon thought when he woke up in a hospital bed was, *Better than waking up in the morgue, I guess.*

Gesell was asleep in a chair next to the bed. She looked worn out, like she'd been up for days, but wasn't wearing the same clothes she was in his apartment, which made him wonder how long he'd been out.

"Hey," she said, rousing from sleep as he watched her.

"Hey."

She reached out and held his hand. "How you feeling?"

"Like elephants decided to use my body for kickball." He gripped her hand tighter. "Are you doing okay?"

She softly shook her head. "No."

They held hands in silence for a long time.

After a few days in the hospital, the doctor asked Solomon if he could stay for monitoring another night, and he replied, "Absolutely not." But Gesell convinced him to stay. He was lying in the hospital bed late at night and playing a Swedish death metal band on his phone when Billie came to the door. Her hands were in her jacket pockets, and her shoulders were wet from the fresh bout of snow outside.

"Hey, stranger," he said as jovially as he could muster. He could already see the deep worry on Gesell's face whenever she looked at him, and he didn't want to see that same look on Billie.

"You got your color back," she said as she came into the room and pulled up a chair near the bed. "You were pale green there for a while."

"Blood loss. I'm good now." He paused the music. "Did you ID the third body?"

She nodded. "Kyle Brotus. He's a football player at the college. Close in size to Alonso. The ME found a complete break in his C7 vertebra. Alonso broke his neck. We don't know the connection or how Alonso found him right now."

Solomon sat up with a wince of pain and leaned back on several pillows. "He must've been planning this for years. Find someone who matches him and burn the body beyond recognition as an insurance policy if everything goes to shit. How'd Alonso even take off?"

"He had a car hidden farther out in the desert and managed to slip away after the explosion. Before everyone arrived. He was more clever than I gave him credit for."

"No way he did this alone. Someone helped him. We need to find out who."

Billie didn't reply but instead looked out the window and watched the snowfall with the hospital lights illuminating the parking lot. Solomon stared at the television up on the wall with the volume turned down. He didn't remember turning it on.

They spoke for a few minutes of mundane things, reporters bugging her for interviews, significant cases in the pipeline, her mother's health. He deftly managed to keep the conversation away from what he was feeling. Though, to her credit, she probably sensed he didn't want to talk about what had happened and purposely didn't bring it up.

"I'm sorry, Solomon," she finally said.

"You have nothing to apologize for."

A silence passed before she said, "I better let you rest." Billie lightly touched the back of his hand. "I'll be by tomorrow."

"Okay." She was halfway across the room when he said, "And bring some Atlantis Burgers, would you? I can't eat hospital food anymore."

"You got it."

When he was alone again, he stared at the television. Some talk show where somebody's alleged father was getting a DNA test. He thought shows like this had gone out of style in the '90s, but maybe trash TV never went out of style? The ability to say *Yes, my life's a disaster, but at least I'm not them* was a powerful catharsis.

He swung his legs over the bed and got his cane. It pinched his elbow to put all his weight on that arm, and he had to stop and stretch for a second.

The hallways were empty at this time of night, and the only voices were coming from the emergency room.

Solomon turned down a long hallway away from it. A set of double doors was there, and he had to physically push them open, which caused pain in his hip. He glanced around to ensure no one else was near and then pulled up his hospital gown enough to look at the injury. Thirty-six stitches and half a tube of medical glue held the flesh of his hip together, giving it a slick, shiny appearance under the bright hospital lights. The meat near the hip joint looked like it could slide apart with no friction.

Each step was slow, shooting a dull pain from his hip down his thigh and into his calf. He had to rest against a wall and could hear someone's breathing from another room. It was slow and rhythmic, and he realized they were hooked up to a ventilator.

A sign told him the cafeteria was down a passage to the right. He could see the vending machines. Food sounded heavenly right now, as he couldn't remember when the last time was he'd eaten. As he pulled the cash out of his wallet, he felt someone looking at him and turned.

Joy Rio was standing with her arms folded. She was wearing a jogging suit with white sneakers, and the right side of her face was blushed red but wasn't burnt.

"Joy? I thought you were released. You okay?"

"Yes. I just needed to talk to you. Just me and you."

He nodded but said nothing.

"Do you remember when you took me to the lineup?"

He hesitated. "I do."

She grinned, but it didn't have any mirth. "I was so scared. I was shaking, and you put your arm around me and told me you wouldn't let anyone hurt me." Tears came to her eyes. "I told you I wasn't sure who it was."

"That's a common reaction, Joy. It's fear. It can warp how everything looks around you."

She shook her head. "No, this was different. I told you I couldn't identify him. That it was too dark. Do you remember what you said to me?"

He put both hands on his cane and looked down to the floor.

"You pointed him out to me. I thought that was a normal thing, but I learned later you're not supposed to do that. You told me that he was evil and that the way evil won is when good people didn't do anything to stop it. That you've been trying to put him in prison for so long, and he kept getting away to hurt more people. When I told you I wasn't sure, you told me he might come after me if he gets out. Do you remember that?"

He didn't respond.

"Do you have anything to say?" she said.

"Why didn't you tell him?"

She wiped tears away. "If I did, he would've killed you right then." She folded her arms again. "Was he really innocent?"

"No, he wasn't. And without your testimony, who knows how many more people he would've hurt."

"You mean like he did now?"

Solomon didn't say anything.

"I swore under oath that it was him. I pointed to him and put myself on the line, and you lied to me."

"I never lied to you. He is—was—evil. One of the most dangerous people I've ever come across. We have no idea what he would've done if you couldn't identify him. You might be dead right now."

"Or maybe he didn't do it and didn't deserve that?"

"He deserved a lot more than that."

"Yeah, probably. But we won't know for sure now, will we?"

Solomon tapped his cane against the floor. "He almost killed that man."

"Are you sure? Because he was damn sure he didn't do it."

"Yes, I'm sure."

"The fact that you can't look me in the eyes says you're not."

He looked up at her, and it caused intense discomfort, and he had to look away.

"Doesn't matter if he did it, does it?" she said. "I don't think that was the point. The point was you couldn't prove it, and you used me to do it for you."

"Joy, I didn't use you. I was protecting you."

She wiped the last of her tears away. "Yeah, well, great job."

Joy left, her arms still folded as she walked. Solomon waited until she had gone before he started walking back to his room.

He didn't feel hungry anymore.

55

The few days he'd spent at Gesell's had been peaceful, but the energy was off. Solomon could sense it and knew that she could, too. Something had been irreparably broken between them. She was loving and warm, but he knew she saw Alonso whenever she looked at him.

She would stay for a while. At least until his injuries healed. How sad, he thought, that the injuries would keep her around out of guilt. But after he healed, it would be constant emotional pain whenever she looked at him. He wouldn't do that to her.

He made up an excuse that he had to get his mind off things and go back to work, so it'd be best if he went home. She didn't fight his decision.

Billie came and picked him up late on a Friday night. He could've waited until the morning, but Gesell was out of town at her mother's, and he didn't want to stay there anymore. He wouldn't say he felt unwelcome, but it didn't feel like a home. It had been tainted . . . like he was to her now.

The sheriff stood outside the truck. She helped him with his one gym bag full of clothes and then had to help him up into the truck.

"Here," she said, handing him a stack of flyers once they were inside. They had Russ's picture and Solomon's phone number on them, along with a $250 reward. "Thought we could hang them up tonight. I figured neither one of us would be sleeping much."

He felt emotion in his throat and had to swallow it down. "Thanks."

As they drove, death metal played. Something he knew Billie hated, but she actually turned it up at one point because she knew he liked it.

She got off a freeway exit near Cottonwood Canyon.

"Where we going?" he said.

"The sky cleared."

"So?"

"So my dad always told me to never let a clear night sky go to waste."

She parked next to a grouping of trees near the mouth of the canyon. They got out, and the air was cold. It sent a chill down Solomon's chest. A stream was nearby, and he could hear the crackling of water against rocks.

Billie helped him up into the bed of her truck, and the two of them leaned against the sides and stretched out their legs as they stared at the sky. There wasn't a cloud left, and the sky was almost a dark blue instead of black because of all the stars and a bright crescent moon.

"Did you ever stare at the sky as a kid and imagine aliens staring back at you?" he said.

"I don't think so."

"I used to all the time. I would sometimes say that I believed in them, hoping they'd come down and pick me up. The first human to live among an alien civilization. I thought that would be the coolest thing ever." He swallowed, and the heaviness of what he was about to say felt like he had cinder blocks tethered around his neck. Weighing him down slowly, grinding away until he didn't have strength left to fight.

"Um," he managed to say, "I . . . um . . . I'll take the number to that therapist."

She didn't follow up with any questions and just said, "Okay."

He let out a long breath and stared at a constellation in a lower region of the sky. Orion. The hunter.

"Do you see that star on Orion? The bright one in the upper left? That's named Betelgeuse. Whenever I see Orion, all I can picture is Michael Keaton spitting into his pocket as Beetlejuice and saying he's gonna save that one for later."

She smiled but kept her eyes up to the sky. "I loved that movie."

"The people were the villains, and the ghosts were the heroes. Never seen that before."

"Do you think that? That people are the villains?"

He was silent a moment. "I hope not. I guess that's all we can do. Try our best and hope we're the good guys."

They were silent a bit longer. Finally, Billie put her hands behind her head and relaxed into the posture more before saying, "Show me some more stars."

ABOUT THE AUTHOR

 At the age of thirteen, when his best friend was interrogated by the police for over eight hours and confessed to a crime he didn't commit, Victor Methos knew he would one day become a lawyer. After graduating from law school at the University of Utah, Methos cut his teeth as a prosecutor for Salt Lake City before founding what would become the most successful criminal defense firm in Utah.

Over ten years, Methos conducted more than one hundred trials. One particular case stuck with him, and it eventually became the basis for his first major bestseller, *The Neon Lawyer*. Since that time, Methos has focused his work on legal thrillers and mysteries, winning the Harper Lee Prize for *The Hallows* and an Edgar nomination for Best Novel for his title *A Gambler's Jury*. He currently splits his time between southern Utah and Las Vegas.